SMOKE SIGNALS

Stories of London

SMOKE SIGNALS

Stories of London

EDITED BY THE
LONDON ARTS BOARD

Library of Congress Catalog Card Number: 93–84650

A catalogue record for this book is available from
the British Library on request.

These stories are works of fiction. Any resemblance
to actual persons, places or events is purely coincidental.

First published 1993
by Serpent's Tail, 4 Blackstock Mews, London N4, and
401 West Broadway #1, New York, NY 10012

Typeset in 11pt Sabon by Servis Filmsetting Ltd.,
Manchester
Printed in Great Britain by Cox & Wyman Ltd., Reading,
Berkshire

Contents

Preface

Smoke Signals is the culmination of an exciting new initiative for the London Arts Board. I would like to take this opportunity to thank those involved, in particular the judges and commissioned writers, all of whom were more than willing to give their time and their work to a project that would give new London writers the opportunity to be heard. The Board has their commitment, and the commitment of the entrants and the winners themselves, to thank for this highly enjoyable and endlessly varied collection.

I would also like to pay tribute to the energy and enthusiasm of the Board's Principal Literature Officer, Lavinia Greenlaw and the Administrator of the London Short Story Competition, Sam Maser.

Clive Priestley
Chairman
London Arts Board

Introduction

Smoke Signals is an anthology of new short stories written by London writers, about the city itself. It includes the prizewinning entries from the 1992 London Short Story Competition together with specially commissioned pieces by renowned authors, Roy Heath, Shena Mackay, Michael Moorcock, Kate Pullinger and Tom Wakefield. While these twenty stories range in subject from cannibalism to spiritual enlightenment, from bigamy to racism, all are clearly rooted in London. They reflect the common experience of a life dominated by journeys to and fro across a metropolis slowly grinding to a halt; where incidental meetings with strangers can influence lives; and where hostility and isolation are matched by excitement, a liberating diversity of experience, and continual change.

Short stories have become increasingly popular in recent years. They are no longer dismissed as the first step towards a novel but seen as an equally powerful and ambitious form of writing, where the drama is often all the more potent for being thus contained. Short stories are more inviting for a reader daunted by the complexity of poetry or the demands of long fiction and, for these same reasons, seem more possible to write. There is no denying the craft and discipline that the form demands, but to someone tentatively starting out on their first piece of writing, the short story at least seems encouragingly within reach.

The London Short Story Competition was conceived as a way of stimulating and promoting new London writers, and also as an opportunity to explore the writers' response to the shared experience of living in this particular city. Run by the London Arts Board, in association with Serpent's Tail Publishers and Capital 95.8FM, the competition was launched in the autumn of 1992. The entries were judged by the writers Ruth Rendell and Maureen Duffy, together with Nick Wheeler, Capital Radio's Head of News and Talks. Fifteen equal winners were chosen and their work is published here together with the five pieces specially commissioned as a celebration of London's particular influence and inspiration on its international literary community. The Competition not only got six hundred people writing but also brought together unknown and established authors, publishers and the media in a way that happens all too rarely. The collaboration proved to be a highly successful one and the next London Short Story Competition will be launched by the London Arts Board in the summer of 1994.

Lavinia Greenlaw
Principal Literature Officer
London Arts Board
June 1993

Sightseeing London

TOBIAS HILL

By Kentish Town things are warming up. Across the aisle there's an old girl with a loose-long necklace and she folds it through her hands, one bead at a time. Vauxhall glass or something. Jet. When she gets to the bottom, there's a roll of yellow paper like a fag, and she winces and reels it off and then inside there's a bone. Old. Could be a finger. Maybe her man's or maybe just some hocus pocus.

Beside me there's a schoolkid with big dog-teeth and lanky hair and she's writing to her mate. Her Mum's had an abortion, she's sure, but it's a secret, maybe even her Dad don't know about it. Plenty more kids dreaming and talking, catching pike in the canal and giving Bowe lip, he's crap and Tyson would slap him down. And then there's the workers, grey suits but inside the lining's purple as amethyst, or crimson. They sigh and cough like pigs at an abattoir. But things are cooking nicely. The sights of London are here today.

At Camden it fills up some and I think, Inspector Time. Not too empty and not too full, just right for the Underground People to comb in a tidy profit. And me with nothing in my pockets but holes and bumfluff: if they catch you twice they do you, Kadi says and I got pulled up some two months back. It could be this time, there's no real reason, it just could. But things are warming up. We are going to see some sights today, I think. I sit and wait for it to hotten up.

Airless sway and roaring darkness. It gets so tight down here that you can smell the nerves buzzing. Hutch-mentality, I term it. Animals patient like down on the farm, expecting the worst. Maybe someone will talk, that really freaks them. Or whistle a song, that happens. Or climb up on the seats and swing on the hand-grips or confess to masturbation and devil-worship. It's like a pressure-cooker down here and when it goes, it really goes. Like a rocket. Everybody knows it.

Two tracksuit blokes get on at Euston and when the doors shut it's grudgingly, dirt in the nice clean grease. They squash in and there's a girl, Garden Suburbs, comes on too. When they see she's got a baby they're all over her.

"Look at him. Lovely sprog, my dear."

"What's his name? Fit as a butcher's dog, isn't he?"

"Bathsheba". Quietly, she doesn't want trouble or conversation, no. She's blushing into her alpaca sweater. There's llamas walking up and down her breasts. Her handbag's open. Silly bitch.

"Bathsheba," says one of them. "Very nice".

We're into the tunnel and the Underground switches him off like instinct. Opposite me there's a woman with leather skin, old stitched-up hare-lip, nice togs. Teacher or social worker. And behind her there's me mirrored, stretched out and shadowed like a freakshow horror.

Pig-bristles and rat-tails of hair. Water was off in the squat this morning and I'm not looking too nice, like a mad old rasta-man. Kadi said that last night. Clear and warm in the stillness between sheets, and she was right. I'm looking dirt-cheap now. If the inspector comes on I'm fucked for sure, they'll string me up. By King's Cross, I've got itchy feet and I'm thinking where to beg lunch round here. And then the blind guy gets on and I know I was right. Some good sights for me today.

Waistcoat and suit, all in dark jade green. He's old, maybe eighty, and shaven real clean. I'm thinking, how's he going to shave himself that good? But his eyes are all scooped out and people are shifting around. Too much blindness for them. Sympathy likes these things understated.

The teacher-woman gets up, says something soft and when he nods she helps him to the seat.

"Thank you my dear", he says. And his voice is sleek too. Like tungsten, yardfowl muscle. Tough and smooth with years. He parks his stick between his knees, doesn't take his hands off it, keeps it where he knows.

He's got his own Exclusion Zone; nobody looks at him. We hit the tunnel and the carriage sways into midnight. When the light shudders back on, his head is cocked and he looks like a parrot, a cockatoo. He's listening. Like I'm looking. Someone else out to catch London, maybe. Me seeing the sights and him, hearing things and thinking. I want to know what he's thinking. This is my routine, doing the Underground. He owes me.

Then the tunnel behind him whites out. I jump and he jumps too, I see him flinch. Another train goes coiling by, faces at the windows turning slowly to look back at us. Lightning fear of collision. Then it's gone again. Sublimated. We come out into the Angel bellowing like a bull.

The teacher-woman gets off. One or two only get on and I think, Son of a bitch I'm going to get done. The way people in the gangway are moving around all of a sudden, like it was an inspector. But it isn't. It's another blind guy.

This is it. It's all mine. Sometimes there's weeks when I don't see nothing much down here except rucks and breakdowns. Then something like this happens and it's all worth it. Something to remember. London trapped like Big

Ben in a little plastic snow-shaker. All mine, if I remember it right; a ticket to the city.

Young, this one. Copper hair and Lennon glasses. But mostly he just looks hard. There's anger grained into him like city dirt, and there's lines round his mouth that don't look like they crack. He's got a big Alsatian kind of dog, big for a guide dog, and when someone tries to take his arm he weaves round like a stoat.

"Take your hand off me. Please," he says. He sits down right beside me. He must do weights; he's seriously built. And on his wrist there's a tattoo. Close to the vein, no good tattooist would do it that close. It's a poker hand. A royal flush, but the suit's been cut out. You can still see the tiny scarred hearts.

The gangway's packed nose-to-neck now, and the doors chew up coat-tails when they close. Right down the other end of the carriage, someone's talking flexi-time and wages, but up by us there's nothing except the Alsatian panting and the train speeding up into the dark. When the old guy speaks, it's like a pistol-shot.

"We are in the same boat, I think," he says. I know him, can't see him through all the bags and backsides, but I know his voice. Sleek and loud. For a long while there's silence, and then he says it again.

"I said, we're both in the same boat, sir—"

"Are we?" I look at Red-hair and his face has gone white like ice-cream. His hands are gripping the arm-rests, and the tattoo is stretched out so that it makes no sense. He's turned his head, he's pointed straight through the crowd at the old guy. You can feel people freezing up, listening. Anticipating violence.

"It certainly looks that way," says the old man. I wait for a time but when I turn around, I see the dog has stopped panting. It's just watching Red-hair, and he's grinning like a

4

donkey. He says nothing. Silence reels out into the seconds.

"What is your guide called?"

"Why?"

"Just curiosity, I suppose." He pauses and I see him through the crowd. His head still cocked like a bird. No one looking at him but me. He tries again.

"Do you live in Islington? Because if you do, I'd like to offer you an invitation." No rise from Red-head.

"I'm having a dinner-party this Saturday. Of people similarly informed as ourselves, twenty or so. You know, we have to stick together. Eight o'clock."

"Yeah". I watch that. I want to remember him like this. Still grinning, but the face has softened now, a little. The dog goes on staring up at him and he puts his hand out and strokes its head. Slowly and carefully.

"Take this, please," says the old guy. Red-hair holds up his hand. Someone passes a blank white card through the sweaty pile of people. When I drop it down into his hand, Red-hair frowns and reads it with his fingers.

The train slows and its roar hollows. When we come out into Old Street, the guide-dog stands up and pants at Red-hair. The doors mutter open.

"Goodbye and good luck, sir," says the old guy. His voice is less, weaker now, hollowed out like it was the roar of the train. "Until this weekend. Do come." Red-head is nearly out of the door. "You know, from the balcony of my house, you can hear all the sights of London."

"Right". He gets out in front of a herd of suits. The old guy cranes up, listening after him for a little moment, but there's too much noise or something because he sits back. He looks washed out. No one sees him. After a bit I can't tell if he's awake or asleep. Dead, maybe. It wouldn't be the only time it happened. All around us in the swaying darkness London coughs and looks away.

5

At Bank I pack it in for the day. Before I get off, I pick the blank calling card from off the gangway floor. Smooth it out. I keep it in my pocket. Like a ticket. It keeps me warm.

Hunger

R L HUNTRESS

You might say I wanted to eat the world.

I ate Chinese. Hakka style, Chiu Chow, Cantonese, Szechuan. Indian (North and South), Afghan and Thai, in the styles of Bangkok and Chiang Mai. I ate of the conquerors and the conquered: Castilian at lunch, Colombian at dinner. Burmese fried noodles and Tibetan dumplings. Cal-Mex and Tex-Mex. Moroccan and Mauritian.

To name just a few.

Now, in a banquette seat in a half-lit restaurant in the West End, I was about to add to the list. From across the table, Copernicus Braxby was trying to dissolve whatever was left of my resistance in an undiluted mixture of syrupy charm and strong-arm persuasion. "Come on now, Clary. It won't bite. Not when it's cooked up all nice like that."

"But what the hell is it, Nick?"

Deep sigh. "Clary."

"What?"

"Eat."

Now this was a switch: someone prodding me to eat. Not that I was fat. A little rounder than I would have liked in a couple of places, maybe, but who isn't? No, it wasn't gluttony. I wanted quality, not quantity, and the more exotic the better. I judged my finds on authenticity and obscurity, and I showed off the results to like-minded friends like trophies: Japanese vinegared octopus, milky-sweet *dulce de leche*, Ethiopian *doro wat* wrapped in spongy *injera*.

For a girl from Buffalo who used to argue with her mother about whether to get the TV dinner with the fried chicken or the roast beef, I'd come a long way. I wanted food to be more than food. I wanted it to be transcendence. I wanted to be the Marco Polo of mealtime, a culinary Christopher Columbus, setting my course for the unknown and coming back with stories to tell.

It was easier back when I lived in New York, the United Nations of food, the twenty-four hour neon-lit pulsing pleasure palace. There the game practically came out of the forest and sat on your doorstep. But London was another story.

London was hard work, as nearly three years here had taught me. We're talking, let's remember, about a town where not long ago you couldn't get something as simple as a decent hamburger. Serious fans of exploratory eating still operated like devotees of some obscure and outlawed religion, swapping urgent tales of the two shops where you could buy the *galangal* you need for a proper Penang curry paste, or the Italian place in Bayswater with a cuttlefish risotto as black as the devil's dinner. Hot tips boosted your status among the faithful like relics from a dead saint.

Nick had promised me the hot tip deluxe, the one I would never forget. Now it was sitting on a plate about a foot away from my mouth, and he couldn't wait for me to close the distance, and then start building a shrine to him. I cut off a piece and brought it to my lips. I chewed.

"I'm not even going to try," I said.

"Try what?"

"Try to guess what this is."

"Just as well," Nick replied. "You'll never get it."

He cut off a piece from his own plate and ate.

"How's she going?" This was Nick's friend Charlie, out from the kitchen in dirty chef's whites. He had an Australian accent that cried out for subtitles.

"She's going," Nick answered. "Just started on it."

If Nick was the patron of my little dining adventure, Charlie was the architect. "I've got a friend who owns a restaurant in town," Nick had told me. "Every now and then Charlie will fix up something special for someone who might appreciate it."

So far, there wasn't much to appreciate. "Why do I have the feeling," I said, "that I'd have to name half of London Zoo before we got to what this is?"

"More than half," said Charlie.

"Is it illegal?" I asked.

They looked at each other, and Charlie said, "Too right."

"Endangered species?"

And they looked at each other again, and laughed until tears ran down their faces.

Nick was the kind of guy who drives half the women in the world mad with primitive need, and drives the other half simply mad. At thirty-four, he made no secret of the fact that he had never held a regular job. Nick was an actor, but definitely a part-time actor, and an unrepentant dilettant. He had what he described as family money, which made him a better date than his CV would imply, but not necessarily a better person. I had a high-pressure job in the finance business, and I suspected that a guy who talked openly about his enthusiasm for kite-flying and Tantric sex might be just what my tired soul needed.

Some of us knock ourselves out to rediscover our inner child. Nick still hadn't found his inner adult. He didn't call to ask you to go out with him; dating was too much like what adults did. Nick asked you to come out and play with him.

On the first night we went out to play, he took me to a cramped storefront caff with wooden tables that needed to be stabilised with matchbooks under the legs. I sat there in the nice outfit I'd chosen specially, building up a real head of steam at being taken to such a place, until they brought out what was probably the only Sudanese food to be had in London outside of a Sudanese household. After that, I was ready to play with Nick just about any time.

This meal, however, was not playtime. This was serious. This was the Fantastic Adventure, but I had yet to come to the fantastic part. There I was, hacking off pieces from a slab of wombat or komodo dragon or something, probably smuggled in on the bottom of somebody's suitcase, and putting them away while Nick and Charlie looked on eagerly and ate platefuls of the same thing.

"It's not happening," I said.

"What's isn't happening?" Nick replied.

"The big moment. After the buildup you gave me, I was ready to sprout wings or see paradise or something like that. I'm no stranger to the strange, you know. I had rattle-snake in the Rockies. I had horsemeat in France. I had camel in Morocco, and it's not an experience I want to repeat, thank you. It's true I didn't eat the brains of the live monkeys in Hong Kong. Not because it's a myth. It's not. But I hate uncooked meat, and besides, I won't eat something that's kicking me under the table. Anyway, fess up. What is this toothsome but otherwise unremarkable meat I'm eating?"

Nick gave me a long look. And then he said, "Do you know the expression, 'you are what you eat'?"

"Sure."

"Well for once," he said, "it's true."

I know you have questions. Everybody does. So let's get them out of the way.

10

First, if it tasted like anything, it tasted like pork. Not exactly, but close. And it wasn't bad. No muscle or gristle. It was tender, and the flesh was pale. There was very little fat. It tasted good. Not fantastic, like I've said, but good.

I stared down at the meat on the plate and I thought: so this is what it's like. I'd rehearsed a scene in my mind, in case this ever happened: I was lost at sea on a crowded raft, sunburned and sick from drinking salt water, making myself swallow a bloody strip of the captain's leg. But it wasn't like this. This was all wrong. It was too easy. I wasn't ready for the low lights of the restaurant, the black and white photo of Paris on the wall across from me, the soft darkness outside, the weight of the silverware in my hands. I might as well say it. I wasn't ready for it to be so *ordinary*.

I probably would have felt better about it later if I'd been sick when he told me. But I wasn't. I just couldn't connect the thing on my plate with anything else. Or anyone else. That would have taken thought. And the last thing I wanted to do right then was think.

And let me get something straight. I'm not a bad person, and I don't think I say that just because I'm kidding myself. I've done some things I regret, but who hasn't? I'm not mean. I cry when I see sad movies. I used to work for a group that did things for the homeless. I've always paid my taxes on time. I love my mom and dad and my sister.

But this to me was almost like a dare, what these guys were doing. I didn't plan it, remember. This to me was like the time when I was on vacation as a kid, and the other kids in the place where we stayed dared me and my friend Kathy to spend the night in the graveyard across the bay. We took them up on it. She was up all night, but I managed to fall asleep, because I kept this picture in mind of the dead people all welcoming us. And I kept saying to myself, "They're happy to see you," and then I woke up and it was morning. After

11

that, Kathy and I were the queens for the rest of the summer.

This time I wasn't disgusted, much. Not yet, anyway. And I wasn't scared. But you can bet I was pissed off. And I decided to be queen again.

They sat and stared at me, Charlie and Nick. They stared like kids who've watched a fuse burn down on a firecracker they've lit and don't understand why it hasn't gone off. They were waiting for me to explode, to yell for help or throw up or something.

And I smiled and picked up my silverware, as though we'd just been interrupted.

And I cut off a piece of the meat.

"You sorry sons of bitches," I said, through a smile I forced onto my face.

And I ate, as proudly and calmly as a queen.

They grinned then, as if the firecracker they'd watched so anxiously had gone off with a harmless pop and a puff of smoke.

"Welcome to the club," Nick said.

"I'd like to say it's a pleasure, but that might be pushing it."

"Well," Nick said, "that's gratitude for you. I thought you could stomach a little adventure, so to speak. Perhaps I was wrong. This is the top of the pyramid, the moment where we reach out with our little hands and grab the privilege of the gods. Look at them out there," he said, sweeping a hand toward the passers-by out the window. "How many do you think have ever done this? There's them, and there's us. We've taken you over the threshold tonight."

Knowing Nick, he probably thought this little philosophy lesson showed off his macabre genius. But I'd been around Nick long enough to realise that he was about as macabre as a pair of plastic vampire fangs. As for the genius part, Nick might know a lot about a lot of things, but that isn't genius.

I said, "Where did you get it? I mean, it was natural causes, wasn't it?"

"What do you take us for? Murderers?" Nick was genuinely insulted. Terrific. Of all the cannibals in town, I had to get stuck with the crazy ones. "Of course the causes were natural. We're as gentle as lambs. Just adventurous."

"As for where we got it, let's just say it's better for all of us if we don't go into that," Charlie said. "We have a sympathetic friend who knows people. Leave it at that."

They had played with me. I decided it was time to play with them a little.

"I've got to tell you, guys," I said, "I'm a little disappointed." I pushed another piece of meat onto my fork. Don't think, I told myself. Chew and swallow.

"I mean, no offence, Charlie, but I would have expected a little more atmosphere. Candles dripping from wrought-iron candlesticks. Darkness and shadows, so I could really get off on the sinister implications of the thing. But this is positively *suburban*. Like holding executions in a shopping mall. It's not daring. It's just kind of strange and, I don't know, common."

"Clary," Nick replied, "for God's sake, don't be so old-fashioned. That's the point. We've made it modern, haven't we? None of the dire circumstances or discomforts. No plane crashes or shipwrecks to endure. None of the religious mumbo-jumbo that used to justify it in other parts of the world. None of this power over your enemy rubbish."

"So where's the thrill?"

"The thrill, my dear, is in doing it like it doesn't matter. Break the great taboo at night, trot off to work in the morning. We've just moved the goalposts a bit. It's always been the point where savagery starts. We've simply redefined it as the place where the gourmand has to stop. You just can't go any further."

I wasn't about to argue with that.

Nick said, "We've taken the practice out of the jungle, given it a haircut, bought it a nice black suit with a good drape from a Milanese designer, and sat it down at the table of a decent restaurant. And that means we can enjoy it like the civilised people we are. With a sauce of irony."

I picked up my knife and fork again. I started to count backwards, like I do when the dentist is doing something painful, and cut off more meat.

"You know," said Charlie, "there's no instinct to stop you eating your fellow man. It's just something we agree not to do, the way we agree that it's nine o'clock because our watches say it is. Used to happen all the time. Just fell off in some parts of the world faster than others. They say there's even a dialect word in Melanesia for human flesh. They call it 'long pig'. I reckon we stopped eating each other partly out of courtesy, and partly because we didn't believe it was right to eat something as smart as we think we are. Even the best of us are just meat at the end, you know."

Yeah. Thanks, Charlie.

"Now, when is the last time you had a dish that generated so much discussion?" Nick said, and he and Charlie laughed.

The strange thing is, I was laughing, too. And nobody had said anything that I found funny. Keep an eye on that, I thought. I propped that smile back up on my face and said, "So, what's to stop me from getting up out of this chair and running outside, and telling the first cop I see what's going on in here?"

"Nothing," said Charlie. "Not a thing. Try it, if that's what you want. Walk out onto the street, collar a copper and say, 'Officer, I've just been served the flesh of my brethren in that restaurant. Do you duty!' And he will, too. Which means that inside of an hour, you'll likely be trussed up in a canvas jacket with straps on the sleeves. And if the good constable does come over and question us, all we have to do is show him a slab of our finest pork, explain the practical joke we've played, promise to apologise, and with due contrition say we won't do it again. Simple."

I had finished it. At last. All hail the queen.

"Well, I'm impressed," Charlie said. "A lot of people would have been out of here like a shot. And don't worry about it, chook. A few months from now you'll have dinner parties in the palm of your hand when you tell about it. Just leave out the names, if you don't mind."

Now, that was scary. Because it sounded like he was talking sense.

"Are you cold?" Nick asked. I looked down and noticed that my arm was trembling slightly. Not simply my arm, but my whole body. I *was* cold. I felt it at my centre.

"No, I'm fine. But it's time I was going." I said.

"Are you quite sure? I'll see you home," Nick offered.

"No, I don't think so. I want to just walk for a while. I need to digest this whole experience." Riotous laughter. Well, I'm always a card after I've committed the unspeakable.

"You shouldn't be out alone at this time of night. I'll run you home."

"No, seriously." There must have been something in my voice then, because he stopped arguing. I gathered my things and stood up to go.

"Nick," I said, "you're a weird guy. Interesting, but very, very weird."

"That sounds like goodbye."

"It's definitely good-night."

'Good-night," they said, almost as one. Like Tweedledee and Tweedledum. Fe, fi, fo, fum, I ate the flesh of an Englishman. Jesus, Clary, I thought. Get a grip.

"And remember," Charlie added, "mum's the word."

Nick leaned over and gave me a strange, hard kiss. There was no tenderness in it. It was the kiss that seals a pact.

Outside, I passed a couple in the street. The man put his arm around the woman's back. I thought: arm, back, leg, breast. Thigh, rump, belly, rib. I remembered what the meat looked like, like you'd remember the face of someone who mugged you. It was a warm spring night, but I felt cold, cold on the inside. I hailed a taxi.

I got home and crawled into bed. Even with the duvet on, I couldn't stop shivering, so I put on an extra blanket. My teeth still chattered. I couldn't get warm. I fell asleep with the light on.

Everyone has bad experiences. Most of us get over them sooner or later. I was determined to get over this one, let time fade it out until it felt like a dream. It had shaken me up, but it hadn't left any visible scars or hurt my public standing. So as far as I was concerned, there was no reason why I shouldn't just put it behind me.

That was my thinking, anyway.

I found myself wondering about people. I had started to look at them in terms of meat. I wondered whether we all have the same meat under our different skins. Does a fat person taste better than a thin one? Young better than old? Which kind had I eaten? And who was it?

I saw the bodies squirming on the crowded Underground and thought about what makes people different from animals. I wondered if we would still eat sheep if a sheep had painted the Sistine chapel. I decided we'd probably get the sheep to paint first and eat them afterward. As long as they couldn't complain in a language we understood, nobody would care much.

Look, it was just a little running debate with myself. Nothing serious. I was sure of it.

Nick left messages on my answering machine. At first they were terse: "It's Nick. Ring me. I'm in all day." I didn't call back. After the first two messages, I started screening my calls. The messages got longer and appeared less often. He came to my office twice. I told the receptionist to say I wasn't in. Later she said, "Don't worry. He'll get the idea. I had a few like him before I got engaged." Oh, no you didn't, I thought.

I realised I hadn't eaten meat since that night. One afternoon I made myself buy a steak for lunch at the office dining room. I hated the food there, but this was eating for purpose, not pleasure. It was typical cafeteria steak, grey and overcooked. I saw my colleague Maire sitting with some others. The heavy flesh under her arm swayed back and forth as she worked her silverware. I imagined the meat under Maire's pale skin, white and sizzling over a fire, and remembered how she had covered for me when I was sick, and had given me a music box on my birthday. I spat the steak I was chewing into my napkin and ran into the ladies' room with one hand over my mouth.

That evening I made vegetarian *ma po dofu*, family style bean curd: white chunks of tofu in a fiery sauce, with plain rice. As I ate, I remembered the Chinese nickname for tofu: meat without bones. I couldn't finish it.

When I left for home the next night I took a detour into the West End. I stood outside the restaurant in the darkness. It looked cosy inside, dim lights with an orange glow. Through the glass, the customers mimed amusement, concern, indifference. There was a thrill in my gut, like I used to get when I drove with my friends past the houses of boys we liked in high school, just to look at them. I stayed for a few minutes, waiting to see Charlie, but scared at the same time that I actually would. Later, at home, I ate a few crackers for dinner, and went to sleep to dream terrible dreams.

SMOKE SIGNALS

I woke up early, with that feeling you get when you're at the end of an illness, like an invisible barrier has fallen, and everything's suddenly all right. "You seem to have your appetite for life back," said Maire, and I smiled at her choice of words. By lunchtime I was starving, and decided to go out to someplace fun. Everybody else was busy, so I went alone.

There were a few places nearby. Tuscan, Malaysian, Provençal; a pub with a pie shop in back. I couldn't make up my mind. "You don't have all day," I told myself. "Just figure out what you want and get it."

You need to listen to your hunger. You need to let it tell you the name of what you want. While I stood there, uncertain, my hunger told me the name of my desire. And I understood then why I couldn't find it. It wasn't on any restaurant menu in the civilised world. You had to know the right people. And by God, I had met the right people. And just like they promised, I would never forget it.

When I got back to the office, they couldn't believe that their number one fund manager wouldn't stop crying long enough to tell them what the problem was. But that was nothing. They finally calmed me down and asked what had happened, and I told them. The whole story. And what they heard, they *really* couldn't believe.

I don't mind the boredom here, the crummy view outside my window, the long silences. It's kind of nice to have a rest. And it's not all dull. Like, there's a woman down the hall who thinks she's Amelia Earhart. She wakes up the whole floor at night, screaming as the plane goes down, but she tells great stories during the day. I don't even mind the pills much. Sometimes I just pretend to take them, to see if anyone notices the difference.

No, what really gets to me is the food. I mean, it's not just that it's institutional stuff. It's the menu from the boarding

18

school of the damned. Non-stop grey meat. Vegetables boiled into submission. And gooseberries. I'd happily tell everything to the acid casualties and part-time werewolves in my therapy group in exchange for a promise that I'd never see gooseberries again.

I suppose, given what they know about me, it's no wonder they all look a little uneasy when I ask them what's for dinner. And when I sit down and poke through the mess *du jour* on my plate, there's always some helpful attendant hovering over me, saying something like, "Come on, Clary. It won't bite. Not when it's cooked up all nice like that."

And I turn away. And they say, "Clary."

"What?"

"Eat."

Tomorrow

ROY HEATH

Fenton had never concealed his terror of hospitalisation, and many exaggerated statements in this connection had been credited to him.

"I wouldn't last very long," or "I couldn't put up with the food ..." or "I hate to be away from my home."

Now it was thus far! Lying on his back in the dark he surveyed the beds around him, the night nurse bent over a book at her desk and the vague outlines at the end of the ward, where its swing doors led into the endless corridor along which he had been wheeled on his arrival, under the cloud of a suspected heart attack.

Apart from the coughing man whose bed abutted the wall by the door, all the patients appeared to be asleep. Fenton pondered on the reason for his own wakefulness. Would it be like this every night?

He had fallen on the pavement outside Willesden Green Underground Station while his head was spinning, or rather the sky spun above him like a grey, insubstantial ceiling. What happened afterwards, the screeching of the approaching ambulance and the awareness of faces peering down, unsettled him less than the knowledge that he would be taken to a hospital and deposited among strangers.

The strangers were now asleep and no matter how hard he tried he could not recall their faces, except for one, that of the young doctor who examined him and belonged to that breed who never slept, yet managed to make accurate diagnoses while suffering from acute fatigue. He it was who drew the terror from Fenton's expectations, even when he stood idly by as the electrocardiograph equipment went through its evolutions. After the medical man went off Fenton felt an emptiness grow in him, as though he had been abandoned by a friend.

"She's not moved since she sat down at that table," he reflected, looking across the ward at the night nurse reading.

The stark figure, hardly lit despite the strong beam directed onto her book, seemed authoritative in its isolation, head cupped in hands, to give the impression of complete separation from the sleepers in her ward.

Many hours must have passed, because Fenton no longer heard the hum of traffic from the street below, the only sound from the outside world, he was to learn later on. Now, feeling thoroughly alone, he thought of standing up and making a tour of his bed in order to test his heart. But this was to be his last enterprising reflection before he dropped off, or even realised he felt sleepy.

Two days later Fenton was on speaking terms with three patients and could recognise the registrar when he made his rounds at mid-morning, accompanied by the junior doctor. He had already exchanged essential details about his life with one of the new acquaintances whose bed, placed directly opposite his, gave the curious impression of being on a slope and in constant danger of running down towards his. A married man, like himself, his wife had visited him both days, having made her appearance before any other visitor and left after everyone else. Fenton had not only shared the grapes brought by the good woman, but also remarked on their sweetness as she went by on her way home.

The first time the man came over and sat on his bed Fenton judged him to be brash, but soon learned that he was the soul of discretion. Fenton, who had not been prompted to disclose his family circumstance, nevertheless volunteered the information in exchange for what the man had said of himself.

"My wife's abroad," he confided. "It was I who urged her to go and see her sick mother. Odd how things happen, eh? No sooner she went than this."

And from then on, every morning after breakfast Mr Leander came over to his bed to enquire how he had passed the night.

On the fifth day, after Fenton had seen for himself what lay beyond the swing doors, he asked Leander why the clocks in the ward and the shop off the corridor told a different time.

"I know five clocks in this part of the hospital, and they all tell a different time. Nobody knows why, not even the nurses."

Inexplicably, a chill ran through Fenton's body, like a premonition of misfortune; and he recalled his terror of being hospitalised. And he recalled how no one seemed to want to consult a clock in the ward; how chronological time had been effectively abolished and replaced by a kind of circular time, measured in meals and cups of tea. He himself no longer wished to know the day of the week, nor noticed the waxing and waning hum of traffic below, as in the first days when he still carried the outside world fresh within him.

"How long have you been in hospital?" Fenton asked Leander.

"Nine months."

"Nine months!" he repeated involuntarily.

"Why?"

Confused by the question, Fenton could only make a weak, ineffectual reply.

The arrival of the registrar and junior doctor was the sign

for Leander to go back to his bed before Fenton could say something to make amends for his non-committal answer.

As the registrar and his companion passed from bed to bed, stopping at each to consult the patient's chart, he made the resolution to enquire when he was likely to be sent home.

"He's not the big doctor, you know," his Filipino neighbour said, as Fenton settled down to wait for the registrar to go by. "The big shot's coming tomorrow. The consultant! Mr Power and Glory. Wait and see how he walks."

Fenton repaid him with an indulgent expression when, in fact, he wanted to ignore him and concentrate on thinking what to say to the doctor.

"Excuse me!"

The registrar stopped, appearing surprised that a patient had ventured to address him.

"Yes?"

"Can you tell me when I'm going home?"

"The consultant will let you know tomorrow. Your heart attack weakened you and we're not yet sure whether we need to operate."

"Oh," Fenton said speculatively, knowing that as soon as the registrar's back was turned he would probably think of another question he should have asked.

He watched him move away, dressed in a short overall, which could have indicated either status or lack of it. The junior doctor followed him, and, stopping at the Filipino's bed, they began an animated discussion about his condition.

Fenton settled back in a kind of daze. Like Leander he could be in hospital for months, cut off, bemused, and even fall prey to the impairment of his appreciation of time. Everything hinged on the mysterious consultant's decision.

Giving himself up to reflections while pretending to be asleep, he lay on his bed until lunch, after which he stretched out once more. Then he saw Mr Leander approach his bed, no doubt ready for his chat; and for a moment Fenton nearly yielded to the temptation to admit that he was not asleep at all, that he had sought refuge in his thoughts in order to avoid facing up to the possibility of a lengthy internment.

"Yes, Mr Leander, it's like this," Fenton imagined his reflections reaching the disappointed acquaintance. "I'm thinking of the time when I was a boy and my friends and I used to steal fruit from a stranger's yard; and the peculiar excitement connected with the entry into forbidden territory, plucking the star apples ... Maybe it was like stealing fire. I'm not extravagant, Leander, far from it. I've been watching you and came to the conclusion there's no excitement in your life and possibly never has been. Have you ever done anything forbidden? One thing, my friend: why do so few people in the ward go to the television room now they're supposed to be bored out of their wits lying around, sitting about, waiting for visits and trying to recall why they were once interested in clocks? Well I'll tell you! Television reminds them of the outside world they'd rather forget. 'Strue! Besides, it's infinitely more interesting to wait for a meal or a cup of tea than a television programme. Don't you agree? No, you won't. You've never had a thought in your life. Nice men don't muse. 'Struth! Look! When I used to sail my paper boats in the gutters of La Penitence I knew something I've never experienced since. What? What indeed! I can't put it into words, Leander. Smoke, fire, clanging bells, women descending steps to the river with unsalted food as an offering to Watermama. I did not understand then, but at least there were my paper boats oiled on the outside so they wouldn't sink. Incoherent? In truth! I can't think of anything more incoherent than what the registrar said to me and what I didn't say to him, and what the consultant might well say to me tomorrow after having delivered me up to his incoherent scanners. I am very coherent. I'm attached to my images. I was not bewildered in childhood when the world seemed like a circus; and I could remain for ages at my window watching the almond trees shaking in the wind. Incoherent indeed! You risk drowning in your abstract words, I'm telling you . . . Tonight you must watch the nurse at her table after the ward's asleep and the lights are out. Tell me what you notice about her. No, I'll tell you. She's an abstraction. Yes, man. Did you know she lives on the compound? She does! But that's not the most interesting thing about her. Come closer, because I don't want anyone to hear what I'm going to tell you. She's institutionalised! Yes! I have it on good authority. She's never lived anywhere but on the compound since her student days. Now how about that! Ah! But you should have noticed before me, since you yourself are institutionalised; you've lost all interest in the outside world and even in your wife. Why're you shaking like that? It's plain for all to see. She comes here day in, day out, bringing you every imaginable titbit and you offend her by giving most of it away. Oh, you haven't noticed! Everybody else has. Why does she stay longer than the other visitors? She comes seeking your soul my friend. It's her visit to the underworld where even time is snuffed out; and if she's not careful she'll lose you, and the only explanation she'll glean from the doctors is that you're the victim of a heart attack. Very convenient. That's coherence for you! . . . My father was a very coherent man, you know. An atheist who never lost an argument. He died clutching at a cross my mother was holding above his head.

> Hold thou the Cross
> Before my closing eyes.

Of course that proves nothing. When a drowning man clutches a straw that doesn't mean that the straw is capable of saving him. But it does make you wonder at all this coherence.

"I've been in this hospital less than a week, but I bet you haven't observed what the Filipino young man in the bed next to mine does at night. You must have seen that his light is always out until about nine. He goes home! He meets his wife in secret at the entrance and she drives him home every single night. She refuses to accept the hospital terms of confinement; and unlike your wife who timidly sits about waiting for the signal to leave she snatches him away to feed him at home. For Heaven's sake don't tell anyone, or his soul will be in danger ... And how would you describe that, Mr Leander? As coherence or incoherence? To tell the truth I'm not sure I know the meaning of the word. Yet, when you come to think of it comparisons aren't fair. These Filipinos live in a different world, a world of fire and smoke.

"I know what you're dying to say: that you've never heard me talk so much before. You're surprised, eh? I'm not talkative as a rule, except when I'm anxious. Tomorrow ... always this damned tomorrow. We're haunted by yesterday and anxious about tomorrow, don't you think? It's this consultant who will come tomorrow and seal my fate. He will appear from nowhere and, with one sentence decide whether I go under the knife or not. A man I don't even know. A woman? It might be. What difference does it make? Except that they're more conscientious than men. They'd cut you up with more gusto, I'd say. Cynical? You've got these words you trot out! Incoherent, cynical. Am I right or not? If I'm right why accuse me of cynicism? And besides none of these fancy terms are decent one-syllable words. Try using words of one syllable for a change and you'll see things you ought to see. All around you the most, the most ... ah ... the most intense dramas are being played out and as far as you're concerned nothing's happening, simply because you're blinded by words of more than one syllable. Have you ever wondered, for instance, what the consultant's attitude to me will be if he quarrelled with his wife in the morning? Damn it, man! Think!

"I've got another secret to share with you. That is, of course, if you're interested. Yes? Well, I only shaved and spruced myself up this morning because all the others did so. I mean I felt a lot better for it in the end; but left to myself I would sit around, unkempt and uncaring. Which sets me to thinking: how much of our behaviour are we responsible for, eh? How much of what we do isn't done out of shame? Now think of that my disyllabic friend! You're not interested. Doesn't surprise me in the least. Your world revolves around the games you and your wife play and nothing exists apart from that. But mark my word, you're in serious danger of being devoured by apathy! Every day you remain in this place you lose a bit of your soul ... And I wonder whether your wife is as timid as she pretends, eh? It may well be she knows perfectly well what she's doing. It ... may ... be ... she doesn't want to save your soul at all. She visits you in the underworld with ... No, it couldn't be. A woman with such good taste in fruit must be the soul of decency.

"I know, I know. I use these two-syllable words as well. Damn it, so what! You're not wise, you know. I'll set you a little task, which should earn you a modicum of wisdom. In talking to people, to a person, say, someone you know well, pay particular attention to what they dislike, what they continually criticise, and you'll notice a strange thing; this thing they abhor in others sticks out a mile in their own personality. An old teacher of mine hated pupils who cheated in class or at games. In fact he hated any manifestation of immorality. Well you don't know this man, so there's no point going on about him. But, my friend, he was a vicious brute and drove his family to despair. 'Strue!

"Anyway, let's get back to our muttons, our mehh, mehh sheep. What I was saying before you accused me of ... something or other, my disyllabic friend. Come to think of it I don't believe it's anxiety about tomorrow that's loosened my tongue. I think it's this hospital. There's something eerie about it. You haven't noticed? For instance that no one hears a clock ticking, or that no one raises his voice, or that the night nurse almost begs you to take a sleeping tablet, whether you're an insomniac or not. You never thought of it? But then how can you notice when you're not trained to notice? The only thing people do that they're not trained to do is suck at the breast ... I'd like to say a lot to you, but the trouble is you've never left home. Oh no you haven't! If your wife didn't come visiting one day you'd weep like a child. Well one thing I'd like to say, whether you understand or not ... Do you know what is the most ... or at least *one* of the most remarkable and damaging inventions? The electric bulb! You snigger ... You always snigger at what you don't understand; but the fact is that the bulb robbed us of fire ... What's the point? You're as ignorant as my uncle Therphelio, who never understood what was wrong with a non-ticking clock. People like you are a triumph of education. You're trained not to notice and you revel in your ignorance. Speak of some royal personage and you'll prick up your ears and grunt as though you're about to enter your seventh heaven ... It defeats me why I enjoy your company, but then there's a certain pleasure in talking down to someone. You're such a good listener. Yet what else can you do? Float away in one of my remembered paper boats? I apologise, my friend Leander. You bring out the worst in me, even when you say nothing.

"Leander, my friend, I wish I felt as superior as I make myself out to be. Fact is, I have great doubts, huge doubts that grow and grow when I'm not talking ..."

Fenton gave up his imagined monologue, feeling suddenly

that he had taken advantage of Leander, who, absorbed in his newspaper, did not suspect that he was the object of his friend's attention. He lay down, wondering whether it would be appropriate to fall asleep in broad daylight in his enclosed world.

The next morning, while the patients were in suspense at the consultant's imminent appearance Fenton pretended to have no interest in the visit. Having had a shower and taken his breakfast he settled in the chair next to his bed with a book borrowed from Mr Leander. And even when the little band consisting of the consultant, the registrar and the overworked houseman irrupted into the ward, Fenton continued reading with an impressive show of indifference. Out of the corner of his eye he noticed that the consultant wore no overall, unlike the other two, thereby banishing any comparison with them. But to Fenton's surprise, his tone was sociable, even indulgent.

"You have a problem of drainage as well, Mr West; that's why you were in eurology before you were brought here . . ."

And he went on to explain to the patient that he was not long for this world; in such a gentle manner that the condemned man must have deemed it an honour to be dispatched to the other side by him.

Fenton, chastened by the discovery that the consultant was human after all, put away the book, ashamed at the need he felt to play-act. He followed the smiling figure with his eyes until it stood over the bed next to his, accompanied by its acolytes.

Mr Leander, who had already been seen by the consultant, kept gesticulating to Fenton from the other side of the ward; but the latter, thinking that his friend wanted to warn him about his dress, could find nothing wrong with his shirt and trousers, the same he had been wearing when brought in.

And before he had completed his examination, the great man was upon him.

"And how are we this morning?"

"Well enough," Fenton answered, irritated by the gratuitous familiarity of the question.

After a swift examination of Fenton's chart the consultant smiled and then began to move off in the direction of the Filipino's bed.

"Excuse me! Excuse me. I've been waiting a long time for your visit."

And here Fenton's rising confidence impelled him along in a way he had not believed possible earlier in the day.

"Can you tell me when I'll be going home?"

The transformation in the consultant's features took Fenton by surprise and he automatically looked over at Leander, who could not have seen the offended expression.

"Home?" said the consultant. "In your condition? ... Mr ..." and at this point he consulted the chart. "Mr Fenton, your heart wouldn't stand your going down to the street ..."

Then, suddenly resuming his affable manner he said, "Your tests were not favourable. I'll be studying them more closely this afternoon and then will decide if we're to operate or not."

On he moved, like the engine of some imposing train, leaving a dismayed Fenton with his right hand placed on his defective heart.

His wife was arriving back in the country the following day and would be coming straight to the hospital. He had hoped to surprise her by being ready to accompany her home.

The drama had unfolded so quickly and the consultant had spoken so quietly, no one except the Filipino young man had witnessed it.

As soon as the doors closed behind the doctors Mr Leander came over to Fenton's bed.

"What did he say?" he enquired.

Fenton shook his head in answer.

"Are you going to have an op?"

"I don't believe so," Fenton answered. "I'm waiting to hear about the tests and then I'll be off. Tell me, how long's the Filipino been in here?"

"Fourteen months, I think. Ask him."

"And the man in the bed next to yours?"

"More than two years."

"I see," Fenton said, turning to Mr Leander with a desperate look. "Has anybody in this hospital ever gone . . .?"

Fenton hesitated to complete the question, fearful of the answer he might receive.

Once Leander returned to his bed Fenton recalled how, that day, he had not consulted the clock once and, like the other patients, had begun to show an unusual interest in the arrival of meals.

Waking up with a start, he looked around him as though he had just realised he was in a place other than his own home, and came to the conclusion that it must be one or two in the morning. Rain was lashing the window panes above Leander's head, lit more by the street lamp than the feeble light from the night nurse's table. Certain that something was wrong he scanned the ward until his eyes fell on the bed next to his. It was empty! The Filipino's wife had not brought him back.

Fenton got up and bent over his neighbour's bed to make sure that what he thought he noticed was indeed true. Then he lay down again, astonished at the risk his fellow patient had taken. His thoughts finally settled on his own fate, which was to be decided that very day by the enigmatic consultant. Should he be going home he would miss Leander, and even the shadowy Filipino, whom he envied for his youth and enterprise. Such a dark night! Such a wind! He would have liked to stand at the window and listen to the occasional car go by far below. Were they not suspended, like the earth itself, like their very lives? He called to mind his wife's little attentions, the many postponements of her trip abroad to visit her ageing parents, and the things he had stored up to tell her about the hospital. He thought of Leander's wife, as familiar to the patients as any day nurse. And finally he found himself engaged in another imaginary conversation with his friend, who would in all probability wake up the following morning and be surprised to learn that there had been a storm while he slept.

"Somebody should tell you a few home truths, Leander. No, let me finish. The fact is you don't appreciate your wife."

Leander had expressed the opinion that his wife spent so much money on him out of a secret longing to be loved.

"No, you don't appreciate her. You're always going on about certain people back home when you were young. And have you noticed something about all these generous people you drool on about? They kept open house! You walked into their homes, said a few words of greeting and then made straight for the fridge. Yes! You told me so yourself! Well, listen carefully to people of your ilk and sooner or later they'll say, 'People *like* me'. Yes, the words will slip out, and sometimes those of your kind who've got some awareness of themselves will put their hands to their mouths to stop the leakage. Oh yes, my friend Leander. You takers want to be loved as badly as the givers you wash your mouth on. Yet you're not fit to lick their boots. My advice to you is to get permission to go out and buy your wife something, some little thing . . . What's the use? You'd sleep through anything. Your whole life's a long, long sleep, full of wrong-headed dreams. Rain? You're afraid of rain? A storm? I like it. It's reassuring. Do you know what the sister in a maternity ward did once, some years ago? When an infant started bawling all the other infants began screaming as well. Then the sister put on a record of a woman's heartbeat ... Boodoop—boodoop—boodoop—. The effect was miraculous! Within a minute the crying stopped. You've ever heard of a thing like that? Why did nobody ever think of the idea before? Rain has the same soothing effect on me. Mind you, I prefer rain on a zinc roof, a resonant deluge that fills the world with its sound. When we had our last conversation I was depressed and could only think of the consultant's visit. Tonight I feel different, calm ... and I don't know why.

"Leander, I didn't mean what I said the last time. I'm not responsible for what passes through my mind. Some of my thoughts wouldn't bear uttering."

Fenton, oppressed by his own reflections, got up and went to a window further down the ward, where he stood looking out at the fugitive threads of rain. Did anything matter? Shadows of people, rocking chairs from long ago, censored words, black nights; some things were buried when we came abroad, old clocks with Roman numerals and December masks. "Does anything matter?" "Read the Upanishads!"

Down below a single vehicle goes by from time to time, almost noiseless through the double windows.

"Will I ever get out? Like the visiting consultant, like the Filipino and Leander's wife? Is this the underworld seen from below? Do I exist? Concrete trees, shorn of their branches stand immobile in the rain. They say two beggars live in the recess of the library doors. Tomorrow Irene will come and tell me all about the mountains and the sea and notice the stench of my unchanged clothes."

On his way back to bed Fenton was intercepted by the night nurse.

"Mr Fenton, have you seen Mr Pestano?"

"Who?"

"The Filipino gentleman in the bed next to yours. Do you know where he's gone?"

"No idea."

"Why are you up?"

"I went to look out at the rain."

"What!?"

"The rain."

"My God! What we've got to put up with!" she exclaimed, walking away in anger.

The following morning the consultant arrived on time, pursued by four other doctors and the registrar and the Sister.

Fenton, who had put on his shoes, remained standing beside his bed, determined to make it clear that he had every intention of going home, whatever the prognosis.

The consultant seemed to be taking twice as long to do his round as the day before, while Fenton tried to appear as calm as possible.

"The rain stopped! The rain stopped!" he kept repeating to himself, in the way yoga adepts intone a well-tried mantra.

The rain had indeed stopped and the wind had fallen. Leander, on catching his eye, gestured that he would be coming over as soon as the consultant left.

The Filipino's bed was still empty, and it occurred to Fenton that perhaps the Sister was accompanying the consultant in order to explain his absence.

Fenton raised two fingers of his right hand and one of his left in an effort to indicate to Leander that he felt there was a two to one chance he would not need to be operated on; and as the consultant approached the neighbour's bed on his left he repeated the sign more emphatically.

"They always do it clockwise," he thought, and with that

drew his sleeve across his forehead to wipe away the sweat.

Then, despite the suspense at the impending visitation of the God-man, despite his vigilance, Fenton found himself unexpectedly surrounded by the group.

"Mister Fenton!" came the hearty greeting. "The impatient patient ... Good news. There won't be an operation. Besides, you can go home as soon as you feel strong enough to walk from here to the staircase. The nurse will give you a prescription and instruct you on how to prepare yourself for a long life ... But isn't that what you desired so fervently yesterday?"

"Yes, yes," Fenton answered, not knowing what to make of his cool reaction to the good news.

"Good! Follow instructions to the letter and we'll meet in Paradise."

Ignoring the Filipino's empty bed, the group passed on to the next patient, then a few minutes later disappeared, like a pack of dogs that had successfully marked their territory.

To avoid facing Leander, who was getting ready to join him, Fenton set off for the washroom barefooted, with a towel over his arm; and on the way he could not help looking up at the clock hanging on the wall.

In the past six days a transformation had occurred within him, a small, but ineluctable change connected with the suspension of time and a certain void belonging to primeval forces. He recalled how he had read too much into the news that some patients had been hospitalised for months and how he had been affected by the disclosure that the clocks were unreliable, as though he *knew* he had already succumbed to a fatal sloth, yet refused to acknowledge it. His professed contempt for Leander and admiration of his Filipino neighbour, like oblique revelations of his own condition, had passed unnoticed for what they were.

When another patient came into the washroom Fenton

left, but went to the television hall instead of going back to his bed. An old woman from a nearby women's ward was sitting alone, her steel grey hair framing her head and her arms stretched out along the arm-rests of her chair. On the television screen a singer and her accompanist had just started Richard Strauss's song "Morgen". The singer stood by, waiting for the long piano introduction to come to an end, and then, abruptly, emitted a sound so pure that Fenton sat down in an empty chair a few feet from the old woman to listen. And at the end, turning to his companion in order to comment on the singer's voice, he saw that she was weeping silently. He stared at her before looking round at the bare walls and the gutted furniture, and remembered that his wife would be coming to see him in the afternoon, straight from the airport.

"Would you like me to get you something?" he asked the old woman.

"No thank you," she said, not bothering to look at him. "Do you know what day it is?"

Fenton could not say what day it was, but promised to find out.

And while going off to consult a calendar he realised, with dismay, that he had walked the distance which, according to the consultant, qualified him to go home.

Just Below the Surface

KATE NIVISON

I am not what you might call a sound sleeper, being somewhat of a nervous disposition when it comes to noises at night, and what with the burglaries and people putting horrible things through letter boxes, you can't be too careful. At least that is what I say when my husband teases me about it.

"Indrani," he says. "You would wake up if a butterfly passes the window." He is more educated than I, and has many good expressions like that.

Not that I was lying there thinking about horrible things through the letter box, because that is why we moved out a little to Wanstead, so as not to worry about all that. You expect that kind of nonsense round Brick Lane and those places, but Kumar says you don't get that sort of thing where the suburbs are green and leafy and the houses expensive— although myself, I'm not sure what leafiness or double garages have to do with it.

So when I heard these scratching and scuffy noises, I thought at first it was next door even though it was the dead of night. Our house is semi-detached, but a fine big one with coloured glass windows and a lot of extensions and modernisings. The kitchen is all fitted very nicely, and there were carpets throughout, which I was glad to see because I hardly would have known where to start with all that, after only the little flat above the shop.

Anyway, there I was lying beside Kumar, who is beginning to snore a little these days, and there it was again for the second night. Then I began to think that maybe it wasn't next door with some peculiar hobby, like doing the decorating only at two o'clock in the morning. It seemed to be coming from downstairs, and in particular our own so nicely fitted kitchen. It couldn't have been the children. Hanif is only a baby, and Laila is six but never wakes all night.

It seemed to scratch and scrabble for a while, then it would stop, only to start again, and I was now thinking that this wasn't anything mechanical like the fridge playing up. It sounded alive. Suddenly I sat up in bed. It was mice! Here in our nice new home, I was hearing mice. I felt so ashamed. It was not the kind of kitchen that should be having mice, and I was sure there had been nothing like this when we had first moved in.

So I lay there for a long time worrying and thinking I would say nothing to Kumar, or he would say I was a bad housewife, and what should I do to get rid of them. Next morning after Kumar had gone to work and Laila to school, I made sure Hanif was safe in his cot and had a good look round. I didn't see anything at first, but when I looked in the cupboard under the worktop beside the sink where I keep the rice, I could see that a hole had been chewed in one of the thick brown paper sacks and there was some grain spilt. Also there was a much larger hole in the wooden floor of the cupboard, so this must have been the rustlings and scufflings I was hearing. We were being burgled by mice, and it looked likely to continue on a regular basis.

Now that my opinion was confirmed, I still didn't know what to do. The lady next door seemed very nice when we first arrived and asked if there was anything I wanted to know about the area and didn't Hanif have lovely brown eyes. But I hadn't seen her since and didn't feel like going to her and saying "Excuse me, I think we have mice and what can be done about it?" She might have screamed and thought we were dirty or something. So I got out the Pears Cyclopaedia which Kumar had bought on recommendation to help me learn about things, but I couldn't find anything on mice, not even under Medical Matters.

Of course I know that you can get poisons and traps, but with Hanif beginning to crawl, I was hoping that there would be something new and civilised. Also Kumar always takes me shopping, and how could I explain buying a mouse-trap in Sainsbury's or wherever?

There was nothing for it but to take Hanif in his pushchair and go out looking for myself, which so far I had not done in Wanstead. It was quite a long walk to the shops past a lot of leafiness which is not safe at night from what you read in the papers they put through the door about men with no trousers in the bushes, which seems a strange and shameful thing to me.

My sandals were not really up to the walk, and by the time I got to the shops, the first thing I had to get was some comfortable shoes to walk back. So I got some trainers at Freeman Hardy's and immediately felt better, although they looked a little funny with my rose-pink sari. The girl seemed so nice that I asked her where I could buy mouse-traps. There were mainly women in there at this time, mostly pensioners or mothers with toddlers and soon the whole shop was offering advice as to which shop to try next. I felt a little embarrassed at causing such a stir, and everything was going fine until one old lady said more or less to the shop at large, "Of course, you have to keep the place clean, otherwise you'll never get rid of them," and I left feeling not much bigger than a mouse myself. "Don't forget some cheese, dear," said another as I went out. "They like a bit of cheese."

From then on, I was too embarrassed to go anywhere except to places where you can help yourself. In the end I found the traps in Woolworth's. As I was not sure how many mice there were, I thought I better get half a dozen, and the girl at the till said, "Got an invasion on your hands? They really give me the creeps, the little buggers," which made me feel much better.

"Are you having mice yourself?" I asked hopefully, thinking that perhaps here was an expert who might even know about which cheese was best, because we are not cheese eaters ourselves.

"Haven't seen one for years," she said. "Not since we got the new flat. Old place, is it?"

"It's in Broadmead," I replied.

"Oh *is* it," she said, and I knew what she was thinking straight away. What are Asians doing in nice houses like those? Turning them into slums by the sound of it.

So I didn't ask about the cheese. Hanif was getting restless so I didn't want to take him round Sainsbury's, but fortunately, I saw some cheese in a butcher's shop, which surprised me. He asked which sort I wanted and how much. Having no idea, I just pointed to one that looked hard and yellow and said, "Oh about a pound, please," and was surprised to see how much there was.

When I got home I hid everything, even my new trainers, which really I was very pleased with, at the back of the next kitchen cupboard to the one with the hole. I couldn't very well put the cheese in the fridge or Kumar would wonder why I'd bought it. Also the catches on the cupboards are the magnetic type, and as Hanif is crawling, I didn't want him opening the doors and finding the traps. So I had to wait until Kumar was getting ready for bed to fix up a trap. I put on a really big piece of cheese and wanted to do another, but my husband was calling me.

"What is that sour smell on you?" he asked when I got into bed, and I had to go and wash my hands again, but really I was quite excited lying there listening to see if my plan would work. Maybe if I managed to catch one mouse, the others would run away and I would be saved any more trouble.

There were a lot more scufflings that night, and as soon as Kumar had gone to work, I immediately went to inspect my trap. But oh the disappointment! The cheese had gone, the trap had sprung, but there was nothing in it. Worse, it looked as if the mice had been having a picnic. Grains were spilling from several holes now, and they had started on the chickpeas and chipati flour. I cleared up the mess and wondered what to do next, thinking maybe two or three traps and less cheese.

Unfortunately that evening, Kumar did something he almost never does, which is look in the kitchen cupboards, but a friend was getting us a good price on some tins of ghee, and he wanted to see how much space we had.

I watched in horror as he pulled out the trainers and cheese, all the while asking if his wife had gone mad to be buying such things without his knowledge and was I going out jogging on the quiet. Bravely I said that cheese was good for the baby, and that my feet had hurt. So he said I would soon be wearing trousers and eating roast beef, and how much of this smelly stuff was the baby to eat, for goodness sake. He got so excited that he didn't check the other cupboard.

The next night was a truly horrible one. I set three traps in the cupboard before going to bed. Maybe I dozed off, but we were both awakened by a dreadful squawking and a thumping noise.

"Whatever is that? Has a bloody cat got stuck some-where?" cried Kumar. "Am I crazy or is the noise in the kitchen?"

Very much afraid now, I followed him downstairs. It was

coming from the cupboard and I yelled at him to take care. He hooked a broom under the door and pulled, and then we got the shock of our lives. Out tumbled the biggest, fiercest rat you ever saw, thrashing about and squealing with its tail caught in the trap, which it was thumping about all over the place.

I screamed, a very loud scream, I'm afraid, and what happened next was worse. The rat somehow turned on itself and began to gnaw at its own tail. Then with a final screech that sounded as much like triumph as pain, it broke free and disappeared down the hole leaving a slimy trail of blood on the cupboard floor.

Kumar dropped the broom and the door snapped closed.

"Oh my God, this is terrible, terrible," he kept saying, and rushed to put everything he could find in front of the cupboard. At least then I could tell him about the mouse-traps and the mystery cheese. "We will tell no one about this," he said. "Or they will think we are responsible. Tomorrow I will block up the hole, and get some poison and some bigger traps. Then we must move all the food to a different cupboard."

All this was done very successfully, but the next night was even worse. At least now, Kumar was listening with me. There seemed to be even more scratching and I was sure I heard one of the traps give a hard click. There was no screeching this time, but the scratchings continued on and off for most of the night.

Next morning we opened the other cupboard, fearful of what we might find. There was a dead rat caught in one of the special traps Kumar had bought, and it wasn't the one with half a tail. A nasty hole just as big as the blocked one had appeared. Some of the poisoned bait had gone and also more food.

"That is enough for me," said Kumar as he picked the

whole nasty thing up on a shovel and put it outside the back door. "There are laws here about this sort of thing. We must call the Council."

How to describe the next week! Two men from the Council arrived and asked a lot of questions about the infestation—that's what they called it. I showed them the holes and the damaged food bags, also the bait and the dead one outside.

I said that it had been a great shock to me, because I hadn't been expecting to see such things, not in Wanstead where everything looked so respectable. Even in Brick Lane we had not actually seen any rats, although the market people said they were there.

"It's with London being a port in the old days," said the senior one. "They came over on the ships, you see. From out East, so they say. Still you'd know all about that, I suppose."

"I have never been out East, as you put it," I said a little frostily. "But I know many big cities have rats. They seem to like cities. But surely not in the suburbs. And why have they come to us? Can it be my fault?"

"Perhaps they fancied an Indian take-away," grinned the young one. "No offence, love—I'm partial to a curry on a Friday night myself."

The boss man was not so cheerful. "Your best hope is that you've got a few strays disturbed by cable laying or road works and they're looking for somewhere to set up house," he said, and explained that, if this was the case, they would expect to find no more than half a dozen rats which could be cleared out by bait and traps if we were careful and patient.

"And what is my worst hope?" I asked.

They looked at each other in a funny sort of way.

"We'll have to see about that," said the boss man.

He said they'd know in about a week. Meanwhile it was very important to keep a count of the rats caught, report any strange smells and how much bait or food had gone and to keep the children out of the kitchen. That week three more rats were caught, then suddenly the catching seemed to stop, and no more loose bait was taken. I reported a horrible smell from the cupboard under the stairs, and they had to take up some floor boards to find it. I didn't look, but it made me glad no more bait had gone.

That very same week, on the Friday night, one of our shops was broken into. Kumar wanted it reported as a racist attack as well as a burglary because of what they had written on the walls. It seemed to him that the object was not so much stealing as to frighten us, which in many ways is more upsetting. After all you can insure against theft but not against hatred. But the police were not interested and said it was just an ordinary burglary.

All that was very bad and upsetting for us, so it wasn't surprising that we were not sleeping too well, even if we hadn't got our little problem downstairs.

Then one night, I heard a sort of click, but it wasn't a trap. It sounded like one of the cupboard doors closing. Since there was no way I could have left one of them open, I was very puzzled, but I didn't want to wake Kumar because the trouble with the shop had made him very exhausted.

By morning I had put it down to my imagination—until I was getting breakfast and noticed a rat dropping right on the draining board and some toothmarks on a wooden spoon. Never before had they come outside those cupboards. I squealed and rang up the rat men, and Barry, the older one, said he'd pop round for a look.

When he arrived he had a rolled map under his arm which he put on the table. He tested the cupboard catches and laughed. "Magnetic," he said. "Do you know what they do?"

I shook my head.

"They've got these sussed out," he said. "If they want to get out for a wander, they just stand up on their cute little hind legs and push. One squeezes into the space as it opens, and the rest walk over him."

"And he stays there until they want to go back inside and down the hole?" I squealed.

"Not always," said Barry calmly. "Very unreliable, rats. Dead smart—but unreliable. Know what I mean?"

It took a moment, but then I saw what he was saying. I looked round the kitchen in horror. He meant there could be one, maybe more, lurking anywhere in here right now!

"Now for the *really* bad news," said Barry and began to unroll the map. "I have to tell you that because of the pattern of infestation, we suspect that these rats are not strays. I reckon they're coming straight up from the sewers." He tapped the map. "I checked. There's a big sewer pipe right under this house."

I sat down very hard on a kitchen chair feeling a little dizzy, but not so dizzy that I didn't forget to look under it first. I said to excuse me but I didn't really understand what he was saying.

"It's quite simple, love," he said. "The sewage from half London comes through this way. Goes through Beckton and finishes up out by Barking Creek. Got to go somewhere, innit?"

"But what about the rats?" I whispered.

"Well, they come along for the ride," he said. "It's like rush hour on the Underground down there. There's millions of them, just below the surface. Makes you think, doesn't it?"

I said it certainly did, but why were they suddenly coming up in my nice new kitchen.

"System can't take it any more, know what I mean?" he said. "It all needs redoing. Meanwhile, when one of the little bastards, begging your pardon, finds a crack, he starts exploring and brings his friends."

I asked him how he could tell all this, and he said it was all quite simple, love. Rats born in sewers learned things from each other. They knew how to open unlocked doors, get out of traps or avoid them, kill cats and not to take bait. Some of them were now actually immune to different poisons, and they seemed to be growing bigger. These were called super rats. As my rats, that's what he called them, *my* rats, were no longer dying or getting caught, but were still around as large as life, taking food and playing tricks, we had to assume this is what they were.

"Do you know what I've seen 'em do?" he was saying almost fondly as I was staring at the cupboards. "A place we went to out West Ham way, the shopkeeper, one of your lot, said they were stealing eggs. Naturally we thought he was telling porkies or seeing things, so we watched one night. One of the little buggers, well, a big bugger he was—King Rat, you might say—he got this egg, rolled over on his back holding it to his belly with his front paws, and the others pulled him along by his tail. True as I'm standing here—they pulled him back to the hole, egg and all. Like I said, a bit unreliable, rats, but they're smart. Survivors. Grafters. You could almost admire them really."

"So what do we do next?" I whispered.

"Like I said, it's very simple, love. The pipe's right under your living room. We'll start there and hope we find the crack pretty smartish. That's it darling, you have a good cry, and I'll start working on how to get the floor up."

Oh my goodness. Here was this man loving and darling me, and saying he is going to dig up my living room, without even my husband here.

"But what will we do when all this is going on?" I asked, feeling as if the rats were already crawling over me.

"That's all right. We'll probably be able to leave the stove and that. You can live upstairs," he replied, as if this was quite the normal thing to do.

"What about the children?" I said.

He was very reassuring. "Don't worry about it," he said. "You just keep them well out of the way. We'll put a grille over the hole at night."

My legs felt wobbly. I asked him how long he thought it would take. He said he couldn't say. It depended if they found the crack quickly and how bad it was. Mainly all you could do was patch it up and hope for the best.

I said all this was quite amazing. I had no idea that there was this sort of thing in a place that was supposed to be civilised and what would the neighbours think.

He shrugged. Then he said a funny thing, this man from the Council who was supposed to be helping us. "It's all down there," he said. "Just below the surface. I know it and you know it. Everyone knows it." He rolled up the map, but I didn't like the way he was smiling at me. "Anyway, we can't kill them all. The main thing is to send them back where they came from, and then pretend they ain't there. Know what I mean?"

Oh yes, this time I knew exactly what he meant.

Rosita Travels by Tube

A story of love and death

CLARE PALMIER

Rosita didn't speak English, only a few words, enough to embarrass other people or make them laugh or make them talk at her slowly and very loudly. She did not want to be in London but arrives in this story out of her own necessity. She appeared on the platform of King's Cross Piccadilly Line (southbound) with her face glued to the glass and her body wedged between several other passengers. She is one of many. She clutched a piece of paper with an address written on it that she couldn't pronounce and a drawing of her with a large hat on by her niece (Will you see the Queen, Auntie?) There were a lot of smells inside the compartment. Enforced proximity made people smell more—almost as a reaction against the anonymity of the streets; odorous come ons and get offs stung the insides of nostrils. Travel peak time and you become suddenly aware of living, sweating, eating, shitting bodies, vying for attention. Right up against you bones lean heavily into your flesh, searching for a raw nerve; pushing you against another body or a flat hard surface. Erections are felt but not mentioned. It is a rigorous anatomy lesson. Rosita had found an elbow that didn't belong to her. It nestled by her side, resting furtively on her hip. She humoured it. It was a family habit to swallow two cloves of garlic a day against aggressive tendencies. She squeezed her precious paper into a gap and showed it to a pair of eyeballs that seemed to belong to each other. (Her name was Rosita which would make English people laugh as they always laughed at anything which sounded vaguely illicit, and Rosita would frown and if she ever heard of the names Jane or Sharon she would know it was preferable to have been called Rosita.)

There were forty people crammed into the one compartment and none of them were true Londoners. Only one of them could truly speak of four British grandparents and another would lie. His mother was Lithuanian and he lived in a very white, working-class area in Bermondsey where BNP graffitied every wall; with feelings of self-preservation he had recreated his history on many a night in The Standard. His parents did not put in an appearance at his local but allowed their son his safety and moved to a suburb in Essex which did not demand any sense of belonging. Rosita, Rosita, what a name he would have thought, clutching blindly at its mystery, hearing it in a Spanish resort on his two weeks off; drowning his fearfulness in the sea, in the sun, in the wine. And then back to London to hide in the betting shop.

Rosita was looking for her sister. She had come from Casares to Gatwick Airport to Victoria Station to chat with a Spanish newspaper seller who told her that London was full of foreign people—it was beautiful and dirty—she was beautiful—London was lonely—people were rude and he hadn't slept with a woman since he came over. Rosita was a little bit afraid in London. It made her heart rise and stick behind her ribs and even when she sat she did not feel like she was sitting but that she was running with someone behind her. It was the feeling that she usually kept for when someone was sick or dying, or when a baby was being born. There were lots of other people afraid in London, but most of them called it stress so that they could get paid for it. She felt sorry for the newspaper seller from Malaga but she was silently out

of breath and a romance at this point would divert her
energies. A calm panic fills her body and almost topples her
from her three-inch heels.

The Japanese elbows precipitated Rosita's departure and
her arrival on the platform. On her knees she arrived in the
heart of London, with a graze on her leg which trickled a
rivulet of warm blood. The Japanese man videoed her body
efficiently before the doors closed and the train moved off.
Later he would make a neat in-camera edit and juxtapose
Rosita with a group of obsolete punks from Poland nestling
around the statue of Eros in Piccadilly Square. Why have you
come here? We saw pictures of it. We wanted to see. We dye
our hair. We harm no one. We like the cinema. We like
British music. We are not angry. It's very good London.
There is always someone who looks weird. Goodbye. We
would like to try ecstasy.

Rosita had come to find her sister who had been living in
London for five years. Rosita had not tried ecstasy. No one
had heard about E or her sister. London had swallowed
Mercedes whole. Mercedes was the married-to-an-English
sister who had been lost to a foreign city and an English
gentleman called Frank. But now, with the death of her
father, Rosita came bearing a home-made cheese wrapped in
a tea towel and a "shop local" carrier bag and an obligation
to pass on the news. Rosita was unknowingly like a character
from a sub-titled film appearing in red skirt, high heels, beads
and embroidered scarf. She was not an innocent when it
came to people disappearing in London. 'Berto had gone two
years ago after a small cruelty on her part. Rosita was very
real just like all the other strange people half glimpsed as they
appear; from out of a dark corner, off the cover of a
magazine, from a memory locked inside the imagination. Did
you see that? Where were they from? What were they doing?
Why were they wearing those shoes? Why did they have dirt

on their face? How strange and wonderful. She had received a card showing a red bus and a policeman and saying that he loved her and when he felt it was right he would come back to love her more closely. For a while she had wondered if the policeman and bus had signified an accident or a brush with the law. Men often gave you big clues to assist in over-looking the specific but after some thought she put these pictures out of her head. She was no innocent and knew that he must have got lost in the machinations of his heart or something to do with money. Both of which take up a lot of time. By which time she might have forgiven herself and got old and ready for black jumpers and knitting for nieces' and nephews' children. (Does the Queen really wear tights all year, Auntie?)

She sat on the platform and took off her shoes and looked unique. One of the heels was broken from her fall. It was a pity. These shoes had never been to London or anywhere else before and when she stood up she would realise the full vulnerability of her shortness within an urban landscape. She remained sitting. The platform was empty of travellers. It was a rare thirty seconds, a moment of peace for Rosita in London when there was no one and she was just herself. There is never silence but there are usually people, all trying to be themselves and each other. To find tranquillity people stay up all night and walk home alone tasting the silence. Or they shut themselves in during the day away from the daylight in editing suites, or flotation tanks or saunas; paying for the privilege of hearing pennies drop.

Jon breaks that moment for Rosita without knowing it. They see each other. She beckons him to her elaborately. She is in no position to be modest.

She is twenty-six years old. He pulls her to her feet. What station is this he asks her in broad Glaswegian. She does not understand. She shows him her piece of paper and her broken heel. These must prove something. Where are you from? Espagne. He spits vigorously on the pavement. He went there once and suffered a stomach upset, manifested by endless symptoms to linger over and rediagnose when he was well. He nearly died. He was in hell. Inglaterra, says Rosita and spits flamboyantly hitting the blob of Jon's saliva and moving it a couple of centimetres along. He is impressed as you would have been disgusted. You bet, he agrees, Inglaterra and he spits again. This is a three spit meeting. They slap hands in a rhythmic fashion like black comedians that they have both seen on TV; Rosita in the kitchen with her late father and Jon alone in his bedsit in Tooting Bec. Then they go their separate ways. They will never meet again. He thinks she is attractive with adequate breasts but he will not remember her tomorrow. If they both lived in London for ten years they might never meet again. Or they might run into each other again three times on the same day, in a bookshop, and then at the supermarket and again at the cinema; and be embarrassed, trying to remember, where?, how?, had it been sex?, were they a friend of a friend?, how nice to, well, see you again maybe, how funny to ... And if they ended up as neighbours—one of those strange coincidences that the higher percentages in London seem to encourage—then they wouldn't talk to each other at all—but perhaps send each other Christmas cards or compete with their display of sweet peas and honeysuckle in the back garden.

But Rosita was full of hope. She has given up on an attempt to hop on one heel. It allowed her the dignity of inches but was both ungainly and precarious. Barefoot she reached the bottom of the escalator. People rode towards her without expression. She showed them her piece of paper. They averted their eyes as they passed. She was polite and then she was insistent. She pushed it towards their faces. The garlic clove shifts in her stomach.

HIJO DE PUTA MADRE. BASTARDO, she says to the faces. They lift their pointing fingers to their lips and indicate silence. SSHHH. They are reverent about their disinterest. BASTARDO, she repeats. A well dressed and guilty looker presses a coin into her hand. And she looks firmly with closed eyes into her disappointment with people. Halfway up the escalator Joseph breaks into a sweat and punches the nearest nose which breaks cleanly without fuss and mends after a few weeks with only the slightest alteration to the face, endowing it with a sense of enigma and enquiry. With a new nose Adrian finds people of both sexes attracted to him and he starts going out leaving a pile of gardening magazines to wither. His window box survives in spite.

Joseph has never talked before with his fists. But he really has been having a bad time. Various incidents. Mishaps. So bad that no one will ever know about it. Secrets. But they enjoy guessing at murder, sex, drugs and a broken home. Some women that don't know him go to Westminster Abbey to pray for him in the inclusive category of "lost souls". What a beautiful church! A good place to believe in God and get warmed up on the same morning. What lovely singing! What a sound that comes from the organ! Earlier a small boy sat and watched him cry as he sat on a bench in Hyde Park. He had never seen anyone cry silently, he had never seen a man cry at all—a mystery unfolds and the sight of these tears make other things seem possible. He decides that Joseph has lost his dog. Perhaps he should tell him about Battersea dogs' home but just at the right moment he is dragged off by his older sister who wants to look for eyeliner. Joseph looks way down to the bottom of the escalator ignoring the wary glances of the frightened passengers. He has never worn make-up. He looks at the dark haired woman who swears in a foreign language and waves his hurt hand. Rosita smiles at his loud pain.

A tug on her skirt makes her look down. Pat from Derry sits on the floor to earn her money with a notice. That's mine. This is my patch for at least an hour. I've only just started. Give me what is mine. She puts out her hand confident of her right. Rosita returns to her quest and shows her the address on the paper. Is this your friend? sister? Spanish are you? Why does your sister live there? It's all Greek up there. It's almost suburban. You can tell that people round there use a lot of toilet paper—great wodges of it wrapped around their hands so there isn't the slightest risk. What's your name? Rosita? Serious? I suppose we all have to walk around with something on our backs. There's always deed poll. Pat smiles through her hostility. She thinks she's quite good with people. Once she thought about being a nurse, and she would walk past St Thomas's hospital each day to bring luck to her career plan. Tell your sister she is living in an emotionally unhealthy environment. Crazy people live around there.

Minutes later Rosita is on another platform pointing the way that Pat has told her, grasping Pat's *A–Z* with the corner of a page turned down to mark her sister's whereabouts and wearing Pat's spare pair of trainers. David stands beside her and thinks about dinner. He has been to the market and has come away cheered by the shouts of the stallholders. Dreary customers break into a smile. Eer y'aar Dahlin Beeutiful bunch of bananas—I'm sure that a girl like you will know what to do with those. Put a bit of custard on it eh? Everyone is smiling, sad hearts are giggling and David has carrots, potatoes, leeks and parsnips and tomatoes. Rosita stands next to him, closes her eyes and smells his vegetables and finds comfort in a daydream about the market—Roberto and Rosita carrying their basket together through life, one handle each.

'Berto is driving the train. By his seat he has a bag full of herbs that he is taking to his friend Jean-Louis who chefs in

Poland Street. He grows them on the roof in Stoke Newington where he also goes to look at the stars with his telescope. Clear crisp nights make him happy. When he sees a clear patch of sky, he remembers who to be and how to do it. It is not possible to be in London permanently without feeling the need to search for a clear patch. At the weekends and during public holidays, the hordes go searching armed with maps and wellingtons. In London everyone has started gardening. Everyone leaves for the sun and foreign food but they always come back. One day, Raoul will go back too, he often says; looking into the mirror to check that he's not lying to himself. He thinks that he is already crazy.

Rosemary, oregano, thyme, coriander and the recently acquired favourite, the bay tree, have given him great pleasure and some interest from Madeleine, the Australian tenant in the flat below; who sometimes bathes without a bikini top in between his herb pots. Her nipples don't look quite real. Jean-Louis accepts the herb with a wiggle of his moustache, proud of the flavours he is able to concoct. He cooks 'Berto regular meals in the kitchen when the manager is out for the night, and takes him along to the South Bank boule club which plays the first Sunday in the month on the gravel in between the Thames and the National Theatre. Will Rosita and Roberto meet without it being an obvious and clumsy reunion when so far everything seems to be falling into place? She is now talking to a vicar who is enjoying the chance to practise community awareness and a few words of Spanish. His County Durham accent makes Rosita narrow her eyes in concentration but she is able to nod at a few words that she recognises; rain, God, tortilla. She looks at his face rather than decipher his words and notes the tight, tense lines and the jutting Adam's apple. He should learn to dance she thinks. He will die young or unhappy, she concludes unfairly. The vicar Dominic, laughs nervously and blushes at a thought that he hadn't invited. The exotic woman is young and attractive. Dom will never lambada at the Club Bahia with the Colombians living in Vauxhall.

Rosita is tired of smiling at people like a happy tourist. Where is her sister? She can smell the cheese warming in its hiding place. She knows the goat that provided the milk. You can't trust them ever.

A terrible screeching of brakes and a resounding thud sends everyone falling into place on the floor. A pile of seven. An assortment of sexes and body types scream and groan. Some think that death has been brought to them courtesy of a politicised bomb and others use this chance to grope flesh. The train has stopped in the tunnel. Gradually the passengers pick themselves up, rearrange their clothing and examine each other for possible blame. A few seconds silence and then everyone is talking, muttering, murmuring, ranting, and a voice familiar to Rosita comes through the internal speakers. Please do not worry, we will soon reach the station. Where has she heard that voice before? She wonders if there is something spiritual going on. Grace Edmunds has lived in London for a long time. It was hot lying under the vicar and she is glad he has staggered to his feet. Moments later and everyone will be busy again. There is laughter and then everyone will be busy again. A few moments of communion and familiarity and then everyone will be busy again. She has a dizzy spell coming on. Is this happening now? Who are all these people? What do they want? They can't be relations. She comes from a good looking family and this lot are shabby with grey, unhealthy skin. Someone sharp-sighted and worthy helps her to a seat forcibly vacated by a boy in a back to front baseball cap. He scowls as the old woman passes into unconsciousness and sneers as she sees again the sheep-covered hills near Abergavenny. Fluffy youngsters that were lambs in the spring.

The train comes into the platform, and the doors open with a united sigh of relief from all the passengers. Hurriedly Roger (who we know nothing about) helps Dom carry the old woman onto the platform. They are both worried that she will die and they have never touched dead flesh before, only on the dinner table. They lay her on some coats provided by other onlookers greedy for the unusual. Roger mysteriously disappears into the crowd before anyone can discover him. Rosita strokes the brow of the old woman's face and hums a little tune, because she can't remember the words. All around people are on the move. Coming from, going to, trying to, succeeding and failing. It all makes a lot of noise and takes up time. The old woman sighs and passes on. Raoul fights his way through the people—he had heard whispers from the back of the crowd about murder and knives. He lays a sprig of rosemary on Grace's chest, slightly disappointed. Rosita taps him on the back accusingly. He's been gone a long time but he recognises the smell of the cheese. He smiles. He is apologetic. He gives her the bag of herbs to smell as he doesn't know what to do with his hands, he feels awkward again. She gives him her piece of paper, opens up the A–Z and offers it to him. In London that day there are four thousand, three hundred and thirty-two people who don't know where they are going, but not all of them live happy every after.

Boom

KATE CLANCHY

Inflation got to Giles in the monstrous hot summer of 1989. As he cut breathless deals for more and more improbable sums, as his tarted-up little flat began to be worth £80,000, then £90,000, as the thermometer, to daily shrieks from the media, crawled relentlessly up to 28 degrees, so his thirty-year-old stomach, brown, a little hairy, his soft-skinned stomach that he still cradled in moments of stress, started gently to swell, opening the buttons of his striped shirt.

It swelled all day under his desk in his high up office in the city, growing taut until his belt cut him as he shouted down the telephone. His shoulders expanded and his shirt wetly grabbed his shoulders as he leant across the desk. In the packed bars after work his jowls inflated as he murmured importantly, constricting his smile. His cheeks puffed, pushing his curling eyelashes together.

In the steamy evenings he sat with clients on the pavements outside expensive restaurants, feeling his wrists puff up and straining his watch strap, hiding his fidgets under the tablecloth. He swelled quietly and privately at night as he tossed on his futon listening to the braying of a Fulham street. His throat swelled just above his Adam's apple, choking him, making him gasp and pant like an old man. The disorder obsessed him, filling him, for the first time for years, since he was chubby and awkward on his first day at prep-school, with self-doubt.

It was water retention, said Stephanie, and it usually happened to women, though not, evidently, to Stephanie who was skinny and hard as a knife. Giles wanted to touch her, but even his hands were swelling, his fingers were stiff, pale, like cheap sausages. He would leave sweat marks on her silk tee shirt, cloy her skin. "It's not as if I'm overeating," said Giles, defensively.

In fact, he ate nearly nothing, for with the swelling had come a sharpening of his sense of smell, the sort you usually have after vomiting or long illness. Stephanie's expensive scent, bought by him in duty free, the genuine article, smelled sharp as neat meths. The most innocuous foods, yoghurt for example, smelt of mould, of old knickers. There was something nasty in his airing cupboard, something that smelled of fried washing powder. It haunted him all day, made him afraid to go home.

On the other hand, he was buggered if he wanted to go to a party with an interior designer. "Where?" he said to Stephanie.

"Spitalfields," said Stephanie, tinny and casual on the telephone. "Darling, it's terribly near, you know, where you go for a curry sometimes. You could walk."

Walk. Giles rarely walked. He worked out on shiny machines, he played squash with chaps in high white courts, he swam in a scentless blue pool filled with slender, intent adults, but he moved in taxis. Walk, indeed.

Spitalfields, besides. Giles had made a deal of money in property, he was all for improvement, but Spitalfields, Bethnal Green, Brixton, these places gave him pause. They were the limits to money, they defined it, they couldn't be money themselves. It was partly envy, of course, fear of some one else with a better deal, but he hated to have these places talked of, it would all end in trouble, end up by sucking at the value of all he had worked for. He had acquired a particular estate agents' patter for the purpose of putting down these property pioneers that ended "Downright unpleasant and dangerous." He was right. The walk to Spitalfields in his distended state was terrible.

It was the hottest day yet, and the high city streets burned and shimmered like a movie of New York. Beyond them, in the sudden slum past Liverpool Street Station, the old fruit market was hot and empty as the Nevada desert. He had never seen it sober or by daylight. It was a battlefield of rotting vegetables, and it stank.

Giles' ankles and feet were so swollen, they felt coated in boots, those squidgy rubber ones people wore on the ski slopes. They burnt with every step. He was covered in fine oily sweat. The sweetish reek of orange filled his mouth with sharp water, and there was a background smell of rotting turnip, the smell of bins, of old school soup.

With a lurch of doubt it occurred to him that perhaps the smell was coming from him. He looked round, then paused in a doorway to open his jacket. His stomach stuck out like a medicine ball, and his shirt was wet to the belt. He sniffed, then almost cried out with shock. He stank of sulphur, the pure distinctive smell of rotten eggs, of stink bombs. What terrible disease did he have? He flapped his jacket helplessly.

"Spare some change, sir?" Giles shuddered with shock. The voice came from belt level. He looked down and saw an old face, deep lined. A dwarf. A dwarf was watching him sniffing his armpits in Spitalfields Market, and he, Giles, was swelling like a water-melon and smelt like a schoolboy's joke. Giles turned his eyes to the sky, which was brownish, rotating round the spire of the Hawksmoor church. That was where he was headed. There were pulses in his neck, and his collar cut him. He was very ill, and the dwarf knew it. He had something on him.

"Got some change, sir?" Giles looked down again. The man's misshapen head was balding, it gleamed pink and shining between strands of nicotine yellow hair. And there was something in his hands, something that gleamed in the sun. He was standing in front of Giles, blocking the doorway. He was being mugged. His heart thudded against his wallet. Water rose in his stomach, the acid water of panic, and he gagged. His collar button popped off and landed with an insouciant twist in the gutter.

It was the last straw, Giles moaned, and brought down his hands convulsively. His big fists hit something horrible, something like old carpet, dirty, dust on his fingers. Something yielded, and there was the heavy sound of bones on concrete. He had hit a dwarf, and was a criminal. His vision blurred.

Then Giles was running, gibbering, sweating, on his fat feet, with his jacket flapping, in zig-zags like a rabbit caught in open country, in the direction of the church. He felt his thighs swell with every step, his stomach was like a barrel he had to carry. He thought about rushing into the church and flattening himself on a cool white marble aisle, but he hadn't believed for years, and besides, outside sat three tramps in overcoats in the heat. He imagined their smell, hot dirt, beer on the carpet after a party, pee. If they noticed him, everything could be up. Giles forced himself to slow to a walk, breathing in the old, used-up air, trying to get enough down his swollen throat.

There was no difficulty picking out the house. It was the one with the shining windows and the elaborate umber doorcase. He leaned on it, breathing in his enriched, horrible smell, considering what to do. It was important to keep up a good front. He tightened his tie as best he could over the missing button, fastened his jacket over the bulge, wiped his face with his hankie. The door snapped open.

"Darling," said Stephanie. "What on earth?"

"Bloody slum," said Giles, surprising himself, and waddled into the poky passage.

"Anne," said Stephanie. "Here's Giles, but I'm afraid the heat's getting to him. He's all pink in the face and talking like his father."

"I'll get him a drink," tinkled a thin woman in cycling shorts.

"Bloody stinks," growled Giles, and Stephanie grabbed his arm and pushed him up the narrow stairs into a small panelled room painted a hectic shade of red. It was hot and damp as fevered breath, and full of people holding glasses. He collapsed onto a high-sided sofa, and the Anne person put a cold gin in his hand. His eyes were on a level with her black lycra crotch.

"Sorry," he muttered to her brown knees. "Bloody heat, terrible stinks out there."

"It simply pongs," she said. "I know, the drains, they're literally medieval. God farting and all that. Part of the charm."

Giles squinted at his gin, and swallowed most of it. He felt giddy. The disease was getting to him, he could feel obscenities bubbling up in him, names for scrawny Anne, for that limp young man, for Stephanie flaunting her legs, all the cool, unswollen people. He rubbed his hands together, feeling the dwarf in the sausages of dirt. He longed to go and wash, but if he did, everyone would see him waddle. He wiped his face with his hankie again. Stephanie was right, he was acquiring his father's gestures.

"Gorgeous place," she hissed.

Giles swivelled his puffy head like a sea lion, taking in the elaborate curtaining, the portraits that he betted were nobody in particular, the baskets full of arty twigs, the red walls caving in on the bright faces all talking of the heat, and when it had last rained. He gulped the last of the gin, and felt it travel immediately to his face, swelling it like mumps. He was furious.

"Fucking awful," he grunted. "Sheer bloody hell."

"Giles!" she squawked, and to Anne, "He's having an awful time in the heat, swelling up, you know, water retention."

"Sounds pre-menstrual," said Anne, filling up his glass.

Stephanie giggled. The man next to her laughed outright. Giles swallowed his drink, then opened his mouth and let out a huge burp.

"Giles!" said Stephanie.

Giles put his hand over his mouth. This was a new thing, another part of the disease. He shut his eyes and imagined his swollen insides as an early chemical factory, filling him up with terrible gas and stinks and obscenities. He would have to puff like a steam train and run forever saying damn. They would all see him. His eyes filled with tears.

"Darling?" said Stephanie.

"God Jesus," said Giles. "Gotta, gotta ...", and he lumbered to his feet, swiping with his arms.

"Through there," said Anne.

Her lavatory was small, but it was white, at least. Giles sat on the mahogany seat, and let fart after sulphurous fart rumble out of his body, He grabbed the soap off the basin and clutched it to his nose, breathing in its smell of money, his mother, department stores. He had to pull himself together. If people like him didn't hold it together, the whole thing could collapse.

He ran the basin full of water and stuck his head in it, then thrust in his arms up to the elbow, and stood gazing at himself in the expensive, old silvered glass. It gave his face cracks. He pouted, turning his face this way and that, trying to believe his mouth had always stuck out like that, that it was the light that gave him those multiple, packed bags under his eyes. With his cool hands, he pulled back his eyelids, exposing round, fishy eyeballs, streaked with red.

"Giles," it was Stephanie, sounding oddly doubtful, knocking at the door.

"All right," Giles let the water out of the basin and ran his hands through his hair. His shirt was splitting almost to the waist: the tie just looked ridiculous. He took it off and was struck, suddenly, by the big man in the mirror. His swollen chest was rather magnificent in a way. He looked like one of the chaps at the gym who had blown themselves up with weights, especially with his hair damp like that. He turned sideways and flexed biceps big as plucked chickens.

"Giles, please come out," quavered Stephanie. Silly bitch. Christ knows what was the matter with her. It was her friend's bloody party, and here he was, and nothing the matter with him. That big chap in the mirror, he'd soon sort her out. He smiled, watching himself, leaning closer until his nose almost touched the glass.

It was the smile that did it. That slow grin in a puffy face, that wobble of double chins, that disappearing of the eyes in swollen lids, they were all sweetly familiar. Giles had grown the smile he'd always known he would have, the smile he had in dreams. It was the smile of a Victorian mill owner in a caricature, the smile of his father in his preposterous forties, the smile of a rich man. The bubble of doubt in Giles exploded: it wasn't poison after all, but a special blessing. He was light with elation. He clenched his fist in triumph, and snapped open the door.

Stephanie's sketchy little face was stiff with anxiety, her painted eyes wide open. In his new mood of cheerful expansion, he slung an enormous arm around her.

"Darling," he boomed. "No need to worry about these people. Not the real thing really."

Stephanie shrank away from him. He actually seemed taller as well as a bit porky. "Darling, this water thing is really getting to you. You're awfully swollen, and there's a fearful smell."

"Drains," shouted Giles, "Fearful drains, full of the shit of generations of bloody foreigners." He strode into the sitting room, trailing Stephanie. "Anne," he demanded, "why do you live in a bloody slum for bloody foreigners, hey?"

Anne laughed her tinkly laugh. "Giles! Because it's charming, it's simply loaded with history, and the bloody foreigners make lovely neighbours. Why, it's so safe round here, I could walk absolutely anywhere at any time, totally safe."

Giles felt tremendous, he was filling the room, all the silly thin people were huddled against the walls. He was bigger than any of them. He raised his arm in a heroic, monumental gesture.

"Ha," he cried, "Ha". The last button popped from his shirt.

He had caused a silence, and filled it gladly with his huge patrician voice. "Just been bloody mugged myself. Right out there, in the market."

"Giles!" shrieked Stephanie, and rushed to put her arms around his waist, but her hands would not reach round the great swelling barrel, and she sunk to her knees, her head on his crotch. He touched her shiny bob absently, flexing his hands. They were pink and swollen as inflated rubber gloves, but they had lost the dwarf's cloying dust. They were grand hands, the hands of a hero; everyone in this room depended on them, and it was about time they knew it. His stomach let out another inch and his trouser button burst. Every eye was upon him. Anne stood frozen with the gin bottle.

"Eight of them," said Giles, "All of them black as the ace of spades." A woman squeaked, and Giles swivelled on her. What a little creature she was! "Black they were, black as Sambo, like everyone around here."

"Bangladeshi," whispered Anne, out of reflex.

"Fucking black," roared Giles. "Huge. But they got nothing out of me, oh no. I faced them down, didn't give them a fucking penny. What do you think of that, eh?" He swivelled his head at the tiny staring people flattened on Anne's red wall.

"Fucking preposterous colour," he added. No one spoke. They were watching Giles grow.

For he was swelling like an airship, his trousers rising to show his neat black socks, ripping over the monstrous hairy hams. Stephanie's crouched form only reached his knees. His hair was a shrunken wig on a head massive as a cow's. It was approaching the ceiling, and as it rose, it went on talking.

"Gave them a bloody good seeing to, I tell you, I told them their place. Just a question of confidence, that's how the whole thing runs, mustn't be afraid to stand up and be counted or the whole thing crumbles. Money, houses, all just a question of believing, all simple. Do it on the telephone." He gave another swipe, cracking his shirt from seam to seam, and his arm touched the further wall, knocking one of the phoney portraits to the floor. The woman standing below it, realising that she was only as tall as Giles' waist, moaned and fell to the floor.

Giles looked at her silly collapsed face, her rolling eyes. Why, this was the kind of woman who had patronised him at a thousand parties, she was like his bloody sister who worked for a charity, and she was lying on the floor meowing like a cat, with her skirt all rucked up. She was the only one squeaking.

"Shut up!" yelled Giles, and his voice was the voice of the

police addressing the thousand demonstrators. "Stupid cow. Shut up if you like the good bits. Bet you do, eh?" He bent over to shout harder, and his trousers broke, revealing a lush bottom, fat as a sofa, wrapped in the sad remains of his boxer shorts. "Who pays for you, eh?" he bellowed, thrusting closer. 'All the same, you bloody women, whingeing about what we should do, but who pays for you? Bet you belong to fucking Amnesty, eh? Bet some idiot pays your subscription, bet you like reading about electric shocks, eh?'

Stephanie fainted, a graceful rag on his foot. Giles picked her up, and slung her over his shoulder. His arms were like a fat man's legs, they were traced with blue veins wide as drinking straws. He was actually bent over now, he was taller than the room. Stephanie's head jostled the light fitting.

Anne was sidling to the telephone. "Don't you bother," shouted Giles. He pinned Anne to the wall with his foot. "Don't you go phoning some hostel, oh no. She's mine. I paid for her, I make money, don't you see? I make it on the telephone. Because I believe, and that's what counts and then you go and spend it on tarting up a bloody slum. You let me alone, I'll take care of her, give her some air. Lovely bloody weather." Giles farted, and the room was filled with sulphur. A delicate young man in black slipped behind the sofa and thrust a cushion in his mouth.

"Open that window," shouted Giles, shaking the floor as he lumbered to it. Stephanie shook like a toy on his shoulder. Anne was fiddling with the festoon blinds. He ripped them down, and punched open the eighteenth-century window, so the ancient wood cracked and lurched open like rags from a line.

He slipped Stephanie off his shoulder, and dangled her out into the air between his hands, then squeezed his massive torso out to thrust her out further. "Soon feel better," he bellowed, then held still. Beneath Stephanie's convulsing twig-like limbs, gazing up at him from the narrow street, small and quiet and true, was the dwarf. His hands still held the thing that flashed in the sun.

"Liar," shouted Giles. He had to sort him out. He draped Stephanie over the window, shook his fist. "Little man. You're little because you want to be, don't you know that? Just like I'm big because I want to be, I earned being this way, I fucking earned it, don't you sit there and think you can have some because you're little, because you can't. You and your sort you drag us down, you don't believe, you bring the whole place down."

The dwarf looked at him through his watery blue eyes. The street sat dirty in the heat, the drunken ancient buildings leaning towards each other. Silently, like leaves on the wind, the three tramps from the church drifted towards the dwarf. In their rags, on the ancient paving stones, they were men from any time, from forever.

"Don't look up at me like that," shouted Giles. "You could be here if you could think big enough, if you'd any backbone. I'll show you, I'll give you backbone. I'll make you big." And he squeezed himself back through the window, and lunged across the room, rucking the rug round himself, scrunching chairs like paper.

He was too big for the door, he had to squeeze through it in parts, losing the remains of his clothes. First he thrust his legs through like great rolls of carpet, then his stomach, piece by piece, like marzipan through an obscene piping tool. The stairs were easier, he slid down them flattening the banister like card. The crowd crept out after him, and stood huddled on the landing, looking at the naked colossus struggling with the door chain.

The door swung open on a block of sun. The three tramps were shadows in overcoats, their ragged sleeves feathery like wings.

"Right then," shouted Giles, stepping out over the door frame. "Let's have it then, who's in charge now? Where's the big man?" The dwarf slipped from behind, the thing glistening in his hand.

"Oi," said Giles, and his grotesque inflated face had for a moment a childish, touching expression, of puzzlement, regret almost. It was too late. The dwarf slipped in the needle, and with the noise they had all been expecting, a noise huge as thunder, but without its glory, a sound with wet in it, Giles popped.

All over parched London, people heard the sound and held up their hands to catch the rain. The juice that had filled him burnt stucco in Kensington, scarred Hampstead Heath, spoilt washing in Tooting, dripped doubt and despondency into the banks, the estate agents, the stripogram offices of the city. Scraps of his skin scattered far and wide on a sulphurous wind, over the proud towers of the city, over the slums that have crouched so long by those cliffs of money, patient in tide after tide. They landed on telephone wires, entwined satellite dishes, clogged ventilators, draped softly over washing lines, invisibly over hands and minds. Wherever they landed things started, very quietly, to shrink.

The Darkness

D A J PEARSON

It's getting late. Chilly too. Still, it's nice and cosy in my little hut. Safer, too, now they've put the new iron gate on the outer wall. That might keep the thieving little bastards out. Doubt it, though. It's all just another game for them. They don't see anything wrong with what they're doing. They even expect me to join in the joke.

Time for my last cup of tea. They left me that this time. That's something. Last time the bastards threw it all round the hut, out of sheer spite. God knows why they bother breaking in, they all know I've got nothing here any more. Just tea, milk, sugar, my battered kettle and my old tin mug. I don't dare leave anything else behind. I'll put the kettle on and get the tea bags out. While I'm doing that, I'll have time to think. I need time to think.

Two iron bars.

One meat cleaver.

And a baseball bat.

Why are they there?

What should I do about them?

Take it easy. I've got plenty of time to decide. One step at a time. First things first. The kettle's boiling. Pour the water out, add the sugar and milk, then go to the door and have a look round. No need to rush things. It's getting dark. Lights are already coming on in the new high-rise estates all around.

Makes the park look like a small, black lake. Completely cut off. Surrounded by the concrete jungle. Funny how the night creeps up on you. Like old age. Go into the hut and it's light, come out half an hour later and you can't see a thing. I hate English winters.

What's out there now? Not a lot. It's not wise to be here at night. I look out past the twisted, spiky shrubbery, all that's left of the flower beds. Nothing grows here any more. They won't let it.

A couple of shapes are dangling on the rusted swings. With their squat, sullen dog. Dark, hunched figures swigging from a bottle. I can make out their young, hard faces, hollow eyes and cropped hair by the glow of their cigarettes. My eyes are still good after all these years. They look up as I come out, and I can feel the hatred in their looks. It scares me, and I thought I'd seen everything. I think I recognise them now. They're the two I saw in the bushes earlier today, when I was chatting to Gemma. She's the one who told me what they were hiding there under the leaves. And why. I still don't know whether I can believe her. As a rule, I never believe little girls any more. They can be such liars.

Two iron bars.

One meat cleaver.

And a baseball bat.

I still haven't seen them, mind. I don't know for sure if they're there. All I've got to go on is little Gemma's word. But if I went to look, and found something, then I'd have to do something. And if I went to look, they'd see me. They'd know it was me who'd found them. And they'd do something about it, I'm sure of that. I don't want any trouble. Not now, after all these years. Not with these new kids.

One of them's passing a packet to the other one. Drugs, probably. No point telling the police, though. They won't do anything. Won't or can't. I gave up telling them things years ago. They used to send a couple of coppers round in the old days, whenever I gave them a call. They'd have a drink of tea and listen, smiling away nice-as-pie. Take down statements, get me to sign them and then go away with their "thank you very much, sir. You may be hearing from us shortly." I never did, of course. But I used to think they liked our chats and pretending to be interested, all the same. Used to make them feel not everyone round here was against them, that we were on the same side. We aren't, of course. I know that now. Now I know they were just humouring me. I haven't seen them here for a long time, but I'm glad really. It's not good to be seen talking to the police.

I won't tell them about this.

They're leaving now, the two on the swings. Laughing about something, I think, or is it just their dog snarling? Swaggering back to their high-rise estate like the park was their private property, which it has been, more or less, since the last big fight. I hear the sound of glass smashing and when I listen carefully, I can just make out some of the words. *Effing* this and *effing* that.

Good riddance.

It makes closing the park a bit easier. But if it's the two I think it is, if Gemma told the truth, they'll be back.

And this time they won't be alone.

Two iron bars.

One meat cleaver.

And a baseball bat.

What shall I do about them?

There goes that police car again, slowly circling the park like a striped shark. I can feel the eyes peering down at them through the curtains of the nearby high-rise estate, the same way they watch me. We're all in the same boat here. Everyone watching everyone else. Off it goes, round the corner. I'm on my own again. They looked pretty fed-up in

72

that car of theirs. I'm not surprised. It's not a good job being a policeman round here.

It's worse being a park-keeper.

You get the uniform, but you don't get the power. Or the respect. Kids used to be scared of me. Or at least they'd pretend to be scared. They used to run when they saw me coming, looking all fierce. "It's parkie! Leggit!" they'd shout. That used to make me laugh. Just like a game of tag, with me as the bogey man. It was fun. Of course, I had to look serious, but, to tell the truth, I loved every minute of it. It made me feel young again. Usually.

Now they play different games.

Two kids I chased out of the toilets once waited till I went to the shops then followed me shouting things. Things they said I'd tried to do to them in the toilet. Liars, the pair of them. I never did any of what they said. But someone called the police anyway and things got very nasty for a couple of weeks.

They had to let me go in the end. Their word against mine, they couldn't prove anything, and the two of them had been in trouble plenty of times before. I kept my job, too, just. The union still has some powers left. But it all left a dirty taste in my mouth. I still get the feeling people are looking at me oddly and I don't use the local shops any more if I can help it. It's true what they say about mud sticking.

As if I wanted to touch any of them, the nasty little things! Diseased, the lot of them. It was them in the toilet all along, them and their dirty friends. I know what games they get up to in there. I've seen the money changing hands. I've heard the noises, the giggling and the sudden silence. Then the panting. I can't help overhearing things that go on. It's part of my job. I have to keep an eye open. Young girls, too.

What was that? Something thrown over the wall. Sounded like a brick. I can hear whispers. Giggling. Footsteps running away. Wait. Let them go. Leave a few seconds before investigating. They might be waiting to throw another one when I come out. They've done that before. They nearly killed me the first time, but I'm wise to most of their little tricks by now. Unlock the gate quietly. I don't want them to hear me. I don't want them to know where I am. Now look round the gate carefully. Easy does it. Nothing in the shadows. It's all clear.

Ah. That's what they've been up to. The playhouse is on fire. They must have piled up some leaves inside it. The flames must be four feet high. Nothing I can do except go and investigate. It won't damage the playhouse, though. It's designed to be fireproof. Not like those new blocks they live in. Double lock the gate behind me. Funny, though, I thought they'd given up trying to burn the old thing down. It's been months since they last had a go.

The flames are dying down already. As I thought, they've had no effect. These old things were built to last. Someone's buried some glass in the sandpit, though. Not quite well enough. I can see bits glinting in the flames. And that's a syringe over there. I'll leave a note for Bob to get them out to-morrow. Some kid could cut themselves wide open or worse.

It's darker than ever now. I can hear someone coming. Better get back to my hut and the warmth. You never know who it might be. Not long to go now. Soon I can go home. I wonder what I'll have for dinner. Maybe I'll just go to the pub for a steak and kidney pie and a pint. I've earned it. There's that phone ringing again. I'd better hurry back.

Someone's written something on the gate. I missed that before. I can see the paint now, trickling down the metal. In the fading firelight it glistens like blood. I can just make out the writing. "White Power". What does that mean? Some pop group, I suppose. It makes a change from football teams and filth.

Missed the bloody phone.

It's always the same; just when I get the last lock off, the bloody things stops ringing. Why can't they wait a couple of seconds longer? Who could it have been? The ex-wife, possibly. Doubt it though, there's no reason for her to ring. Probably the supervisor checking up again to see if I'm out working. That should keep him happy for a bit. I might as well sit down and have a breather and another think.

Two iron bars.

One meat cleaver.

And a baseball bat.

What can I do about them?

I'm going to have to make up my mind, but there's no real hurry yet. What's the time? Five o'clock. Half an hour to shutting time. I'll go and have a last look around. It's odd. There's usually someone in the park at least. But not tonight. There's definitely an air about the place tonight. I don't think I'm imagining it. You develop a nose for these things after all this time. Something's going to happen. The last time I felt it was before that big fight a few months ago. Whites beating up blacks, this time. Last year, before they built the new estate, it was the other way around. I went back into my hut, locked myself in and let them get on with it. It wasn't any of my business. If they wanted to fight each other, let them. I couldn't be seen taking sides. There was nothing I could have done anyway. Someone called the police in the end. I heard there were some bad injuries.

At least no one got killed.

Still, it seemed funny, them fighting over this smashed up old park like that. It's not like it's anything worth fighting for, really. And it isn't as if they look after it. Just the opposite. All they were fighting for was the right to smash it up even more. Kids'll fight over anything or nothing. If it wasn't over the park it'd be about football or something else.

I haven't seen many other blacks in the park since, though. And they don't hang around long when they come. I've seen one small group in here sometimes, that's all. Smoking drugs and carrying on. It beats me why they and the whites fight each other. They're all just the same, as bad as each other. I've seen one of them walking through the park a few times, last thing at night. I told him the other gates were already locked the first time, but he just swore at me, then walked on like I wasn't there. He's had a girl with him the last two times. White and nice-looking from the back. And it's that that makes me wonder if little Gemma's telling the truth, after all.

Two iron bars.

One meat cleaver.

And a baseball bat.

They're going to use them on his head.

That's what the little girl told me. She'd heard them talking about it while they were hiding them. A whole group of them were going to wait till he walked through the park tonight and then they were going to give it to him. Teach him to mess around with a white girl on their territory. Their girls would take care of the girlfriend.

Five twenty. My tea's gone cold. Serves me right for thinking too much. Time to pour it away. It tasted bitter anyway. Then I'll go and close the park down. I've still got a bit of time to make my mind up what to do. First things first. One step at a time. No need to rush things. I'm going to put on my jacket, lock up the hut and go out into the park. It's pitch-black outside now. I can hardly see my hand when I hold it up in front of my face. As I go up to the northern gate, I can make out a group of kids huddled whispering on the street corner just outside the park. They turn, suddenly silent, their eyes boring into me.

In the dirty, orange street light, they look like ghouls.

My hands shaking slightly, I lock the gate and turn my

back on them, half expecting them to throw something. Nothing. I'm in luck tonight. Clenching the keys tightly, I walk down the park to the eastern gate, sure they're still watching me, waiting for them to shout something, and as I do, I pass the bushes where the things are meant to be hidden.

Two iron bars.

One meat cleaver.

And a baseball bat.

What shall I do? What shall I do?

Are they there or aren't they?

I half turn to look. Behind me, I hear the sound of stealthy footsteps, clambering over the railings.

They're in the park now.

I walk on hurriedly and don't look back. I take a deep breath. I've reached my decision, as I always knew I would.

I'm going to do nothing.

It's not my problem. Whatever I do won't change anything. I tried to do my bit and got nowhere. It's up to someone else now. I wash my hands of the lot of them. I walk past the bushes and make my slow way down to the southern gate. The last gate and then I can go home to my cosy house and my supper. It's a long walk and it seems longer tonight.

I don't know why.

I can see two people coming, dim figures in the street light. For a second I hope it isn't them, but it is. Why do the men wear their hair like that? Something to do with their religion, isn't it? He's got his arm round the girl and they're laughing. It's the first real, happy laughter I've heard for ages. They're nearly up to me now, but they don't really see me. They only have eyes for each other. For a second I'm almost touched by it. It all looks so innocent. I've still got time to warn them. I can still do something.

I half-open my mouth, then I recognise the girl. She's one of the ones I chased out of the toilet. She doesn't look at me. I freeze and as I do, they step aside to go round me, the boy's shoulder clipping mine as he passes. We look at each other for an instant, two dark faces in a blacker night, but he doesn't apologise. I didn't expect him to. He just mutters something sounding like an insult, then carries on laughing, as if he hasn't got a care in the world. I'm invisible to him, not really there. I'm locking the gate behind them now. For them there's no way out.

There.

It's done. It's too late to turn back.

Relieved now the responsibility's taken away from me, I turn and walk quickly away from the park. Behind me I hear the mocking sound of laughter being swallowed up by the darkness.

Angelo

SHENA MACKAY

The long brown beans of the catalpa rattled in the wind, brittle pods dangling in bunches among the last flapping yellow leaves of the tree, so ancient and gnarled that it rested on a crutch, in the courtyard of St James's, Piccadilly. Splintered pods and big damp leaves littering the stones were slippery under the feet of the friends, enemies and those who wished to be seen at Felix Mazzotti's Memorial Service. Drizzle gave a pearly lustre to black umbrellas and brought up the velvet pelts of collars and cashmere and cloth, moistened hats and vivified patterned shawls and scarves.

Violet Greene settled herself and her umbrella in a pew beside a stranger. The umbrella's handle was an ivory elephant's head, yellow and polished by time like a long old tooth, the grooves in its trunk smoothed by generations of gloves. The heavy white paper of the Order of Service in her black velvet fingers, thick gold leaf braid trimming white stone, glittering brass; Violet concentrated on these, and caught the little black eye of the elephant's head, which *was* an old tooth, taken from some Victorian tusker too long ago to worry about, and carved into little replicas of its original owner. Round her neck Violet wore a string of jet beads, mourning jewellery, which Felix had given her forty years before. Felix's mother had been English, his father Italian and although he was officially a Catholic he had never felt the slightest twitch on the thread. Hence this church rather than the Brompton Oratory or Farm Street. The lapse of time between the news of his death, the funeral, which had been a private affair in Italy, and the memorial service had accustomed people to his absence from the world, and time in any case rushes in as the sea fills holes in the sand. When someone is shot, Violet had read, they often feel no pain at first; she had waited, after the bullet's impact of the news, for the wound of loss to bleed and burn, but she had not seen Felix for five years—which was good because she had no picture of him as the really old man he had become suddenly—although they had spoken occasionally on the telephone and it was hard to remember that he was dead. One day she had decided to believe that he was still in his terraced garden among the olive trees that gave the beautiful green oil of which he was so proud, and felt a release. It was so simple she wondered why she had not thought of it sooner. He had told her that his olive oil gave him more pleasure and sense of achievement than all the books he had written. It had seemed such an arrogant remark, one that could have been made only by somebody as successful in the world's eye as he was, that she had felt irritated for days. Even though she refused to recognise his death, questions would persist: What were we like? What were we like together? Who was I then? She had been sixteen when they met, he a much older man of thirty. A mere boy. And was that girl herself, Violet Clements, in a silky dress printed with pansies under a cheap black cloth coat, shivering in the March wind on the steps of a house in Gordon Square? On her way to the church in a taxi this morning she had passed a bed of blue and yellow pansies, and watched the colours quivering, trembling with the taxi's motor, the dyes running together in the rivulets of the wet glass.

Her black velvet beret, with its soft pleats like the gills of a large field mushroom, was skewered with a black pearl clasped in two tiny silver hands, and she wore an emerald scarf of fine wool in a loose triangle across the shoulders of her black coat. Violet Greene she was now, and supposed that Greene, her fourth surname, would be her last, although she would not quite have put money on it. She rather liked it, the Pre-Raphaelite purple and viridian of her name, the hectic hues of Arthur Hughes, or bright green Devon Violets scent in a round bottle with painted flowers. Or Cornish, Welsh, Scottish or Parma violets—the cachou odour was the same, and a sniff of it would recall seaside holidays with the boys, salt-caked plimsolls and rough sandy towels bleaching on the rail of a wooden verandah. A present for the best mother in the world bought with pennies saved out of their ice-cream money. Today a delicate waft of toilet water was all but indiscernible as she moved.

The organ was playing a medley, a melancholy fruit cocktail in heavy syrup, as the pews filled. Violet was clasping her hands, not in prayer but to restrain them from plucking a silver hair from the coat in front of her, when a finger prodded her own back. She turned.

"Hello. I like your hat. Is it what's called a Van Dyck beret?"

Violet had made a decision long ago not to dislike a girl simply because she was young and beautiful, so she smiled at the whisperer under her hooded eyes, still violet but faded, as the flowers do. Someone's daughter or granddaughter, some child in publishing or from a gallery, in PR, met at some party she was still invited to more than she bothered with; a fixture on some guest lists after so many years on the sidelines of the arts. All black lycra and red lipstick, with long fair hair that required to be raked back from her face every few seconds, the sort of girl seen at the cinema with a giant bucket of popcorn, climbing over people's legs, drawing attention to herself.

"It's my first time at one of these," the girl confided in her loud whisper. "I s'pose you must've been to hundreds ..."

"Thousands," Violet confirmed drily.

The girl's hat lying on the pew was the kind of crushed velvet thing you would see on a stall at Camden Market between racks of discarded dresses that might have belonged to Violet long ago, and she had evidently lost confidence in her ability to wear it. Violet never went out without a hat, linen and straw with a rose or cherries or a floating scarf; canvas, wool or feline print; she was known for her amusing and assured headgear in a time when so few women knew how. Her ear picked up a few bars of *What'll I do* interwoven plaintively through strands of *Sheep May Safely Graze*, *Voi Che Sapete*, *Memories* and *For All We Know* ... *For all we know, this may only be a dream. We come and go like ripples on a stream. Time like an ever rolling stream bears all its sons away. They fly forgotten as a dream ... Imagine there's no heaven* ... she was aware of the girl behind her slewing round in her pew, and the velvet hat was proving useful, she saw as she turned her head a fraction, waving frantically at some young people hesitating noisily at the back of the church, flapping them into the seats bagged for them. They should have been holding enormous paper cups of Coca Cola rattling with ice cubes, and straws to hoover it up, rather than those unfamiliar prayer books with which they had been issued. *Here we are, out of cigarettes ... two sleepy people by dawn's early light, too much in love to say goodnight* ... who had chosen this music? Felix's third wife, the charmless Camilla over there in the Liberty hair band, in the first flush of middle-age but still young enough to be his granddaughter, with children from her first marriage, who took none of his references, responded to his jokes with serious replies, mirthless barks or groans, didn't smoke and bridled at the mention of Violet's name. There were bits of bridle or snaffles or some piece of harness across her shoes, vestiges of the nurse she had become to Felix cling to her as if demanding respect for an invisible uniform of self-sacrifice. It was hideous to imagine Camilla snouting through naïve old letters, selecting the worst photographs of Violet for the authorised biography. The only redress would be to write her own memoirs, but Violet lacked the energy or inclination to do it, and although she had given up poetry many years ago, she remembered the torture of trying to recreate the truth in words, even when only trying to describe a landscape or a lampshade.

Her uncharitable thoughts about Camilla were prompted by Camilla's hostility to her, concealed today for appearances' sake. She resented being cast as a witch, an *old* witch, because Felix had loved her best. Violet Clements had been orphaned at fourteen and a year later had left her aunt's crowded house to make her own way in the world. She had got a job at a small printing press whose decorative hand-blocked volumes were collectors' items now, and at night she had filled notebooks with her own verses by the gaslight of her attic room. She had met Felix at a teaparty given by one of their poets, where absinthe was offered in rose-painted cups. The poet, killed in the war and his work forgotten, had called for a toast to "the green fairy" as he poured the romantic liquid. Violet took only a sip or two of infamous anise but she was under the green fairy's spell, in love with and in awe of the shabby glamour of the bad fairy's court. Felix's invitation to coffee to show him her poems filled her with joy and terror for he was an established novelist and man of letters and so she was trembling with awe as much as from the March wind when she rang his bell. Shocked, for Felix wore a spotted dressing gown, she backed down the steps, blushing and starting to apologise, not looking at his bare legs, thinking she had got the wrong day. He laughed. He lead her into a room with an unmade bed.

"But it's the morning!"

He had laughed again.

The poems in her bag, so carefully selected, wilted like wallflowers at a party. It was cold, painful, and above all excruciatingly embarrassing. Violet's face had blazed for hours like the gas fire he lit afterwards, and drinking the black bitter coffee which he had made at last, she could neither look at him nor speak.

"Violet Greene has a string of lovers," she overhead somebody say years later, and she saw herself on Primrose Hill, against a yellow sky, pulled across the horizon by the pack of dogs whose leashes cut into her hand. Four of her former lovers were in the church today, she counted, and Felix, if she were to admit it, was scattered over the grass at Kenwood where leafless autumn crocuses shivered on their white stalks like girls gone mauve with the cold. Camilla had brought his ashes home in a casket.

> Who would true valour see
> Let him come hither;
> One here will constant be,
> Come wind, come weather;
>
> There's no discouragement
> Shall make him once relent
> His first avowed intent
> To be a pilgrim.

Violet's eyes blurred, and she had to control her mouth which was unable to do more than mime the words. From Kensington nursing home and Oxford, Sutton Scotney, Bloomsbury, Maida Vale, Hampstead and points south, the pilgrims had come this wild morning, old playmates summoned by the cracked bell of Fitzrovia.

"Bloody Brighton train!"

Maurice Wolverson edged into the pew beside her, knocking her umbrella to the floor, in a fury about leaves on the line.

"Not a bad house," he commented, looking around.

Mingled smells of damp wool and linseed oil came off the camelhair coat whose velvet lapels were stippled with flake-white, and then an amber peaty aroma as he unscrewed the silver top of his cane and drew out a long glass tube and offered it to Violet, who shook her head. His last part, four years ago, had been a walk-on in a television sit-com set in a seaside home for retired thespians and he had taken to daubing views of Brighton's piers to block out the sound of the swishing tide while waiting for the telephone to ring. A cluster of tarry shingle was stuck to the sole of his shoe and a red and white spotted handkerchief in his pocket made a crumpled put at jauntiness.

"They'll have to paper the house when my turn comes," Maurice muttered. Violet patted his knee.

"Choirboys. On a scale of 1 to 10 ... ?"

Violet slapped his knee.

Looking back, she was incredulous, and indignant on behalf of all foolish young women who took themselves at a man's valuation, that her fear and distaste had been compounded by worry that her body might not meet Felix's high standards, for he and his circle were harsh arbiters of female pulchritude. She had been half afraid that the jaded gourmet might send back the roast spring lamb.

"Well, what did you expect?" he had asked, "turning up on my doorstep looking like that?"

Apologies came years later. Even now, Violet knew that she brightened in men's company, became prettier, wittier, revived like a thirsty flower, with a silver charge through her veins. She had never succumbed to sensible underwear or footwear and no giveaway little pickled onion bulge distorted her shoes.

Her eyes closed as she listened to the anthem, and she felt a pang of affection for Felix's olive oil, and let the viscous yellow-green drip slowly from the bottle with the label he had designed, until it brimmed the spoon, sharing his pleasure in it, not arguing. She had hated him often as he pursued her down the years like Dracula in an opera cloak or a degenerate Hound of Heaven, and she had carried a bagful of grievances against him about with her, but now the drawstrings of the bag loosened and all the old withered hurts, wrongs and frustrations flew out and upwards to the rafters, unravelled and dissolved in the gold and amber voices of the choir. As they knelt to pray, she ran the jet beads through her hand like a rosary, feeling the facets through the fingers of her gloves.

A nudge in the ribs jolted her.

"Was it Beverley Nichols or Godfrey Winn who had a dog called Mr Sponge?" came in a stage whisper.

Violet squeezed her eyes shut tight: "O God please bless Felix and let him be happy and reunited with his family and—" if there were a heaven, it was a good thing for her and most of this congregation that there was no marriage or giving in marriage there—imagine the complications.

"Which of them got Willie Maugham's desk in the end?"

"Oh God, *I* don't know." She didn't know, didn't know if her prayer would get through the myriad, innumerable as plankton, prayers eternally sluicing the teeth of Heaven's gate. A snowball's chance in hell perhaps.

"Ask them yourself—later!" Her words hissed like sizzling snow.

A teenage boy, perhaps one of Camilla's, was standing at the front of the church, clearing his throat. He read badly, as if he had never read any poetry until this public occasion; it was Francis Thompson's "At Lord's" that the boy was murdering but could not quite kill. Violet's eyes filled again, and her unshed tears were brackish with bitterness. The poem had brought her back to Felix once when she had been on the point of leaving him. They were in a taxi, his coat was specked with ash and she had recoiled from his tobacco-stained kiss. They must have been passing Lord's for she had mentioned the poem, that she thought was her own discovery, a manly poem that had touched her girl's heart, and Felix had at once recited it, word perfect, and she had felt an overwhelming tenderness for him. How dared Camilla know about it? He had spread himself thin, rich pâté eked out over too many slices of toast. Desolate, small and old, she would have given almost anything to be riding in that taxi through the blue London twilight now. But Felix was in Italy, she braced up, pontificating over a bottle of young wine or extra virgin oil, holding it up to the light.

She forbade the tears to spill, it would not do for people to see her—unmanned. A man's woman—yes, she had always been that. Her women friends had always taken second place to the man in her life. "Flies round a honeypot," Felix would snort with jealous pride after every party. Had the essence of herself been dissipated, though, and nearly all her choices been made for her, by some man's or boy's need which outweighed her own? At a splash to her right she stared at Maurice. Tears were rolling down his cheeks and dripping on to his Order of Service. She gave a sharp nod towards the handkerchief in his top pocket. Upstaged. She swallowed an untimely giggle that threatened to turn into a sob.

As Denzil, Sir Denzil Allen, ancient ousted publisher, began his address, Violet thought, this is odd. Very odd, if you come to think of it, as she did. She referred to her Order of Service to confirm her suspicion: all the speakers and readers were men. Felix had been such a lover of women, many of his closest friends had been women and yet those women he had loved and who had known him best, herself chief among them, were to sit in their pews and have him expounded to them by these men. Well, that was the way of a world which she had made no attempt to change, and she could have been Violet Mazzotti and have organised this service herself, and made a better job of it. Women had not always been nice to her. She remembered the resentment, the thinly veiled spite of some of Felix's old friends when they were living together. Men too. Had she really expected them to say "Welcome, Violet Clements, lovely and gifted youthful poet. We embrace you as one of us?" She could understand them now, but she had often been hurt and she stuck to her resolve never to snub a young girl, however pretty or silly, in whom shyness might be mistaken for arrogance. Across the church she could see Sibyl Warner, the novelist, making a rare appearance. Heavily veiled, once a great beauty, she had long been a recluse from a world which assumed the right to comment on time's alterations.

"My God, I didn't recognise you! You've changed!" That wound was inflicted twenty years ago by Jill Blakiston, in an affronted tone which hinted at betrayal and that the photographs on the jackets of Sibyl's books must have been forgeries. She sat behind her today, a retired editorial director, rummaging for a tissue in £1,000 worth of crocodile bag, quite unaware of what she had done, but Violet had been there and seen Sibyl flinch, gulp her drink and leave.

Something had shocked Violet almost as much as the revelation that people could go to bed in the morning. "Mind if I pee in your sink?" Felix had asked. It was a year after they had met and she was living in a respectable boarding house in Mornington Crescent. She most certainly had minded. There was her cake of carnation soap on the rim of the basin and her sponge and toothbrush in a glass. "This is intolerable," Felix said. "The sooner you move in with me the better."

Her landlady, catching Felix tiptoeing down the stairs at one in the morning, told her to pack her bags at once and so, in a cloud of disgrace and defiance, she departed to Gordon Square. Living in sin entailed, she found out, a great deal of scrubbing shirt collars and darning socks and hours of copying out manuscripts and typing. But it had been fun too. Fun—what a funny, bizarre, orange paper hat word. After a while afternoon drinking clubs and hangovers and cooking for Felix's drunken friends wasn't fun any more. Felix sailed to America in 1938, for which some still condemned him. Violet refused to accompany him and when he returned she was Violet Morton, a widow with two children, the younger boy born posthumously after the Battle of Britain. She had married George Maxwell-Smith to give the boys a father, and divorced him after he had gambled away his father's furniture factory and fled with the girl in accounts. Bobby Greene, a painter, had succumbed to cancer after just eighteen months of happy marriage. His pictures hung on her walls and there had been intimations recently of a small renaissance interest in his work.

> Hold Thou Thy Cross
> Before my closing eyes.
> Shine through the gloom
> And point me to the skies . . .

An amethyst cross, grown huge, loomed gleaming through swirling mist, suspended above Felix's bed; Felix rising vertically ceilingward with feet pointing down. An amethyst cross on a silver chain that had belonged to her mother, pawned and never redeemed.

As always after one of these occasions Violet was left with the thought that all that really matters in this life is that we should be kind to one another.

"Imogen, there's no Heaven!" she heard a boy say outside, under the Indian bean tree leaning on its crutch.

"Ha, ha, Very funny,' said Imogen, the girl who had been behind Violet, and blew her nose, saying "Has my mascara run all over the place? You know, I really quite enjoyed that."

A group of black-coated youngish Turks was lighting cigarettes, and one of them cast a satirical eye at the knot of Violet's friends moving towards her, and made a remark at which the others laughed. Violet wondered when the power had passed to those young men with sliding smiles and snidey eyes; when had they staged their coup? She glanced around and thought: you—girl in a black dress squirming away from the poet you had thought to flatter with your charm—you have read none of his work but someone told you he is a poppet, and now he's threatening your cleavage with the dottle from his pipe. Who are all these rouged dotards, you wonder, boys and girls, these deposed Old Turks who sidle up to you with swimming eyes like macerated cocktail cherries, pleading for a reissue of their mildewed masterworks, a mention on the wireless or a book to review, that you will never send? Who are they, these mothballed revenants that you thought dead for years, these relics of whom you have never heard. Who? Well, my dears—they are you.

Violet was weary: wake up, Denton Welch, Djuna Barnes, Mark Gertler, Gaudier-Brzeska, Gjurdieff et al—it's time for your next brief disinterment. Angels were warming up to dance on the heads of pins. A bored miaoaw from Schroeder's cat. Stale buns, duckies. It was reassuring to be kissed by old kid and chamois leather, badger bristle shaving brushes and paintbrush beards, comfortable if elegaic to be surrounded by elegant decaying warehouses that had stored fine wines and cheeses and garlic for most of the century, and some were as stout as their sodden purple-seeping vats and others as frail as towers of round plywood boxes that might topple and be bowled along by the wind.

"Are you coming along for drinkies?"

"No, Maurice dear, my grandson's taking me out to lunch."

He was, but on the following day. Violet had had enough. It had been gracious of Camilla to invite her today, perhaps, but enough was enough. She disengaged herself and started to walk towards Fortnum's, rather worried about Maurice. Who would pour him into the Brighton train in the frightful gloaming when the lights of shops and taxis blaze bleakly on wan faces and all souls seem lost? Would some sixth sense carry him along, a buffeted buffoonish bygone with the cruel and censorious commuters, or might he find himself alone on the concourse but for a few vagrants, Lily Law bearing down on him, the last train gone and all bars closed, or would he wake without a passport at Gatwick Airport or in a black siding at Hassocks or Haywards Heath? She consoled herself with the knowledge that it was the drinks afterwards which had persuaded him to make the journey, and that after a certain hour everybody on the Brighton train was drunk. Deciding against Fortnum's, she turned down Duke Street into Jermyn Street, making for St James's Square. The shop windows were lovely, still dressed for autumn with coloured leaves and berries, nuts and gilded rosy pomegranates, but behind the glass of one display an aerosol forecast snow.

Violet loved the symmetry of the gardens, that square within a circle within a square within a square. She sat on a bench with a sense of being alone with the equestrian statue of Gulielmus III at its centre and the birds that fluttered in the foliage and pecked about in the fallen leaves on the paving stones. An obelisk marked each corner of the inner square and a tiny-leaved rambling rose had captured one of them and held it in its thorns, and a wren emerged from a bush, saw her and disappeared. Her eyes were still sharp enough to identify a bird; she was fortunate in that. She was fortunate in having a tall fair-haired grandson. Had there been a touch of smugness in her tone when she had spoken of him to poor lonely Maurice? Well, she *was* proud of Tom and delighted that he should want to take her to lunch; too bad, why should she temper her feelings to Maurice's sensibilities? She did try not to condescend to those who were not the mother of sons and had only granddaughters instead of big handsome boys who made one feel cherished and feminine and even a little deliciously dotty and roguish at times, and it was pleasant to bring out carefully selected stories from her past as if from a drawer lined with rose and violet pot-pourri spiced with faint intriguing muskier fruitier notes. Maurice had been involved in some unpleasantness in the bad old days, she recalled, but he must have put aside all such foolishness now, as she had. The long windows of the London Library glittered, reminding her how once she would have hoped love lurked there, playing peek-a-boo round the bookstacks. She toyed with the idea of a cup of coffee in the Wren, the wholesome café attached to the church, or something worthy to eat, but putting that aside in favour of her own little kitchen and bathroom, along with the unpleasant image, like a grey illustration in a book, of Maurice in a suit of broad arrows breaking stones in Reading Gaol, she decided to take the Piccadilly Line to Gloucester Road.

There wasn't a seat and Violet had to stand, but just for a moment or two until a rough-looking lad heaved himself up and nodded her into his place. Violet thanked him courteously, giving a lesson in manners to any who should be watching, and a rueful, apologetic little smile to the dowdy woman left standing. It doesn't do to judge by appearances, she thought, of the boy, while acknowledging that he, naturally, had done just that. It didn't surprise her because it had always been so; men had never stopped holding doors open for her, and even when she and the boys had been marooned in that rotting-thatched cottage in Suffolk after George's defection, there had been some gum-booted Galahad to dig her out of a ditch or rescue a bird from the chimney.

A startlingly beautiful boy was sitting opposite her. She couldn't take her eyes off his face. About sixteen, with loose blue-black curls, olive skin and a full, tragic mouth. He must be South American. Venezuelan, she decided, in a city far from home. He had the face of an angel. She named him Angelo. There was a panache, a muted stylishness, about his black leather jacket, dark charcoal sweater over a white T-shirt, black jeans, silver ring and earring, the black-booted ankle resting casually across the knee. Fearing that he might imagine there was something predatory in the way she drank in his beauty, she averted her attention to the ill-featured youth on Angelo's right, but she was drawn back to Angelo's almond-shaped, lustrous, long-lashed eyes. Hyde Park Corner came and went. Violet shut her eyes, abruptly suffused with a sadness she didn't know what to do with, and a statue came into her mind, a little stone saint in a wayside shrine whose lips had crumbled, kissed away by thousands of supplicants' desires. She wanted to warn the boy: Angelo, beware. People will prey on you, want to possess you, corrupt you, exploit you for your beauty until there is nothing left of you and you are destroyed; but there was a wariness about Angelo's face which said that he had learned that long ago.

She opened her eyes. A sudden instinct told her that Angelo and the youth who had given up his seat and the lout on his right were connected, and pretending not to be. A lunge of silver, her bag ripped from her hands, fingers tearing at her rings, and as he grabbed the necklace, black against a blazing yellow and grape-purple flash of anguished desire to snatch back and relive her years, she was aware of a knife at her throat and that Angelo was a girl.

93

Zone O

DAVID ROGERS

After his wife died, Channon was unemployed for three years. During that time Andromache, his claimant adviser, had tried unsuccessfully to fix him up with a number of jobs. In the end she dropped his file into a little black cabinet by the side of her desk and said: "Right, well we'll bung you down the tube then."

His interview for the tube was conducted in the foyer of an Uxbridge hotel by a Captain Harper, who had a hearty Essex accent and wore a tweed jacket with leather elbow patches. He apologised for the secrecy but explained that it was in the nature of the job.

"What job is that?" asked Channon suspiciously.

"Revenue Protection, m'boy," said Captain Harper, stroking his moustaches with a brown gloved hand. He pushed a long buff envelope over the little coffee table. There was a job description inside.

Every year LRT lost an estimated 35 million pounds through fraud. Revenue Protection had the task of stopping this very serious leakage of capital from the system: by (a) locating passengers who had failed to pay their tariff of travel, and by (b) ensuring that any monies recovered were paid in full to the appropriate authorities. His job, should he choose to accept it, was to get caught without a valid ticket. When this happened he was to tender the correct fare, memorise the inspector's identity number, and report number, time, place and amount to—here there was a blank space with the name "Cpt Harper" added in biro—at St James's Park HQ. Or, if he were arrested, as he might well be, he would play along until delivered into the hands of the transport police, whereupon at a suitable moment he would show them his secret identity badge, and they would let him go.

For as long as he could remember, Channon had lived in a stunned silence with himself. He enjoyed no more than a vague nodding-acquaintance with the face he met each morning in the bathroom mirror. After he began work with LRT, however, he would spend hours staring with a thoughtful frown at the metal loops laid flush to the floor of the carriages. When his shift was over he posted Observation Form RC145 to Control, went home to his flat, drank a bottle of Bulgarian country wine, ate a Safeway chicken curry, and watched television.

Channon's secret identity badge was a black leather purse containing a bas-relief of a tube train entering a tunnel over a motto in Latin. Next to this was a rectangle of plastic with his photo and name on it: Revenue Protection Officer Channon. He liked to carry it in his left breast pocket, where he could feel its tug through the fabric of his shirt. He no longer felt he ought to be ashamed of the salt and pepper stubble on his chin, his abominable footware, his tobacco-margarine aroma of long-term poverty, the horned moons of dirt under his nails. These were nothing more than the elements of Revenue Protection Officer Channon's cover; his real identity—well, that was a secret so secret that he himself only had it on good authority that it existed at all.

In the first few weeks of his employment he tried conscientiously to travel over as much of the system as he could. But after a while he noticed that he tended to avoid the overground periphery. It seemed somehow thin and insignificant—the prosaic ankles and elbows of the system. He had a tropism for the deepest parts of the network, where the air was stalest and most metallic—to the great complication of connections within the ring of the Circle Line: this was, he felt, your actual Centre of Things. He liked to gaze at the walls of Charing Cross, at the germinal matrix of History in the making, Power in the darkness, Big Money, Beauty, Sex and Myth known as Zone One. It would be quite useless to tell him about the romance of the outer stations—Turnham Green, for example, where the Earl of Essex gathered 24,000 Londoners to defend their revolution against the Royalist army, or to suggest that power was not generated in the centre, but had retreated there, as the blood of a hypothermic animal withdraws to the body's core—Channon didn't know much about the Underground, but he knew what he liked. Perhaps in another incarnation he had been a woodlouse, or perhaps there had been no other incarnations, perhaps this was a first attempt.

"Well Channon," said Captain Harper at the end of his probationary period, "you're doing a fine job. You may like to know that your figures are the best I've ever seen for a newcomer. We've all got a pret-ty high opinion of you in Control." Channon shrugged and apologised for not doing even better. "One thing, though," the Captain continued, "you might do something to change your appearance from time to time, hmm? We move two million people a day but you can't be too careful, m'boy, if they once get wind of you, well that can severely limit your value."

"Yes, Captain," he said, and bought a personal stereo and a tape of Frank Sinatra singing "Songs for Swinging Lovers".

By the end of his first year, Channon was a changed man. Once he had so closely resembled a baton of continental sausage that he might have hung himself upside down in the window of a delicatessen without arousing comment; now his skin was pasty, his eyes hemeralopic, and his small, brittle frame had slackened and swelled. In his dreams he travelled on a ghostly facsimile of the Underground, alone, on a bridal train of ashes that sighed through long exhalations of church-grey corridors, from station to station, each with platforms made from cake-layers of moss, dead leaves, and pink crematorium gravel.

Channon's hermetic existence was only punctured by the ticket inspectors, whom he grew to hate and fear. It was the way they appeared in the carriages, thunderclap and cloudburst of creatures he—floundering for a noun to bundle up the vicious verbs—strutting, flapping, hissing, stabbing—always mistook for enormous birds. When this happened he always experienced the same sequence of sensations: of waking from a warm reverie drenched in dread, his heart crashing gears and kangarooing into his stomach which refluxed the gastric acids that burned his throat, squeezed tears from his eyes and gasps from his lungs. When the inspectors reached him to begin his ritual humiliation (a trial in which it was pre-ordained not only that he would lose, and should lose, but also that he be complicit in that loss), he crossed his arms tightly against the brass and leather of his secret identity, to confirm who he was, but also to stop himself from ripping it out and waving them away, as a scarecrow waves away birds with its outstretched arms.

One day a couple of ticket inspectors boarded Channon's eastbound Central Line carriage at Mile End. He was listening to "I've got you under my skin/I've got you deep in the heart of me" when he looked up to see the inspector unfurled above him, like a black Babylonian death-pennant. That particular week he'd been instructed to trawl for Age

Misstatement Frauds, so he'd bought a Child's One Day Off-Peak Travelcard. Dumbly, he held out his ticket with his thumb over the price and the "C" designation. The inspector took the ticket from his hands.

"This is a child's ticket Ssir."

(Don't you know, little fool, you never can win)

"Is it?" asked Channon. "I didn't know."

"Might I assk how old you are, Ssir?"

(Use your mentality/Wake up to reality)

"31. It's my birthday."

"In that case I must assk you to accompany me off this train when we reach the next sstation. Happy birthday."

When Stratford station arrived the inspector took Channon to a small room marked "Private" in a corridor labelled "No Exit". The room contained a row of metal chairs, and a table. On the table was an ashtray, above it a video camera. Channon was told to sit in one of the chairs. An hour or so later, he was smoking the last of the butts in the ashtray when, instead of the transport police, two tall pallid men entered.

"Would you fill this in please, Sir," said one. (His face the pink-grey-white of uncooked chicken skin.) Channon blinked stupidly at the form, it seemed to be some kind of market research questionnaire.

"What's this for?"

"It's a market ressearch quesstionnaire," said one of the men.

"Revenue Collection try to provide a professional sservice for our clients," added the other.

Channon could not decide how to take this remark. Nothing like this had happened before. He filled in his name and address, assessed how politely and efficiently the RCS had performed, stated how often he used LRT, which lines, how often he evaded payment, which methods he used, his work record, what academic qualifications he had obtained, his political views, his idea of a good time, the names of two referees, and so on. There were fourteen pages, and some of the questions were pretty odd. Channon noticed that the inspectors wore silver pins in the shape of caducei in their collar-lapels, and that their teeth were long and brown. When he had signed and dated the form they took it away and led him back to the platform.

Looking along at the lines of motionless, unsmiling strangers, sheltering from a heavy drizzle, silent, or conversing in whispers, Channon was reminded of a scene from a Cold War thriller: a scene shot in underlit monochrome, an Eastern European capital caught in the overlapping penumbra of East and West, where every third face belonged to a spy or a secret policeman... But these faces expressed nothing but the differently resolved struggle between anxiety and fatigue; a separation each from the other so grotesque that any one of them could be raped, mugged, or garotted by thuggees while the others stood by and, insulated by that indifference they called individualism, pretended not to notice. What day of the week was it? He didn't even know that: he had long since exchanged sun-time for system-time. Nobody would hear him if he cried. Panic blew up in his chest, like a life raft: the panic of being picked out from the sleepy herd, which lives forever in a dream, to become a lone mortal, shaken suddenly into consciousness.

The next train arrived. The inspectors each took hold of an arm and pulled him back into a niche. The foetid stench of their breath coiled around him. When Channon moved up to secondary school he had to take swimming lessons. The class was divided into those who could and those who couldn't swim. Channon, who could just manage a width with a dive, claimed he could, but when they went for their introductory lesson he had to take a test: two lengths of the biggest pool he had ever seen. He swam a quarter-length with his eyes closed, then, when he turned his head to gasp his first breath, sucked in only super-chlorinated water. Straight away he lost the stroke and had to struggle for life, with deoxygenated muscles, in a world stripped of everything but pain and the imminent presence of death. Oddly, Channon recalled this twenty-years-forgotten episode entire while he floundered among the overcoats, limbs and umbrellas of entraining/detraining commuters. He staggered through one partial collision after another, fumbling as he ran as he fell for the badge that would save him until his elbows found concrete, his badge went skipping under the train, and the doors hissed shut. He looked a moment at his own puzzled frown in the glossy flank of a lawyer's attaché case between the bars of ivory-stockinged knees, as from behind hands took his arm and yanked him savagely round; he pirouetted on one knee, the inverted V of shadowed thighs jump-cut to a bootcap that appeared from nowhere, like a falling piano in the middle of a garden party, and he saw, balanced a painless instant longer on the fulcral moment between anticipation and recognition, his own two top front teeth spat across the platform like thrown dice.

Channon sat in a room similar to but smaller than the one where he'd filled in the form. There was a phone on the desk beside an ashtray recharged with butts. A woman wearing the starched cotton tulip wimple of a Great War nurse was picking pieces of grit from his face with a pair of tweezers. He remembered fragments of what had happened: being wheeled aboard the special train, handcuffed to a metal loop in the floor, and taken to St Giles (a station which didn't exist), then to this room. How long had he been asleep? shivering slumped forward head on the tabletop, manacled hands between his knees, until roused by this kindly angel.

She'd brought a bottled gas heater, a couple of aspirin, and a mug of sweet tea, which he'd managed to drink by waiting until it was tepid, pooling as much liquid as he could under his tongue, adding the aspirin, opening his throat, and jerking his head back so it all went down at once.

St Giles was the largest and strangest station he'd ever been in. The walls were covered with cracked, discoloured white tiles, like a morgue or a public toilet; the staff wore green gumboots. He could hear, in the vast scary hinterland of echoes, accelerating/decelerating drill-whines, high-pressure hosepipes, ten-second buzzings, the steady clangour and vibration of machinery whose purpose and action he could not picture. While half-asleep Channon heard voices arguing in an adjacent room, too blurred by the toilet acoustics to make much out, but distinct phrases came through from time to time: "kingdom of evil" for example, and "in the Government of the Night", and "you're nestled in the devil's cleavage".

"You've been in the wars incha, love?" said the nurse, patting his cheek with a cloth that smelled of pine resin. The water in the bowl balanced on the heater turned a thin sepia. His face began to sting.

"You've even got it in your ear."

He stared steadily at the red cross pattée on her dazzlingly white pinafore. The stinging was promoted to a lancing.

"Wha's in uh wa-hub?" he asked.

"What's in the water? Just something to kill the germs."

The fragrance of pine began to burn his nose. He repeated his question with greater urgency.

"Well ... we're a bit low on antiseptic so I used toilet cleaner—but in actual fact it's better, it kills everything there is."

Channon's face burst into flames. He tried to pull his head back but the nurse had one hand knotted into his hair.

"Almost finished," she said, encouragingly, rubbing a little harder. "Come on, darling, we're almost there." Channon braced his knees against the edge of the table and forced himself backwards with all his might, detaching a handful of hair, a patch of Australia-shaped scalp, and striking the back of his head against the corner of the gas heater, then, a little while later, the white tiles of the floor.

A telephone began to ring.

"Allo yess," said a man's voice. "Yess, I've got him here now. No, no point we don't think, no, no use at all. I couldn't tell you. Ang on a mo." A seamed and pleated head rose over the horizon of the table-edge, eclipsing the strip light into which Channon was staring. "It's for you, Mr Channon."

A man in a black uniform stooped to fit the phone between Channon's shoulder and chin where he lay on the white tiles. There was no pain any more, he could jam his stiffened tongue right into the gum where his teeth had been, he didn't feel a thing.

"Hello, Channon? This is your Captain speaking m'boy ... Look here, Channon, you've got yourself into a bit of a pickle I'm afraid. They've found your badge at Stratford, and we think there's been some jiggery-pokery with the Post Office sorting staff, they've been intercepting your RCI45S ..."

Only his eyes moved, picking out the thorns of a compass rose, slow and untroubled, shapes seeping into blur over a black horizon tracked out as red bootprints in the empty offing. There was blood in a tube coming out of his arm, but he couldn't tell which way it was flowing.

"To tell you the truth there isn't much we can do at the moment; we're in negotiations."

There was a warm sense of floating—of ascending in light. Everything was shrinking at the rate of one millimetre a minute, and the ceiling was getting closer. He was nobody

any more—all the nonsense was knocked out of his head—
he recognised he'd always been nobody, just like everybody
else, torn scraps of faces in career from station to station
forsaken again, groping the vast edges, crawling down the
Black Hall to the dark door opening to the box provided, for
office use only—but Channon could no longer understand
his thoughts, so he listened instead to the random sounds of
nearby industry, tempered and orchestrated into the machine
that was hoisting him higher—and draining him away.

"Now I expect you're wondering about the police,"
Captain Harper's voice continued regardless, 'well they're
neutral m'boy. We might have done something with the fire
brigade while you were still at Stratford but they won't go
near St Giles. Just sit tight and await developments. And no
more heroics, you'll hurt yourself. Remember the motto! *Sic
transit*, m'boy, *sic transit*."

The Salt Bins

PATRICK CUNNINGHAM

In the first months of my retirement I found many ways of keeping myself amused. My bus pass took me in search of adventure from Tulse Hill to Muswell Hill, from Tooting Bec to Bexleyheath. But after a time travel was not enough. I needed something else to add spice to my days. So in the evenings I sometimes wrote hysterical letters to myself from the daughter I never had, demanding money, accusing me of maltreating her or threatening to put me in an old people's home. On my bus trips around London I dropped these, in addressed but unsealed envelopes, in the salt bins so solicitously left on the kerbsides by our caring local Councils.

It was quite by accident that I discovered that the salt bins did not sit neglected and unloved by passers-by. I was surprised to find that they had a secret life apart from their main function of being receptacles for municipal salt. It was when I was invited to take afternoon tea with my cousin Agnes at Brown's Hotel that I made the discovery.

Agnes went up in the world when she married a man who is a wizard in the shrink-wrap-film industry. My mackintosh, which I wore to keep out the April drizzle, was not a garment which would have added lustre to my entry into Brown's Hotel, so at the corner of Albemarle Street and Grafton Street I slipped it off, rolled it up and, when no one was looking, popped it into a convenient salt bin and arrived at

Brown's Hotel looking respectable, if not bandbox new, in my jacket of herringbone Harris tweed.

Cousin Agnes is a kind soul and even though not a true cousin to me but a cousin of my late wife, she never fails to look me up on her visits from rural Cheshire. She invites me to stay with her in the country but I tell her that I do not care to leave my house to the depredations of burglars and vandals. That is the correct response, for her invitation is part of the delicate web of family etiquette that binds us together; its acceptance would be to break a filament of that web.

Brown's do a good tea: little triangular two-bite sandwiches, cakes with French names, the different textures of flaky pastry and sponge, sugar-glaze and marzipan, the softness of whipped cream. Afterwards I came out into the street restored by Agnes's kindness and cosseting. A little luxury does one good. I walked to the corner of the street, lifted the lid of the salt bin—my mackintosh was gone. In its place was a bundle of out-of-date magazines carefully tied with string.

I did not mourn my loss for long. There was no point. I have trained myself to take life's blows in my stride. Someone needed a worn-out coat more than I, I thought. In my wardrobe was an old blue Pac-a-mac that would do me just as well. But I took the bundle of magazines as compensation for my loss.

On the bus I sorted through them: *Country Life*, the *Burlington Magazine*, the *Yachtsman*—rich people's magazines. I did not think at the time that their owner was the person who had taken my mackintosh, but I must have been wrong, for something happened that was wonderful and strange. In the pocket of my mackintosh was my gas bill, received that very afternoon as I left the house. I had put by the money to pay it, but now it seemed I would have to wait for the reminder to tell me the exact amount. But the weeks passed without bringing me the warning letter and when, worried that my supply might be cut off, I rang the gas company, they told me the bill had already been paid.

"The computer doesn't lie," they said.

Next month I popped the electricity bill into the salt bin in Sloane Square; I deposited the water rates demand in Hampstead High Street. Nothing happened. The final demands were lying on my mat within weeks.

It was a combination of boredom and the receipt of three pages of blandness from my son Kevin in Brisbane that prompted me to write that first letter to myself. There was something missing in my relationship with my son. Perhaps I did not have a talent for parenting or perhaps it was that Kevin was his mother's child. When he was four he worried that she might die, and she did die, though not until he was fourteen. Afterwards he acted as if I had no function in his life, as if by my failure to keep his mother alive I had shown my unfitness to be the father of a family. I was a redundant relative. And when he was twenty-two and I had not set him on the path to riches, he left for Australia. I did not miss him a great deal—what was there to miss? But we continue with the courtesies of a father-son relationship: we are dutiful about that. He telephones or writes at the appropriate times. At Christmas he sends me a sweater with an Australian motif—a kangaroo or a boomerang—embroidered on the chest. His letters read like a digest of the headlines of his local paper: "There was a plague of insects at Wattamatu," he writes. "There was a four-car pile-up at the corner of Brunswick Heights and Fleming Street. Two people were killed."

He has become a fireman and twice he sent me newspaper photos of himself and his crew in action at fires, but because the reproduction was poor and the men were half hidden by their protective gear, I couldn't pick out which one was my son.

On that Sunday afternoon I was thinking that perhaps it would have been different if I'd had a daughter. I thought of the letters she might write, affectionate, funny, gossipy. But when I pondered it, the question arose in my mind: if I had failed with Kevin, why should it have been any different if I'd had a daughter? She might have fared even worse. I might have soured her life completely. And so that first letter was a letter of blame. It blamed me for the chances she'd never had, it blamed me for being a bad provider. It accused me of being overly preoccupied with my own comforts. I wrote it well. There was real feeling behind it. It even convinced me.

It lay on my table for several days before the idea of leaving it in a salt bin came to me, but once the notion presented itself, it seemed the right thing to do. I wanted there to be the possibility that these faults of mine might be exposed to at least one other random person. So I addressed it to myself and slipped it, unsealed, into a salt box on the Embankment, near the Houses of Parliament.

And once the letter had gone out into the public domain, so to speak, it seemed to make her real, this daughter of mine, this shrewish, complaining girl. I composed more and more and posted the letters in salt bins all over London.

She sounded angrier, more resentful, as the weeks went on. "I could have been another Margot Fonteyn," she wrote, "but you wouldn't stump up for the lessons." She had a slangy style and wrote on cheap lined paper, with "Number 34" scrawled at the top, by way of address. What else could I expect, since I had neglected to have her educated nicely?

"My Billy was right mad when I told him you was refusing to move into a Home," she wrote. "He wanted to go over there and give you a talking to—and you wouldn't like that.

You'd get a good price for that house, even though you keep it like a pigsty, and then Billy and me could have a proper place of our own. You owe it to your only daughter who you never treated right. Yours truly, Babs."

This one, placed in a salt bin in Holland Park Avenue, came back to me with a message written in pencil on the margin. "Stay in your own home," it said. "Don't give them a penny. You won't be thanked for it. I've been through all this, so I know." It was unsigned.

I was cheered by this evidence of a sympathetic heart beating somewhere in West London, so I tried a few more variations of the theme, giving more prominence to the thuggish Billy my daughter was shacked up with. "Billy is taking it out on me for you being so stubborn," she wrote. "He gave me a load of verbals when I told him you wouldn't move. He'll be over there to give you a going over, no way can I stop him."

I deposited copies of this one in Mornington Crescent, St John's Wood and Primrose Hill. Primrose Hill responded. It was a proper letter this time, in neat, well-formed hand-writing. "I couldn't help scanning the contents of this letter," it said. "My heart bleeds for you. I urge you to seek help from a social worker, or, failing that, to see a solicitor. It will be money well spent." And then, in capital letters underlined: "DO NOT GIVE UP YOUR HOME."

That reply seemed to bring out the worst in my daughter Babs. In her next letter she sank to new depths of nastiness. "You broke my mother's heart, but you won't break mine," she wrote. "Is there no end to your lies and mendacity? (Her vocabulary was improving.) The only way you can make amends is to sign over the house to me. Even that would be little enough recompense. And my Billy's temper is at boiling point. He's not a man to be crossed."

This one I left in the salt box in Kensington Gore. I waited two weeks, but there was no response. It was a disappointment.

My daughter's next letter was, frankly, abusive. "You snivelling old git," she wrote. "An excuse for a father. If you haven't made arrangements to hand over the house by the end of the month Billy's coming round to beat you up and I'll be there to cheer him on."

I made two copies of this letter, one for King Street, Hammersmith, the other for Shepherd's Bush Green. But when I got off the bus at Hammersmith the February wind whipping around the new office buildings chilled me, so I left one letter at the Broadway end of King Street and the other farther along near Ravenscourt Park. I was glad to get home again for there was sleet falling and I missed the old mac I'd lost when I visited Brown's Hotel.

It snowed in the night and there was a thin slick of snow on the streets in the morning and the sky was so dark I had to have the electric light on to read my paper. It was nearly four in the afternoon when the couple turned up on my doorstep. "I'm Mike," the man said, "and this is Mrs Brownlow— Elaine. We're from the Social Services and we wondered if there was any trouble—if everything's all right."

"Well, so far it is," I said, "but if it freezes up those footpaths will be treacherous. The Council ought to . . ."

"That's just it," Mike said, interrupting me. "The Council roadmen found something—two things, in fact—two letters—that led us to believe you might have been threatened."

So there it was. I'd forgotten that the salt bins' main function was storing salt to be spread on the snowy streets. I'd felt so safe, but now I was cornered.

I denied everything. I said I didn't know what they were talking about. I said I had no daughter, only a son, and he was in Australia. I showed him the Australian motif on the chest of my sweater. I said I knew no one called Billy or Babs.

I couldn't tell if they believed me or not. I could see them glance uncertainly at one another. They asked me a lot of questions and gave me leaflets about day centres and luncheon clubs and chiropody services. To get them gone I agreed to have meals on wheels. And they did go at last and I shut the door behind them. They'd shaken me up. I'd always kept officialdom at arm's length before. I had to sit for a long time before I got my nerve back. There was no reason why I should be frightened, but I was.

There were no more letters from my daughter. It was another thing missing from my life. Babs was not the best daughter in the world, but I missed her nonetheless. Her Billy was a rough diamond, but they worked well together: they were a pair.

Mrs Brownlow from the Council called on me from time to time, making light conversation, asking questions. I did not like to think that someone had opened a file on me, however kindly meant. I thought of ways to avoid her attentions.

"I may soon be remarrying," I said to her one day.

"How nice!" said Mrs Brownlow. "A local lady, is she?"

I shook my head. "From the West Country," I said. I pointed to a framed photograph of Cousin Agnes on the sideboard. "That is my intended."

Mrs Brownlow admired Cousin Agnes's abundant jewellery.

"She is a Lady Mayoress," I lied, to explain the four strands of pearls around Agnes's throat.

"How nice!" Mrs Brownlow said again.

When she had left, I thought about my new love, the West Country Lady Mayoress. If Mrs Brownlow continued to call I would have to explain why our nuptials were delayed. I knew at once who was the obstacle to our happiness. In my mind's eye I saw him, a fat man, florid-faced in his scarlet Mayoral robe, with a false smile for all and sundry.

Almost without thinking I took out pen and writing pad. The anguished words of the Lady Mayoress appeared almost without my willing them: "He spends all evening in the Mayor's Parlour," she wrote, "and I serve out my sentence in the kitchen, ironing his white shirts and pressing creases into the trousers of his pinstripes, when all I want is to be with you ..."

Back

SUE GEE

At a time in my life I prefer not to think about, I used to make a bus journey each week across London, travelling on the upper deck. I was living at the time in the house of my friend Elizabeth, in an area of the city close to one of the great parks. Tall white terraced houses lay street upon street behind the main road which ran past the park, and my memory of those streets, which I had visited since childhood, when they were rather different, shows sharp spring sunlight, bay trees in pots, dark ivy trailing over the walls of secluded gardens. My memory of those days is in certain respects unreliable, but I can see the delicatessen on the corner where Elizabeth bought her cheese, and the dry cleaners where American women quite unlike either Elizabeth or myself took their husband's suits and shirts and their own silken dresses, collecting them at the end of the day in candy-striped paper bags. Women in pressed clothes and narrow shoes, having a nice day now, while I went to pieces. That is how I think of them, of it.

I unreliably remember sunlight: in fact it was very early spring, and often cold and sometimes raining, and the journey I made on the top of that bus was through a winter of the spirit.

Seasons are important; weather and houses are important: I dream about houses all the time. They are never houses I know, but they must mean something. Elizabeth's house meant something.

Elizabeth had been at school with my mother. In the way that schoolfriends sometimes do, they stayed in touch long after they had ceased to have anything real in common, and so it was that as a child I used sometimes to be taken for supper, and sometimes for Sunday lunch, to a tall dilapidated house quite unlike our own, in what was then a rather rundown area. Elizabeth was square and solid, with heavy dark hair and a strong, well-set face, and she lived with another woman, a painter called Louise. Naturally, when I was a child, the exact circumstances of their relationship were not revealed to me. I simply knew that there was Elizabeth, and there was Louise, who had a studio up at the top of their dilapidated house, where she painted, while Elizabeth went out to work. She was also doing the house up, bit by bit.

I liked them both, and I liked the visits, going up dangerous front steps to the front door, squeezing past boxes of tools and paint tins in the hall, glimpsing a trestle table for papering the huge, barely furnished sitting room. We went down narrow stairs to the kitchen, smelling fresh plaster and Sunday roast. A wall had been knocked down, floorboards had been taken up, unpainted glass doors led out to a small neglected garden. Elizabeth was working on it, bit by bit.

She and Louise lived, it seemed, in harmony. I think I was always aware of their devotion, liking the way they walked round the garden together, after lunch, Elizabeth's arm round Louise's shoulders as she talked about beds and plants and paving stones. I liked the way they looked at each other. Somewhere I was aware that my parents did not look at each other like that.

An only child, I was used to spending much time in the company of adults, or in my own company. When we went to supper, I would be put to bed in the dusty spare room, still with its original wallpaper, up on the landing across from the studio. I lay beneath a heavy paisley eiderdown, listening to the voices from downstairs. Next morning, I was allowed to sit in my nightgown on a high stool in the studio, watching Louise at work. She painted interiors, and views from the studio window; she painted Elizabeth, often, and once she painted me: we were both in an exhibition. I used to talk to her as I talked to Elizabeth: about everything, as children do. Then I grew older: I talked less and noticed more.

I noticed that the easy flow of conversation which Louise and Elizabeth shared, and which I had shared with each of them, was not something which went on at home between my parents: they were polite with one another. I noticed that the dilapidated house became, over the years, bit by cherished bit, a warm and well-ordered home. It made our house in Wimbledon feel too tidy, as if the furniture itself were being polite. Later, I realised that my parents' manner towards each other masked a deep dislike. Later, they divorced. By this time I had begun to think too much. By this time, Louise had died.

My mother moved to Edinburgh, where she had a cousin; she did not remarry. My father bought a flat in the Barbican; neither did he. Elizabeth and he had dinner from time to time; from time to time they went to concerts. Then these outings stopped. She was still in mourning: my father understood. He told me this one autumn Sunday afternoon, as we stood on the tiny balcony of his flat, looking down upon the lakeside terrace, where the fountains were.

I had not seen my father for months: by now I had my own adult life, which was proving difficult. I was too pre-occupied with my own affairs to think of other people's. I was working, I was married: things were going wrong. I did not like the direction my thoughts were taking.

I told my father nothing of this. At the end of the afternoon we kissed goodbye and I walked along the grey brick corridors past dozens of studio flats where people lived alone. I went down the spiral of concrete steps to the street near St Paul's, and caught the bus back to my own house.

Then what had been difficult became intolerable.

My husband and I tried to make things better. We tried to have children, and found that we couldn't. Then he found someone who could.

It did not occur to me to go anywhere else. I rang the brass bell by the green front door, and Elizabeth took me in. She made me a bed in the room of my childhood, next to her lover's old studio. I lay beneath the heavy paisley eiderdown beneath a painting of rooftops; I turned my face to the pillow and slept, waking in the small hours as usual.

I was off work; I was given pills; I was going to pieces. So. This journey. I came out of Elizabeth's front door and down the steps; I walked through those white streets and up to the main road, crossing to the bus stop when the lights changed. People were still in their winter coats. Mine was absolutely straight and black, long, beautifully cut: the last thing my husband bought me before his departure. Clothes are important, too: when I am well, I notice everything.

People queued, shivering; they hurried through the park and took refuge in restaurants. The bus came; I climbed to the top, wanting to be above the press of traffic; I sat at the front, looking out, seeing nothing. I truly can remember nothing, until we drew near to my destination.

A four-lane road, a roundabout. White road signs hung just above the level of the upper deck. Miles and fractions of miles—to the river, the railway station, to the East End—

passed above my head. We moved into the far left lane. I did notice now, I noticed everything. Racing heart, tight chest, empty stomach churning. An enormous Victorian building engrimed with dirt, paint peeling on every window frame. Litter blew in the wind; pale young women pushed babies in plastic shrouds. If the sun shone I do not remember it. I remember the dusty windows of the bus and a leaden sky above the roof of the hospital. I remember my appointment card, a pale spring green, and a list of dates and dates and dates.

Dr Morgan had private consulting rooms in a street in the heart of the city: I could not afford to see him there. I pictured leather chairs, the discreet closing of a heavy polished door. Here, I sat not in a waiting room but a waiting area, a space. A girl at a desk had a computer screen before her; a large box of toys stood on the floor for those who had come with children.

I had no children.

Each week, I had half an hour with Dr Morgan. I entered his little room and sat down; the black coat, unbuttoned, fell away to the sides of the low chair opposite his; on the table between us was a box of tissues. Once, as I talked, I remembered a woman sitting before the long illuminated mirror of a very expensive hairdressers I used to go to in the days when my husband loved me. The woman was a few seats along from me: I became aware of disturbance. I turned, I saw her weeping, her hands and her long wet hair covering what I could see, when at last she looked up, was a fine and lovely face. Scissors stopped, coffee was brought; Lenny, attending her, was all concern. Cheer up, he told her, no man is worth it. I saw her try to smile.

Why are you telling me this? asked Dr Morgan. What is that woman to you?

I liked her, I told him, and I knew why she was crying. She had been trying not to cry for years.

Have you been trying not to cry for years?

Perhaps. Probably. Yes.

About what?

Everything everything everything—

Then it was time to go.

I climbed the steps to the house of my friend Elizabeth and unlocked the green front door. It was starting to rain, it was after four. Elizabeth was still at work: I was still off work. A letter from the second post lay on the mat: I picked it up and went through the hall, with its paintings by Louise and faded blue and ochre rugs, and down the stairs to the kitchen.

A bowl of hyacinths stood on the table and the air was full of them. I put on the light above the cooker; I propped Elizabeth's letter by the hyacinths, I put on the kettle and let in the cat. He left blurry wet pawmarks on his way to the fridge; I fed him, and stood at the glass doors to the garden as the kettle came softly to life behind me. I watched the rain fall on to the paving, mossy here and there in the cracks; it fell on to clay pots of bulbs, still tightly in bud, on to variegated ivy and leafless shrubs. A dark walled garden, just the right size; a little stone statue: a girl, an urn.

The kettle boiled. I made tea in Elizabeth's blue and white pot and sat at the table and drank it. Rain trickled down the glass doors, the heating came on with a leap like a cat; the cat, beneath a radiator, washed and washed. It grew dark. Above us the house was absolutely quiet.

Rain falling as darkness fell; an empty house; a marriage ended.

I put my head on my arms on the table and waited for Elizabeth to come home.

I woke to see her standing on the other side of the kitchen, reading the letter. She had switched on the low lights above the worktop and for a moment, still half-asleep, I saw on her well-set face an expression I had never seen there before: closed, clouded. Then she put the letter in her pocket, came across and sat down opposite me: she smiled, and her face was as it usually was.

"All right?"

"All right." I touched the cold teapot. "I'll make some more."

"No—let's have a drink."

We opened a bottle of red and she drew the curtains. She asked me, as usual, about my day: I told her, as usual, that there was little to tell. She described her own: I sensed it was somehow an effort. We sat listening to the rain; she refilled our glasses. I wasn't supposed to drink with the pills.

"What shall we have for supper?" she asked.

I shook my head. "I'm not hungry."

It was what I said almost every evening: I waited for the usual kindly coaxing. She said, in a tone which was flat and weary:

"Please—"

She looked suddenly tired—more than tired, exhausted; and watching her I saw again the fleeting expression I'd glimpsed earlier pass across the face which her lover had painted: such a strong, beautiful face. Now it was not just tired but older, much older, aged between morning and evening.

I thought: she's had enough of me, she can't be doing with all this any more, I'll have to go—

Panic began to rise in me, I got up quickly, turning away, turning on the radio, hearing myself say in a high, faraway voice—

"It's all right, I'm sorry, I'll get supper, you must be—"

Bach was on the radio, I do remember that: a harpsichord, I do most clearly remember, repeating a theme which ran over the keyboard up and down up and down up and down up and down relentless and cruel, as if the containment of passion were something so simple and plain—

"Jo—"

Behind me, a hundred miles across the room, Elizabeth was getting to her feet. I opened the door of the fridge and could not recognise how to put one thing with another. I took out the box of eggs and put them on the worktop beside me, I swung the door shut, shaking; I put my head against the cool door of the freezer and tried to breathe. I thought: there are pills and pills and pills upstairs, I shall swallow the lot and they will save me—

A time in my life I prefer not to think of.

"Jo?"

I could not look at her.

"I'm sorry," I said to the eggbox. "I'm sorry, I'm sorry, I'll go, it isn't fair on you—"

'Darling," said Elizabeth, "It isn't you. It isn't you, it's me."

'What?"

The harpsichord had finished, and now there was a play.

"Come and sit down. Please?"

I switched off the play and sat down: I looked at her. Not just older but thinner—she had grown thinner: how had I not noticed that? What else had I not noticed?

"What is it? What is it?"

I'm sure she would rather have told anyone but me, but she had to tell someone, and I was there.

Next morning, when I woke up, things were rather different.

I got out of the bed with the paisley eiderdown, in the house where I had spent some of the nicest days of my childhood; I put on my dressing gown and went downstairs and made us both tea. I took the tray to Elizabeth's room and drew back the curtains and kissed her. She was already awake, and the cat was sleeping beside her. We drank our tea together, and then I left her, and went downstairs and made a telephone call. And then that part of my life was over.

I am sitting at a table on the terrace at the Barbican. It is mid-morning, midsummer, a Saturday. Ducks drift across the green-black water of the lake, between the fountains; the church bell strikes on the other side. People come and go, in no hurry, enjoying the sunshine; they push open the heavy glass doors of the building carrying trays of coffee and Danish pastries, and as they do so phrases from a string quartet in the foyer float out, and are shut in again. I think they are playing Bach, but it does not sound as it sounded on the radio harpsichord that terrible evening—relentless, merciless. It sounds okay. I stir black coffee in a white cup, look at the paper, and wait for my companions.

The church bell strikes the quarter hour: I look up. Families are feeding the ducks, restraining toddlers at the water's edge. At the far end of the terrace a couple are walking slowly, arm in arm, looking for someone: he tall, with a bit of a stoop, grey-haired, wearing glasses; she shorter, thin in a way anyone can see is not natural—the way her clothes hang loose, the original square shape beneath clearly needing more flesh to fulfil itself. She wears a straw hat, dark glasses, leans on him.

They are looking around: I rise to greet them: I wave—to my father, who raises his hand, to Elizabeth, who smiles. I pull out chairs for them as they draw near; we kiss, and Elizabeth slowly sits down.

"More coffee?" asks my father, seeing my empty cup. "I'll get it."

Elizabeth and I sit next to each other, watching him go. She will have tea—coffee does not agree with her now. There are quite a lot of things which do not agree with her: with her illness, her thinness, her skin beginning to draw tight across her face.

In spite of all this, she is more beautiful than I ever remember.

"How are you?" I ask her. "How did you sleep?"

"I'm tired but I can't sleep," she says. "It's a bloody nuisance. Never mind."

I put my arm round her; she leans against me, watching the glass doors. We wait for my father to rejoin us.

There are people excluded from this little company we make. My mother, walking her dogs in Edinburgh, writing me brisk letters. My one-time husband, with his new wife, new baby. My one-time self: restless, anguished, making a bus journey across the city so that I could cry, counting up stored-up pills.

She's gone.

I stepped back from the brink.

Sitting there now, my arm round Elizabeth's thin shoulders, I think about marriages, which sometimes work and often, if the truth be told, do not. I think about Elizabeth and Louise, who loved each other always, and I think about friendship, which seems, in my present state of mind, to be the thing to aim for.

Then my father comes out through the glass doors, making his way towards us. We sit with our drinks in the sun, watching the ducks, the children, the rise and fall of the fountains, seeing Elizabeth through.

The Glass Citadel

ALISON LOVE

It was half past three, and the 73 bus was lumbering along the Euston Road. I was sitting on the top, at the front, where the schoolkids go, staring across the city. The winter sky was streaked with dark blue and apricot: a perfect backdrop for my last view of London.

I don't know if you've ever noticed it, but they've only cleaned half the frontage of the St Pancras building. There's a line, arbitrary but quite distinct, between the grubby blackish part and the clean red re-pointed part. Except that even the clean part is getting dirty again now, and the whole place is like Cinderella in reverse: a fake fairy palace covered in smuts, sent back to the kitchen to earn its keep.

You only look at a city properly three times: once when you arrive, once when you're leaving. The third time is when you're in love; but let's not talk about that now.

When I first came to London I couldn't stomach it. I mean that literally: I was sick with excitement, in a fever of bliss and suspicion. I can remember when the coach passed through Hendon how my heart began to thump, its beat growing faster like a demon war-dance as the traffic knotted up and I caught sight of signposts to those exotic unknown places: Kensington, Knightsbridge, Pimlico. Forgive the naïvety. I'm a Northern boy: London to me then was both

Paradise and Babylon. Every stranger I met was going to make my fortune, unless he decided to drug me with illegal substances instead, and turn me into a reluctant rent-boy, a sort of rogering Artful Dodger.

Visions like these I had inherited from my poor parochial mother, who imagined that I would be brutally seduced, with a puff of brimstone, the moment I stepped out at Victoria Coach Station. From my father—no less parochial, but not so paranoid—I got the notion of the conquering hero, Dick Whittington, the Marquis of Carabas. I would penetrate the magic circle of wealth and fame, storm the citadel, armed with the great sword of my talent. You'll show them, was his phrase. (Other conquests, other penetrations, he was too pure-minded to contemplate.) I had to laugh at my parents' fantasies but that did not stop me from believing them. If I scoffed at the idea that the streets were paved with gold, it was only because I was too green and too cocky to realise that it was a metaphor.

The bus turned heavily into New Oxford Street, and I noticed a *Standard* billboard, proclaiming "Art Theft Latest" in big letters. On impulse I stood up, hauled my bag from between my feet, and ran to the back of the bus, down the stairs. You can do that on a 73 bus: they still use the old Routemasters, like solid red dinosaurs. On one of the new buses you'd lose your balance running; the stairs are in the wrong place, and the buses are too light, aluminium instead of iron. I hopped off by Tottenham Court Road station, and bought a paper in the flimsy cramped booth. The air smelt of pollution and fast food. This time tomorrow I would be out of here; this time tomorrow I would have a new landscape to contemplate. I could taste in my mouth the nearness of departure: it was sweet and haunting and faintly corrupt.

I rolled my paper under my arm, the way serious

commuters do, and began to walk down Charing Cross Road. I hadn't walked through London like this for months: I had stayed in my parish, trekking to work, coming home to my bedsit, going to the pub or the curry house three or four times a week. That's how people really live in London; people like me, anyway. The folks back home would never believe it. I strolled past the sex shop, with its discreetly shaded windows, past the corner where Foyle's stands, a drab familiar relic. Like every street here Charing Cross Road is changing all the time; changing so fast that it's really not worth remembering what used to be there. The newcomers, the Body Shops and Burger Kings, usurp the old places too well, like sleek androids. I sometimes think death is like that: the world so quickly becomes seamless, and you can't see the join where the dead person used to stand.

As I reached the corner of Old Compton Street I caught a great whiff of coffee, and I decided to walk down to Valerie's to sit and read the paper. When I got there the café window was full of intricate pastries, bright as a fantasy tuck shop; sliced kiwi fruit and glazed cherries glistened like subtle jewels among the whorls of cream and choux pastry. I went in and sat down at one of the smaller tables, at the back of the room.

I had stopped to buy the *Standard* because I wanted to read about the art theft. I'm something of an artist myself. It's what I'm known for, back home: Derek Marsh, who ran off to art school in London. The only place where you can make your name, unless you're L.S. Lowry. It's all right, you won't have heard of me. Don't worry your pretty little heads about that. I've only had one minor exhibition, and hardly any of my pictures have sold, and I've never been reviewed in the treacherous velvet prose of the *Guardian* or the *Independent*. In my time I've worked as a courier and a bouncer and a Betterware salesman, and nowadays I can hardly raise my spirits to raise my paintbrush. But old habits run deep. I still think of myself as an artist; I still think I have the right to a special interest.

The waitress brought me milky coffee and an éclair. I unfolded my paper and started to read. The stolen picture was by Holbein: a miniature, but worth a bob or two. It was the bequest of a rich American to the people of London, and I had read about it before: there had been the usual guff in the papers about national pride and cultural bonds. The picture had been housed with some hot-shot art dealer in Mayfair while the academics and the critics argued about it; and then, last night, it had been quietly stolen. I couldn't help grinning; I suppose it's what the Germans call *Schadenfreude*. The burglar alarms had gone off, but no one had taken any notice. No one ever does: this is a city which has been crying wolf too loud, too long. The police had a couple of leads on the theft, but nothing conclusive.

Carefully I ate my éclair, and looked out at the darkening sky. Once again I felt the sharp thrill of change. London had spoiled enough of my life; time to move on. Fresh woods and pastures new.

I suppose I'd always known, or suspected, that the London art world was a mafia, but in my starstruck ignorance I had assumed that I would be admitted to it. In those days— foolish boy—I thought that talent was enough. I didn't know the mechanics of getting on, the right people, the right places. The right parents too, if you can wangle it. In certain circles it's called schmoozing. I was a lousy schmoozer; I couldn't see the point. Besides, I didn't like any of the people I was supposed to be schmoozing: they made me feel crass and hairy and provincial, as though I couldn't be trusted not to spill the champagne or to fart at private views. They had the gloss all Londoners have, without realising they've got it.

None of this had anything to do with painting, and I said so; rather too noisily, perhaps, but it was the truth. And that's how the citadel simply closed against me, its walls as slippery and forbidding as glass. You couldn't see them necessarily, you couldn't prove those walls were there, but every time you got close you just bounced off them. Through the glass you could see work no better than yours being paraded and praised, but that didn't help you to get inside.

"Do you want anything else?"

The waitress was standing over me, her notebook in her hand. I hesitated.

"No, thanks. Just the bill."

When she had gone I looked at my watch. Six hours to kill before I was due at Victoria. Those hours seemed to stretch ahead like the grim threat of a sleepless night. Then, quite suddenly, I knew what to do: I would go and say goodbye to Nicky. As soon as I thought of it, it seemed that my whole day had been arranged for just that purpose: my final act in London, my unheard swansong, my last rites. I shook some coins from my pocket to pay the bill, and strode out of the café, swinging my canvas bag.

Nicky lives in a little house in the sky, above Gerrard Street. It's not really in the sky, of course, but it feels that way. You ring a silver bell in the wall of a red brick building, and when you've identified yourself Nicky buzzes open the door. Then you go up in a tinny lift, and step out into the open air, to a wide paved square with houses all around it, and a playground at the centre. Nicky's house is on the far side of the square. From her kitchen window you can see across Chinatown, the little pagoda telephone boxes, the lanterns at New Year.

I was sorry about the entryphone because it meant that I

wouldn't catch the surprise in Nicky's face. On the other hand, it meant that if Colin, her husband, answered, I could forget the whole thing. Don't misunderstand me. It's a long, long time since Nicky and I were lovers. I didn't want to see Colin because I don't like him. He's one of those people inside the citadel; one of the people who keep the glass walls intact. We were at art school together, in the far-off days when I thought all men were equal, but even then Colin had advantages of which I never dreamt. He was born into the art-establishment, in a genteel part of Greenwich; his father was a novelist and his mother taught at the Courtauld, although he tried to hide his lineage beneath a faint camp-Cockney accent. The accent's grown stronger as he's grown more famous. You see him all the time now, on the box and in the papers. He's been artist in residence at the National Gallery, and he's won the Turner Prize, and he's designed *Salome* for an avant-garde opera company. Whenever he sees me—which is always by chance—he says, don't be a stranger. As if I could be anything else, when he's in the circle and I'm outside, one of the many, the indistinguishable, the replaceable ones.

Nicky's voice through the silver grille was feathery and uncertain.

"Hello?"

"Nicky? It's Derek."

A silence; then:

"OK. I'll buzz you."

The lift was dirty and covered in graffiti. Nicky's little house is part of a council estate; Colin got the place because he's a Socialist. (All right, I know I shouldn't sneer. It's just that where I come from "Socialist" means something else.) I walked across the square, listening to mothers calling their children home from the climbing frame and the slides. Nicky is the only inhabitant without a child; but that's another story. The gate creaked as I opened it, and there she was, at the door, her face tired and composed. I painted her once looking like that, after a long sleepless night. She is a very beautiful girl; so beautiful that you can't help thinking of her as a trophy. I can't help thinking of her as a trophy, anyway.

"Well, hello," she said. "I'm afraid you've missed Colin."

I stepped into the hall and dumped my bag.

"I haven't come to see Colin."

"He's been called out to talk about this Holbein theft," Nicky went on, as if she hadn't heard me. "He's been on Sky and BBC South East already. What *have* you come for, then?"

She squinnied at me through her lashes.

"I'll tell you later. What does Colin think about the Holbein theft?"

"Oh, he thinks it's terrible. All this stuff going off to the States, and as soon as we're given something back it gets nicked."

"I think it's funny," I said, letting myself drop into the squashy sofa in Nicky's living room. Her house is pretty and light, with sponged walls and Liberty curtains. She walked into the kitchen and swung open the fridge.

"Don't be stupid, Derek," she said, with a laugh. I could see into the fridge from where I was sitting: it was full of Australian wine and Marks & Spencer's ready-made meals.

"Well," I said, "it's one in the eye for the London mafia. Don't you think?"

Nicky took out a bottle of wine and started to open it.

"What are you up to these days?" she asked, in an amiable voice. "Still being a bouncer?"

"Nah. I gave that up ages ago. I've got other fish to fry."

Nicky came back into the room, carrying the bottle and a pair of tall gilt-rimmed glasses.

"I don't know why you don't teach," she said. "You'd be good at it."

I gave a snort, and watched as she poured the yellow wine.

"I don't think so. Why should I be? I'm not interested in other people's paintings; I'm only interested in my own."

When I was with Nicky we used to sit for hours in Trafalgar Square, holding hands like teenagers. I could have painted that square from memory, right down to the litter bins and the grubby wheeling pigeons. I knew just how the light fell on Nelson's Column; I knew just how the students looked as they flocked into the National Gallery. I used to feel the pulse in Nicky's thin wrist, and imagine—no, believe—that I had my finger on the pulse of the city, that we were at its centre, she and I, bright and indispensable.

"I'm taking you out to dinner," I said, when we had drunk the wine. Nicky was curled on the carpet, hugging her knees in scarlet leggings.

"What for?" she said.

"A farewell gesture." I said, standing up. "That's why I came. To tell you I'm off. Up and away."

Nicky's eyes widened.

"Are you? Where are you going? Back home?"

"No, no. Nothing so defeatist." I stretched out my hand to pull her to her feet. "I've been offered a job abroad. A bloke I met at the club has offered me a job."

"Derek," said Nicky, frowning at me, "it is kosher, isn't it?"

"Of course it's kosher. What do you think I am? He's got a nightclub near St Tropez. Wants a bit of extra muscle. That's all." I reached into my pocket to show her the ticket. "See. I'm catching the boat train tonight."

She stared at me, her face still shadowy with doubt. There were slate-grey circles beneath her eyes. I wondered how many nights she spent on her own here now that Colin was famous, with her cold white wine and her chicken Kiev and her view of Chinatown.

"Come on, then," I said. "Chop, chop."

"All right," said Nicky. "Just let me get changed."

Outside it was black and glittering with cold. We walked down the street past the tube station, and into St Martin's Lane. I suppose I was rather drunk, but it didn't feel like that: it never did, when I was with Nicky. I felt instead as though all my senses had been heightened, each sight, each smell a first-and-last experience. I only drank to keep up with myself.

"Where do you want to go, then?" asked Nicky, prancing ahead of me. The fresh air had enlivened her like a shot of freedom.

"I don't mind." We were passing the awnings of the Café Pelican. "This will do."

We sat down in the corner, at a clean white table, my canvas bag wedged against the wall. The waiter brought us glasses of Kir Royale: Nicky's idea.

"So," she said, "do you think you'll come back?"

I grinned at her.

"Oh, I doubt it. There's nothing to come back for."

Nicky examined her glass of pink froth.

"The trouble with you, Derek," she said, "is that the chip on your shoulder's much bigger than your brain."

"Not to mention other parts of my anatomy," I said, brightly. Nicky scowled.

"Don't get cute. I mean it. It's crazy: this fantasy that everyone's against you."

"Not everyone. Just the people who count."

"Oh, yes, of course. The London art establishment doesn't admit snotty little Northern upstarts, does it? Honestly, Derek. You're living in a B-movie. It's not like that any more."

"Isn't it?" I said. Nicky pushed the hair behind her ears and stared at me.

"No, it's not. Believe me. You're using that as an excuse: because you're afraid that in the end you're just not good enough."

"Bullshit," I said, swallowing the last of my Kir. "That's bullshit, Nicky, and you know it. I'm as good as—well, Colin, for instance."

For a moment Nicky was silent; then she said.

"Colin's still painting. You're not."

"Of course I'm not. What's the point when nobody wants the damned things?"

Nicky gave a cool smile, and sipped at her glass.

"Well," she said, "there you are."

"Oh, for God's sake, Nicky. I don't need cheap philosophy. The truth is, I came down to London full of hope, full of talent. And bit by bit it's been knocked out of me."

"My heart bleeds," said Nicky. "Derek, if it's been knocked out of you it's your own fault. You're not the only one whose dreams have gone up in smoke. Your trouble is, you like being rejected. You like pretending you're the outsider, that no one will let you in. Well, fine, if that's what you want, but let me tell you, you'll never do anything that way."

I looked across the table and smiled at Nicky, a long slow smile. She had been expecting me to shout, and you could tell that the smile disturbed her: her eyes, which had been sharp and zealous, grew cloudy, lost their focus, drifted away from mine. I reached out for my canvas bag.

"Let me show you something," I said.

I groped among the soft mass of old shirts and came out with the Holbein miniature. It sat beautifully in my hand, as though it belonged there.

Nicky gave a little hiss of shock. Then, enthralled, she reached out to touch the frame.

"Careful," I said. "Fingerprints."

Her hand withdrew. We both looked at the picture, at the self-absorbed face, the brown and cream tints, painted four hundred years ago.

"What will you do with it?" asked Nicky.

"I don't know. Once I'm in France I might be able to sell it. My friend in St Trop. knows some useful people." I paused, and glanced at the miniature once more. "Or I might keep it. I've grown quite fond of it."

Nicky's fingers lay on the table, just within striking distance. She was still transfixed by the painting.

"Do you want to know why I took it?" I asked.

"I know why you took it," said Nicky. She moved her head and looked at me. "Was it difficult?"

I gave a shrug.

"Not as difficult as you'd think. I've learned a trick or two, in my chequered career. Of course, I was lucky with the alarms, I mean, that everyone ignored them till the police arrived."

Quite suddenly Nicky raised herself in her chair and kissed me on the mouth.

"Well done, Derek," she said. Then she began to gather the folds of her coat around her.

"What are you doing?"

"Come on. Let's walk down to Trafalgar Square." She grinned at me. "For old times' sake."

"But what about dinner?"

"I'm not hungry." Nicky glanced over her shoulder. "Let me find the loo, and then we'll go, OK?"

All the way to Trafalgar Square Nicky hung upon my arm, her face tilted up towards mine. We passed the statue of Edith Cavell, cold and blue, like the Fortitude card in the Tarot pack. The Holbein, safe in my bag, seemed to radiate like a hunk of plutonium, or the bleeding heart in the Catholic pictures of Christ: my great deed, my revenge, my bid for immortality.

We crossed at the traffic lights and stood there, by one of the lions, staring. Far away a siren was wailing. I could feel Nicky's light breath against my ear. My rage had fallen from me: I was somehow purged, like the hero of a Greek drama. For the first time in years I felt that I was at the centre of things, not some sad whirling meteorite on the outskirts of space. I had got my own back, and now, at the moment of leaving, I could feel the city acknowledge me, enclosing me within its magic walls. The grey and white dome of the National Gallery glowed before me, distant and benign. It occurred to me that I might even start painting again, once I was in France, once I was away from here. I was just turning to tell Nicky so when I realised that the sirens were growing louder.

Out in the Community

TOM WAKEFIELD

"Mark is a pleasant, amiable young man who is popular with other students as well as members of staff. Naturally, we are as disappointed with his academic results as he is himself. However, we are in no doubt that he will achieve a good measure of success in the profession he has chosen to follow."

In most respects, Mark Breakwell would have agreed with this final benediction from his public school headmaster. It was true, his good looks, level temperament and vapid geniality had borne him in good stead.

Yet he had not been surprised or even disappointed by his poor academic performance. It was just as he had expected. Never at any time had he ever been interested in reading or writing. At school his correspondence with his parents had been limited to postcards—and even now just more than a decade after this leaving report on a seventeen year old, his written words were limited to filling in the occasional form (thank God most of them required "ticks" nowadays) or sending a postcard with a telegrammatic message. For reading interest, he scrutinised the figures in the *Financial Times* and sometimes went wild and bought a tabloid newspaper which specialised in pictures of women's breasts.

Like the few other semi-literate pupils that left his school on similar terms, he laid claims to being dyslexic in his

adulthood. So few children suffered from "word blindness'
on council estates—one of the peculiarities of this affliction
was its affiliation with privileged background. The poor
always seemed to be retarded.

Mark could conduct a fluent conversation as long as it
involved no deep reasoned discussion and had no difficulty in
his office explaining away his atrocious spelling and rudi-
mentary grammar.

"One just has to accept these things," he would smile
engagingly, stroke his firm square jaw—and reveal his even
teeth. "I don't believe in self-pity. One simply has to make do
for oneself. If one didn't make special allowances for
cripples, I'll bet at least a third of them would jolly well
walk."

Mark could deliver such barbarous opinions so pleasantly
that few of his colleagues ever disagreed with him—if they
had chosen to argue with him he would have laughed politely
and changed the subject. He disliked soft or mushy options
and any conversation which took on emotional overtones he
quickly absented himself from—"I'm a paratrooper in civvy
clothing. You'll have to let me pass on this one."

His work as a dealer seemed entirely compatible with his
outlook, indeed, there were several young men who often
mirrored or vaguely supported his point of view. The market
place—as far as they were concerned—would cure all socio-
economic ills.

At the moment, things weren't too good but talks of
recession and unemployment did not deflate his buoyant
demeanour. As he made his way out for lunch he even had
time to exchange a few words with one of the security guards
who had given him a somewhat dejected glance just as he was
passing through the heavy steel and glass doors.

"Not looking too bright this morning are we, Sam?
Caught your fingers in the door did you?"

"Well, they've never been caught in any cash-till. Never, that's for sure, Sir. I received my redundancy papers this morning—you can't expect me to be full of smiles and 'Land of Hope and Glory' today."

"Oh, I'm sure something else will turn up for you. The market is bound to pick up soon. It's certain."

"Market! Market! It's all any of us ever hear in this place. The one certain thing your market will do for men over fifty like me is to sell us off as though we were slaves," the man grunted bitterly, "perhaps I should get my eldest son to place me up for auction—along with his house—get rid of some of his debts for him."

Mark hastened away. He did not feel the man was entitled to such rancour, let alone express it in such an uncouth manner. As Mark's uncle had said, "You give some workers and inch and they take a mile."

In the past few months zealous credit card companies and harsh mortgage commitments had forced Mark into practising one or two painful economies. He strode purposefully past the El Toro tapas bar. The guitar music seemed more resonant nowadays on account of the drop in the number of customers. Today, the empty chairs and bare tables gave the music a plaintive appeal as it drifted from the open doorway.

His route took him down a narrow street—of which two-thirds seemed to be up for sale. Before crossing the street he experienced a momentary flash of irritation on seeing the sign on the opposite side. "You are now entering the London Borough of Hackney. This is a Nuclear Free Zone."

This road, this parochial boundary, had forced him to lie to his close relatives, his mother and his father, who all resided in large houses in Reigate.

"Not many people can say that they *live* and work in the City—I can walk to the office."

His extortionate poll-tax bill plopping through his letter

box verified this lie—a distance of twenty yards had dealt him a penalty which should have been rightly delivered to state scroungers. What services did his shoe-box proportioned flat demand? Besides, he went home to Reigate most weekends. His bed-sitting room now hung about his neck like an anchor. No one wanted to buy. His side of the road was definitely the wrong side of the track as far as he was concerned.

He had never ventured northwards to view the rest of the London borough which claimed him as a resident.

"I'm about as curious as to what goes on there or who lives there as a dolphin migrating to the Sahara Desert. One would gasp for air. Apparently, there are still some decent church buildings to be seen there—apart from mosques, synagogues, and tabernacles."

His three fellow workers—all in blue and white striped shirts—had laughed with him on his witty appraisal. They all considered themselves to be very patriotic. So patriotic that their squash and badminton club was closed to any outsiders.

"We will just have to raise fees again. Keep them too low and we will just open the flood-gates to Asia, Africa and Eastern Europe. And where would one shower then?"

Botto's Eating Place with its apple green and white window frames and brightly-painted sign stood fresh and vivid amidst the air of dirt, desolation and neglect which the surrounding failed businesses and empty properties seemed to exude.

On discovering the place some two months previously he had hovered in the doorway. The menu was diverse, appetising and reasonably priced, it appealed to both his stomach and his pocket. It was the beautifully scripted addenda at the foot of the poster which caused him to pause and consider whether he should give the place his custom.

Saint Botolph—Patron saint of this establishment—was renowned for his concern and hospitality towards travellers and the itinerant displaced. All our profits go towards helping people who are in one way or another physically, socially, intellectually or emotionally impaired and without proper means of support or shelter. Reg. Charity

"Registered Charity?" Mark had felt somewhat piqued with the idea that in some way he was offering an extra measure of support for "down-and-outs". He paid his taxes and had no qualms about supporting a heavy defence budget—one could see the result of expenditure on a tank, rocket or bomb. But throwing money at people who only had themselves to blame for their situation exasperated him.

His appetite and bank balance had conquered, or at least modified, his irritation to the extent that Botto's now received his regular custom. As a customer he had (on occasions) stated his rights and opinions to the counter assistant and cashier.

"As you can see, I've only managed to eat half of my mushroom quiche."

"I'm sorry about that Sir, we've had no other complaints, in fact we've sold out of it today. I'm very sorry if it wasn't to your liking."

"Oh, the quiche was perfectly all right—but your seating arrangements don't leave much room for choice of table partners."

Mark had turned away from the counter and with a short nod of his head indicated the pine table with seating-pews where he had been sitting.

"I suppose in Sweden they are fine—but if one has to eat one's meal facing customers like that, one ought to be provided with blinkers. Ought you to let that kind of flotsam and jetsam in off the streets? It won't do anything for your profit margin."

"It won't affect me Sir. I work here on a voluntary basis," the young man tugged angrily on the sides of his apron as he spoke, "the people who you are referring to are valued customers—they have been here every day since we opened."

Mark was about to offer a further rejoinder but the assistant moved quickly from behind his counter and had made his way towards the couple who had sat opposite Mark. He spoke to the woman.

"How are you today, Rita?"

Mark had left immediately, such social point scoring only increased his contempt—do-gooders positively sickened him. His table companions had put in him mind of two grotesques from a Grimm's fairy tale.

The man in grey, shiny suit, off-white nylon shirt, looked fraught and drawn—he had rocked to and fro as he had ladled soup into his mouth. The liquid had dribbled incessantly from his bottom lip over his chin and on to the front of his shirt.

The woman Rita—whose body seemed to balloon out in all directions—had chumped and chomped her way through a great, green mound of lettuce, looking this way and that as she munched noisily away like some huge, threatened animal.

At this point, Mark had reached the severe conclusion that such people should not be seen. Could anyone seriously suggest that it was in order for a young working man to spend his lunch hour sitting opposite a pair of mental cases?

Yet today, Mark's glance about the room sought Rita out. Yes, there she was—she could hardly be missed. In spite of the midday heat, she wore a cream-coloured fishermen's-knit woollen cardigan. This heavy garment was decorated with numerous incongruous-looking gossamer butterflies. Tiny sequins sparkled from their wings. They were settled—wings outspread—on her shoulders, back and left breast.

From time to time, she would fondle one of the inanimate creatures as if to check they had not flown away. Mark watched her tongue move about her thick protuberant lips. Was this hunger or was she about to metamorphose before his very eyes?

With some relief he let his gaze drift slowly towards Rita's new companion of five weeks or more. Sitting opposite the human gargoyle was a girl in a yellow dress.

The girl seemed unaware of her ugly chaperone and of all that went on about her. The dress had a square-cut neckline, the top button (left undone) revealed the contours of high, firm breasts. The slender young neck was devoid of adornment. The face—high cheek-bones—large green eyes—full pink lips—light brown eyebrows—was un-painted. The skin—lightly tanned—seemed to have a luminous glow. The fine blonde hair was scraped back away from a wide brow. An elastic band held the pony-tail in place. Her fingers, arms and legs were bare—her feet be-sandalled.

Each weekday Mark had marvelled at the girl's natural beauty. Now it had begun to take up much of his private thinking and at times, thoughts of her had caused his loins to ache.

"I'll have jam roll and custard, and I'll have apple pie and custard," Mark listened to Rita's odd expressionless voice, she spoke loudly as if a small microphone was part of her voice box. She always ordered her meals backwards.

"And I'll have my diet first. Have to stick to my diet."

"That's green salad, pork pie. Followed by jam roll and custard." The counter-assistant seemed to offer Rita positive discrimination in that she always received table service.

"No, I'd like the apple pie and custard before the jam roll

and custard. Save the best until last, eh?" Rita then spoke up for her companion.

"Janet will have sandwiches. Give her four and she'll eat three. Cut them small though—she eats like a canary. Don't give her meat. Don't give her any animal flesh—she won't eat it. It makes her sick."

Janet paid no attention to this gruff solicitude. Her eyes looked on a world that was not here, her mind was entirely elsewhere. Her pale, pink lips moved in animated conversation—directed towards a hearer who could not be seen. Sometimes, she would smile or shake her head in disagreement as though she was hearing a response.

Mark had become fascinated by her—if someone had suggested that his fascination bordered on obsession he would have greeted such an observation with scorn. He tended to be free with his opinions but secretive about his neuroses.

He lingered at the entrance, he had thought out every sequence and move he was about to make as though he were a film director who knew precisely what the players had to do.

Mark set his camera whirring as soon as the food was placed before the two women. He placed his jacket on the wooden pew on the space next to Janet who sat near the wall, he ordered a glass of wine and two ham rolls from the counter. Within a minute or two he had collected his food and drink—and—and—and he was sitting next to her.

At first, he could barely pick up courage to steal a covert glance at the girl. He felt intensely excited. Electrified. Even his breathing seemed to have taken on a different pattern. He watched as the two women surveyed the food that had been placed before them.

It was almost a relief or at least a welcome diversion to pay some attention to Rita who sat opposite him. She was unaware of his observation as she attacked the great mound of lettuce and cucumber that lay before her as though she were performing some kind of duty on which her life depended. She seemed to be driven—not by pangs of hunger but some kind of internal mechanism. The process looked austerely rhythmical. Robotic.

Mark watched as Rita slashed through the crisp lettuce leaves with her knife and marvelled as her mouth opened and chewed and opened and chewed. Her cheeks expanded as more and more of the shredded salad was piled in—her eyes bulged in a fixed, glazed stare.

Enjoyment didn't seem part of the process. Was it possible to enjoy lettuce in this way? Mark smiled to himself. If only Rita's nose might twitch he could imagine he was sharing his table with some kind of gigantic rabbit. A desolate, ageing, barren doe—storing up food for her last winter. Mark sipped his wine and looked towards Janet.

He could do this now without anyone perceiving his interest. The place had begun to fill up and he slid closer to the girl, his pin-stripe trousers were only a matter of inches away from Janet's knee. She ate little that was set before her—for the most part her lip movements were taken up with talk. Rita's noisy mastication acted as background to her conversation. Conversation? Mark studied the pink, limpid lips as they moved and eavesdropped on a sweet-sounding monotone.

"The oval in the heart represents the world and the curse is on me to find out what's wrong with the world. But I'm so unaware (that's what I seem to be), I'm not really because the curse makes me aware. The curse isn't known about until I'm dead. And because I'm aware and people don't think I am, I wonder and pause and meditate on why they talk to me the way they do—I've just worked this out. I never realised it before. A force of field of electricity all around me stops people's vibrations from reaching me. But I don't know why it is there. Other people's vibrations never touch me (Tut-ankh-amen's my guide). The message never really registers in my brain. People all over the world must listen when I show them what is wrong. Oh Mum, look what happened to Jesus. Poor Mum."

Mark moved closer, he pressed his leg against her knowing that the madness of her preoccupations excluded her from making any remonstration. He justified his predatory behaviour by blaming her for his temporary loss of appetite—women—beautiful women—were there to be consumed. Not understood. Not fed. His two ham rolls remained forlornly untouched.

Rita continued to slash, shred, and gorge the last few lettuce leaves on her plate as Janet chanted on, she sniggered nervously and Mark saw the dawnings of a smile about her face. He took this as some sign of encouragement. Janet spoke more rapidly.

"Sorry I didn't get my 'O' levels, Mum. Put that in your pipe and smoke it, Dad. It's not good for you. Smoking's not good for you. I'm a tea-leaf. Do you know what that is? I'm reaching for the best. Richard-the-lion-heart not half. I'm at my best so put that in your pipe and smoke it Tut-ankh-amen. I get the picture and the exorcist. I'm corrupted. I'm going to heaven when I die. I don't need to be forgiven, Mum. You do, Mum. I forgave you before I was born. Oh well, Tut-ankh-amen isn't dead."

Rita smacked her lips, she had finished off her apple pie and the male counter assistant had replaced her empty bowl with one containing two double portions of jam roll. The pudding was partially lost under lashings of very hot, bright orange custard.

It was too hot for Rita to savour but she let the rising steam enter her nostrils as though it were some kind of magical brew. She stared intently at this offering and licked her lips with impatience.

Mark hated the whiff of vanilla flavouring that invaded his nostrils, he conquered his nausea of the pudding and its owner by resting his left hand lightly on his left knee. he had decided to wait until Rita had started eating again before his next move.

He watched as she dug into the pastry nearest the edge of the bowl. She lifted a small portion to her protuberant lips, blew on it, tasted a little, blinked as her tongue scalded to the taste and returned it to its bowl.

Damn the stupid cow—he thought—hot or cold what did it matter to someone like her? At last, desire seemed to overcome transient pain and Rita began to ply one hot spoonful after another into her mouth as though she were assuaging a hungry furnace.

Janet's schizoid meanderings seemed to have gained momentum. Mark raised his hand from his knee. Moved it slowly to his left and let it gently fall.

He was reminded of a deep affection for a machine that he had constantly been drawn to when he was a child. Every time he entered the amusement arcade he was immediately captivated by it. The coin had entered the slot and one was given partial control over a miniature crane which swung from its moorings to settle its claws on some delectable bar of chocolate or a plastic toy and lifted it tantalisingly into the air before delivering it to him.

His hand now rested on Janet's knee. She did not respond. She conversed with her "voices".

"Mum, I love you. I feel like Laurel and Hardy. Kiss me Hardy." (She giggles) "A Viking wants to marry me. If I say yes, he'll leave me afterwards. After what? What would you say, Mum, if I came home with a red-headed baby? No 'O' levels. I'd love any kind of baby. I'm afraid I'm going to ignore you, Mum. If the price of bacon goes up, pigs will fly. Pigs should be left alone. You'd better be careful, Mum, there are people in my aura who will rob your place. Turn it upside down if they know where it is. I don't need a telephone—my head is an exchange and no one gets through to me unless Tut-ankh-amen lets them. Leave me alone Tut. Just leave me . . ."

Mark held his wine glass to his lips in his right hand and sipped, his left hand gently massaged Janet's knee. He'd bide his time. Wait for the right moment. Wait until Rita had stoked up with even more food. Then, he would let his hand travel. What a journey that would be.

Rita gulped on another large spoonful—he commenced travelling. "It's not right!" Rita spluttered. "It's not right."

Mark withdrew his hand as though someone had stubbed a cigarette on the back of it.

'It's not right," Mark's shirt was spattered with spittle and custard, Rita had risen from her seat and towered like some ogress opposite him. Huge, ugly, forbidding she pointed her spoon towards him accusingly.

Like some terrible kind of ectoplasm, custard trickled over Rita's bottom lip and on to her chin. In the face of this unearthly rage he felt unable to move.

"It's not right," Rita's repeated flat tones boomed all over the café; "It's not right, he's trying to put his hand up Janet's frock."

She held the spoon in the air not a foot away from his face. The café had become silent, the drama had even stilled Janet's other world ramblings.

Mark rose swiftly from his seat and propelled himself to the counter; "There! Keep the change," he cast a five pound note on the desk before the cashier, "I'm never coming to this place again. Never. Such people ought not to be allowed out in the community. They ought not to be in our society." He felt that moral indignation was the best form of defence.

The cashier eyed him coolly, she took his money and said, "Yesterday, you said there was no such thing as 'society', Sir. The present community isn't good enough is it Sir? Of course, I'm only speculating."

He turned quickly from her and left the place with his eyes fixed on the floor two yards in front of his feet. He transported himself away in this manner until he was at least fifty yards away from the café. Then he paused, lifted his head and breathed in deeply as prisoners do when they are released from captivity. He felt better, he would visit his squash club, have a shower, wash all trace of the place away.

Rita looked lovingly at what remained of her pudding. It was a difficult decision she had to make. A great struggle. She buried her spoon into the jam and pastry, allowed some custard to trickle over the top of it. Raised it to her mouth— licked her lips—paused for a further moment—blew gently on it—and then proferred it to Janet.

"Try it. Go on. Just a bit. Try it."

The girl craned forward, opened her lips and let herself be fed.

"There. Is that nice, Janet? Did you like that?"

"Yes."

The answer was faint but clear enough. Everyone heard it. And, with this brief affirmative, Janet entered the real world for the first time in months.

Second-hand City

MAGGIE HEWITT

And the next day it was all still there. Not that they had thought that it wouldn't be. You can't really get rid of stuff that easily. Not the accumulated clutter of years. For days they had sorted through it, allowing themselves to keep only what was useful in their new life, to remember that there was no point in taking a lot of it anyway. Box by box they carried it out to the front garden and left it there.

"I never could see why you kept so much junk," he said.

"Well I thought it might come in useful."

"Just cluttering the place up."

"Well I liked it. I'm only chucking it out because we haven't the space."

"But you could have thrown it away years ago, it'd be just the same."

"I think some of it could be useful. It's too good to just throw away. Shall we get a jumble sale to collect it or a dealer?"

"Wait for the dustmen, I'd say."

"I'm not sure I should throw away all my university notes."

"Oh for God's sake, you never look at them. Be decisive for once can't you? Are you going to stand there all day moping? What about this walk then?"

They set off for their last London walk before leaving for

the Oxfordshire countryside. It seemed like a good omen to be having such a clear out, she thought, the sign of a new life as though without the past cluttering up their lives things would be easier between them. It was bad to hang onto things, unhealthy, too much like clinging to the past. She felt like the snail carrying her past on her back. She needed to think about the future, his new job, their new house. The strangeness of it all would bring them together, wouldn't it?

Returning envigorated and in a better mood, they could see their garden from a long way off. Where their neighbours grew flowers, they appeared to be growing lampshades with bundles and boxes lined up along the fence like stalls in a market. As they got nearer they could see that someone was in the garden intently examining one of the boxes. So intently that she scarcely noticed the others walking up the path and was suddenly surprised by their arrival. There was an awkward pause. The couple clearly didn't expect a complete stranger to be in their garden closely inspecting objects which until the day before had been part of their possessions, some of them possessions which she at least didn't really want to part with. And yet by throwing them out hadn't they publicly declared they didn't want them, so just what did they feel was wrong? The intruder rallied first.

"Hello," she said, "you've got some really nice stuff. D'you mind if I take it?"

"Help yourself, it's all got to go."

"D'you think you've got a box I could put it in?"

He went indoors and returned with a box, one of the ones they had been saving for the real job of packing when that began.

"Great! I can get a lot in that."

Systematically she began sorting through all the boxes that they had just filled, examining everything carefully and exclaiming as she went.

"This glove is better than the ones I've got. Do you have the other one?"

"I think I did."

She began rummaging too. Why had she thrown those gloves away, she wondered, they were perfectly good ones.

"Moving are you?"

"Yes, we're getting out of London."

"Oh," she said disapprovingly, "why's that?"

"Oh, well, you know. It's got such a hassle here—the noise, the traffic, and of course the rubbish."

"Like this lot you mean." She laughed.

"Well, no."

"Me, I love it. Never buy anything if I can help it. You can get just about everything from skips or jumble sales. These gloves are much better than mine. You don't mind if I leave mine instead?"

She came into the house bringing back into it a pair of gloves, a damaged sleeping bag, a coat, and an old address book with a clasp.

"This is great!" she said, "I've always wanted one like this. I'll have to get the coat dyed. I only wear black or red. I've got a friend I think will like the address book. D'you have any coffee?"

They sat round talking.

"Look, I hope you don't mind me commenting but your hair would look better with the fringe cut. I'll cut it for you if you like. I won't make a mess of it. I know what I'm doing."

And somehow she did.

No, she wouldn't stay to eat.

"I like the idea but not the event," she said and left.

"What a strange person."

"Yes, I suppose so."

"I mean she seemed so . . ."

"So at home. I suppose she did."

"You know she looked rather good in that coat. I rather wished I'd not thrown it away."

"It didn't look like that on you."

"Like what?"

"Well, she is rather glamorous."

"So you did fancy her then?"

"I didn't say that."

"Well, did you?"

Next morning they were lying in bed relaxing in the warm glow of a Sunday morning when the bell rang. Slowly he got up to answer it, stubbed his toe on the bed, swore and groped round to find his dressing gown. Wrapping the belt clumsily round him he shuffled to the door.

"Who is it?" she said when he came back.

"It's Belinda. She's come back for some things she couldn't manage yesterday. She's brought you some flowers. She says she got them from a garden up the road. I hope it's no one we know. She's got her bike this time. D'you mind if she brings it in while she sorts the stuff through? I've invited her in for coffee ..."

Turning over in the bed she moved across towards the other side where the warm patch was already cooling fast.

London Shoes

JOANNA ROSENTHALL

She had only been in London for six weeks. Rita didn't stop her going out. She had half expected an intrusive but solicitous enquiry casting doubt on whether she was well enough, and whether she could find her way. Esther walked slowly down the tiled hallway, straining to listen to some faraway noise. She hovered at the door as if she had forgotten something but couldn't think what.

The house was completely quiet. It reminded her of being ill as a child, lying in bed like a small corpse, her whole body stretched and rigid, listening, listening for life. The noise of distant footsteps in a faraway part of the house still stood out in her mind. She could see a figure, broad and active. Moving, always moving. The kitchen, the living room, back to the kitchen, the backyard. Some unknown person like a shadow. Her mother? Or a housekeeper? Someone who if called may not have heeded the little girl in bed so far away. She had no idea who it might have been. No idea at all.

She paused at the front door and tried to peer through the crack that shouldn't have been there, where the door was attached to the lintel. Stoke Newington. There was a brownish haze, removing clarity from her view. Was there someone walking up the path? Probably not. She could see moving shapes and something big and black. Waves of fear rushed through her. She should not loiter like this, it brought up the memories. She opened the door. It was heavy. It must have been there a very long time.

This isn't the East End proper, Rita had told her, we've done well to get out here, it means we're not bottom of the pile. It's the first step to being English and there are some Jews here. You'll see, you'll soon feel at home.

Esther had doubted this, but it did seem possible to leave the house and walk. I'm in a Jewish neighbourhood, she told herself. This is Stoke Newington. Such a long name. It will be all right. There was something embarrassing about staying all day and all evening in Rita's house. They had made her so welcome. "You must stay until you find your uncle," Rita had reassured her again and again, "and if you don't find him you will also stay." Rita's house was overflowing with refugees from all over Europe. Whenever there was a new boat, they would squeeze in just one more, even though the beds were long ago occupied, and mealtimes were chaos with everyone vacating their seats as soon as they had eaten.

In the first week Esther had been appalled. She held herself stiffly and made sure she didn't brush shoulders with anyone. It was only as the weeks went by that she realised they had taken her in and she really could stay. The next time Rita said, "If you don't find him of course you will stay, you will be in our large family. London is good. The English are good. It is very safe here." Esther had kissed her formally on the cheek. "Danke," she said, 'sank you very much." It was only later on, much later on that she had realised Rita had seen fear in her eyes. Rita was holding out a hand.

The streets were lined with tall thin houses joined together, they looked flat and stiff, each one the same. They reminded Esther of the carriages of a train lined up at a platform, grey and patient, waiting to be pulled off by the big puffing engine. A train took Heinz away. A train took Mama and Papa away. Trains stuffed with Jews, stuffed with everyone she had ever known. She mustn't think. The longer she was in London the harder it was not to think. She looked again at the houses. Every so often the shape changed. Look. Now she was passing two broad ones, with wide-eyed windows and big inviting steps up to each front door. They reminded her of two large peasant women she had once seen from a train window, squatting to urinate, their voluminous black skirts hoisted, large pink bottoms exposed. How Mama had laughed! She must concentrate on holding her head and her back straight. She must learn to put the past aside. It infused her with pain each time it flooded her mind, which was often. Very often.

Rita had given her the directions to Walford Road, it was a short walk and at least she could look at the synagogue. She might bump into someone and have a chat—there were always one or two hanging around. Rita was being kind, advising her. She might even find out something about Uncle Morris. There were many others like her who had got out of Austria at the last minute, straight after the Nazis had come in. They were all looking for each other. It wasn't just her. She would be surprised how many people find each other by accident, someone you were at school with or a local shopkeeper. Esther had listened. For some reason this kindness, this help made her feel hard and angry inside. She wouldn't find Mama or Papa or Heinz. Not them. But at least she might find Uncle Morris. Yes, she would have to talk to people, that was the only way.

The synagogue was disappointing. A yellow brick building, with dark, ugly windows, squatting on the corner of two nondescript streets. She could have walked past it. She lingered and walked down the side, where she felt relieved to see a row of five perpendicular windows. Just plain, with no masonry-work or tracery. Someone had wanted to make the building beautiful. They hadn't succeeded, but the intention raised the value of the building in her eyes and she was pleased.

It started to drizzle, and a fine sheen of water droplets were sitting on her coat and hair. She looked up and there on the roof was a large stone circle painted white, with a magen David inside, the points of the star straining to be released. She felt a pang. She needed to walk. She quickened her pace, not wanting to see anyone. Not wanting to talk. Just walk. It was too much effort. If Uncle Morris was in the East End, she would find him but not today.

Stoke Newington High Street, Kingsland Road. Long names. Long streets. She noticed a bagel kiosk, then a Jewish tailor. She didn't stop. Her feet relaxed into a pleasant rhythm. She looked down. The low-heeled shoes were padded inside, comfortable, leather. They were womanly yet cheerful, brown leather lace-ups, so different from her old life. Her old life? The earth had not stopped. She was in London living a new life. She told herself this over and over. The litany was arrested by a memory of the shoes. Damn the memories. This one she could not stop.

The woman on the boat. They had exchanged small talk. Not really small talk, but the most basic information that fleeting people pass on to one another. "Where have you come from?" "Where are you going?" "Is there anyone there for you?" Both of them were non-committal and vague. There was too much to say. Far too much. Every time Esther talked the ache came back. She couldn't afford to talk. The woman seemed to understand. There was no pressure. Little was said.

Esther had felt momentary guilt. She should talk to her, she had nobody left, she was alone. She reassured herself with the thought that she couldn't look after everyone now, it was enough to manage herself. No one could expect it of her.

Then she realised that there *was* no one to expect it of her. She wanted to weep, to call for Heinz, for Mama. Mama would have told her to pull herself together and behave with dignity. Mama would have been worried about what people were thinking. What would Heinz have done? She didn't know. The threatening tears receded.

They had been lucky in the boat, sheltered from the wind and rain by a canopy over their bit of the deck, and something to lean their backs up against. They were both shifting endlessly on sore, aching muscles, but neither of them left that spot. It was too good a space to lose. After their exchange the woman had grasped Esther's lower arm and squeezed it. Her fingers were weak. Something intended as firm and reassuring ended up as a caress, or was it a plea? It was a gesture beyond words, one of solidarity that springs up between people when there are no resources left. Nothing left except to understand each other and be there. Esther felt angry. She didn't want to be touched. She didn't want sympathy. She didn't somehow like this woman. There was something about her.

The woman fell asleep and Esther's body gave way a little too. The kind of rest though that offers no real freedom, a semi-sleep where worrying dream-thoughts are followed by tense jerks into the waking world.

Eventually Esther sat upright. She had had little rest. Everywhere hurt. The woman had slumped, her head leaning on Esther's shoulder, her torso half smothering Esther's chest. She shook her angrily. The woman did not stir. Esther slapped her hard on the arm.

"GET OFF!" The German words rang out into the sudden silence of all the people. So many floating people, all half asleep, but dangerously alert to something even worse.

"Help me . . ." Esther begged, crying now, looking around for a pair of eyes that would hold with her own. An older man, he would have been about her father's age, squeezed through, treading on trailing garments and small bundles of hastily gathered possessions. He helped her pull the woman off. Together they propped her up, she was upright. Thank God she was off. Her body was off. Thank God. Thank God.

Esther looked into the woman's face. Her head was slumped onto her own chest at an awkward angle. The side of her face that had been leaning on Esther was deep red, and the other side was entirely white, even grey. Her skin had started to tighten. She was dead. The woman had died on her shoulder. The bloody woman had given her a new nightmare. It was not strange. It was to be expected. Everything had gone bad and there would be many more things, things like this. All she knew was that she must not cry. She must never cry. Another woman had died and she must not cry.

At that moment Esther was pleased she had not allowed herself to relax, to believe she was safe, to think that nothing worse could happen. Now that she knew what life was like, she knew that there is always something worse. Always something worse. That is how it will always be. Here was something else worse.

The man who had helped her was lurching through the choked boat. He was going to summon help to get rid of the body. She looked at the face again, already inhuman in death, and even ridiculous in its division by colour. Esther quickly leaned forward and untied the shoe laces. They came off easily as if the woman's feet had already shrunk. Just as quickly she removed her own worn out pair, put them on the two alien feet pointed and sticking upwards with their own rigidity. The brown leather lace-ups felt good. They were padded, slightly big and even stylish. She was just wondering where the woman had bought them, where exactly did she say she had come from, when she noticed with a chill that the inner soles were slightly warm.

It was a pleasant day. A London day. It could have been a Vienna day, but thank God it was a London day. She was safe in London. The sky wasn't exactly blue, but not grey either and the air was warm. The drizzle had been momentary. There were leaves on the trees and they were green, or mostly so. Autumn had touched them solely at the edges, a delicate tainting, a mere whiff of what was to come. Esther pounded down the pavement, breathing, moving, holding her body firmly straight, determined not to look at her feet. Every so often a little smile played at the corners of her mouth. She walked fast and confidently as if she knew where she was going. Somehow she did. This way then that, straight then turning. She had been walking for a good hour before it occurred to her that she was looking for the East End, but she didn't know where she was going, where she was, nor even how to get back to where she had come from.

Where was she? Where was she? She would ask the way. Would they understand her English? The way to where? She closed her eyes and breathed slowly deeply. She had to tell herself to stop as she felt ripples of dizziness affecting her head, between her ears and behind her eyes. You must stop, you must stop. It was a welcome litany, a phrase that had helped her on many such occasions in the past. This was what Heinz, her fiancée, had complained of, her ability to just breathe and push things down. As she did it, she was filled with a familiar sensation of all going dark, black inside. But not a blackness that was empty. It was a space so filled and full of movement that she frequently had the impression of a rich and fertile place, thick and shifting but entirely without light. It was a place that needed preserving.

She felt a bit light-headed. She might be hungry. She had not eaten. She couldn't just go into Rita's dingy kitchen and help herself. Everything seemed borrowed or second-hand.

Bea was sent to the shops several times a day for a loaf, a jar of jam or a few potatoes. It depended a lot on what they had. Things were so scarce. Each day it seemed like today might be the day when there would be nothing. And then what?

With relief she noticed a large junction ahead. It gave her the incentive to walk for a little bit more. There would be a restaurant. Already she pictured the elegant chairs with matching tables, delicious cakes small enough to pop in her mouth one at a time. She could have fainted with the thought. She couldn't go on walking. She felt weak, tired, the sky looked white, all white, light but grey. She sat down heavily on a small wall. There wasn't a restaurant, but she could see a little tea kiosk set back from the road. She would walk to that.

She knew from Rita that it wasn't worth asking for coffee in London. They couldn't get it here, and they didn't like it. In London it was tea. They drink tea.

"Can I haf a cup of tea?" she phrased the unfamiliar words carefully, and was examining the English pennies in her hand, that Rita had given her. You'll need a bit of money, she'd said, help me with the house and I'm sure we can spare you a bit.

Esther started when she looked up. The old woman had strained her body to lean right over the kiosk and was peering into her face.

'Are ya Jewish?"

She stiffened and nodded. So Rita had been wrong about England. She would be picked on here too. The unfamiliar Cockney drawl frightened her.

"Just come?" Again she nodded, not really looking up. This time the old woman took her hand, squeezed it, pushed away the money and gave her a cup of sweetened milky tea.

'This is how we 'ave it 'ere, it'll do ya good," she explained, indicating a little wooden stool at the side of her.

Esther wanted to laugh and cry all at once, because of the kindness. She sat down stiffly. The tea was hot and sweet, enlivening her whole body as it found its route down, down. It was reaching every little part. Her hands cradled the cup, while someone like a mother was standing next to her, looking after her. She hunched herself in on the cup and felt safe for the first time for as long as she could remember. Maybe she had never felt like that before. London *was* a very good place, with its funny villages. London was safe.

It was a very strange thing. Her mind was lulled, her body was warm and she felt at peace. She had lost the state of danger. She had allowed herself to be fooled.

As the old lady had served customers with tea, she had sat on the stool feeling as if she had just arrived home. It was a delicious sensation. Her eyes had been wandering around, looking at the road, the occasional tram, all the people walking, women wheeling prams. Then she had looked at the large silvery tea urn, and back to the incongruous but pleasing delicate china cups with non-matching saucers. Everyone else she had met or known about was through Rita, but she had met this woman all on her own. She had just been about to ask her name when she noticed the shoes.

The old woman's shoes were identical to her own!

First she had seen the rough woollen coat, shapeless, peasanty. How nice it would be to go to Heinz's father, her father-in-law to be, and ask him to make this kind old lady a coat. Nothing too smart or fashionable, she would feel silly. A *bubeh*'s coat. Then she had seen the shoes. The death shoes. She went cold. How could she have let this stupid woman pretend that all was well? This old woman had on the dead woman's shoes. The boat, the pain, the cold, the icy feeling inside, the doom and the brown leather shoes came back to her. She could feel a swelling rage, it might spill on this woman. She must not let it. The air was shimmering and thin. She shivered deeply.

The old woman was peering at her again, this time with concern.

"What's up?" she asked gently, stroking Esther's head. She could see something was wrong.

"It's your shoes. They're the same as mine." The woman grunted with amusement.

"What's an old woman like me doing wiv young shoes like this? It's a joke, what could I do about it?"

Esther had to explain. She told her about the boat, about the dead woman and her face that was two colours, and about the man who had helped her get the body off. Then she squeezed all her life into one spot inside her stomach and she told her about the shoes. Her face burned with the memory of removing her shoes and slipping on the comfortable new ones. She even told her about them being a little warm. She couldn't look at the woman. She waited for the torrent of abuse.

There was a pause so full of feeling that neither of the two women moved. Then the older placed her hand on the young woman's head and stroked, long soothing strokes, firm but gentle. When a customer came she turned and served the tea, then turned back and attended to the girl she didn't know.

When she sensed there was calm again and Esther's face looked a little pink, she indicated that Esther should stand. She sat heavily on the stool, leaned down and undid her laces. Impatient with Esther's incomprehension, "Give 'em 'ere." It was a command, adult to child, not angry.

The old woman ignored Esther's hesitation and explained, "My shoes are London shoes, they're from 'ere, not bleedin' death shoes. I'm old enough, I don't mind 'em, it's easy for me."

Esther stood up straight in her new brown leather shoes.

They were older than the others, a good size, roomy, a little battered.

"You vill vear zem in?" she smiled at the old lady and hugged her fiercely for a few seconds.

"Course I will," and she shrugged as if to say, you child, don't even think about a worry like that, leave it to the adults.

"You are my first friend in London," Esther felt nearly safe enough to cry.

"Good on ya girl . . ." her voice trailed for a moment and then it was strong again. "Go now, go home, but come back and see me." She smiled as she watched Esther walk up the road in her new London shoes.

The Brigadier

JAMES SINCLAIR

Like many of its kind, the number 13 bus progresses in lurches. On the straight it travels at dizzying speed and, when stopping to embark or disgorge, the manoeuvre is accomplished in a series of savage jerks which have its passengers flung about in heaps. Even the young have difficulty in keeping their feet: the old must rely on good luck and Providence.

Thus it was that the Brigadier ended up in the Royal Free Hospital, Hampstead, one Tuesday morning, having set off on a journey to the West End. The number 13 was in an ugly mood that morning. Having rounded the circle outside Lord's at its usual perilous angle, it straightened up, and then screeched suddenly to a halt at a zebra crossing, catapulting the old gentleman from one end of the aisle to the other. There was a good deal of blood, and his face had assumed peculiar angles, but these, in the end, proved to be by no means the worst of his troubles.

The tall, distinguished figure of the Brigadier, slightly stooped over a walking stick, was a familiar sight in the pubs and bookshops of Hampstead and its environs. Few knew his name, but his rank so exactly fitted his deportment that this hardly mattered. He said little, but listened with a courtly politeness, stroking his moustache and nodding gently at even the most bizarre philosophies, common in that parish.

Since he was so often there, everyone assumed that he lived in the neighbourhood, but when the medical orderlies searched his pockets in the ambulance, they found the address of a flat in Fulham. This was the first of the surprises.

The young constable detailed to notify the relatives dialled the number, which was answered immediately.

"Hello?"

"... Er ... good morning. This is the police station, Hampstead ... is that Mrs Horton?"

"Yes, speaking, but I'm afraid the Brigadier isn't here. You can get him at the weekend."

A comfortable, somewhat fluttery woman in her fifties, Mrs Horton was inclined to plumpness, and had a taste for flowered prints which made her look rather larger than she actually was.

"Mrs Horton, I'm very sorry to have to tell you ... your husband ... has been injured ..."

"Injured!? ... where has he been injured?" There was a sudden note of panic in her voice.

"In Park Road, St John's Wood ... in a bus ..."

"I mean, what part of him ... did you say St John's Wood?"

"Yes, in Park Road."

"Good heavens! ... What on earth was he doing there? How bad is he? ... Where is he? ..."

By now thoroughly alarmed, Phyllis Horton paused only to leave a message on her son's answering machine, and sped off to the Royal Free in a taxi.

The journey seemed endless but, in the foyer outside the lift on an upper floor of the hospital, a nurse took her in hand and conducted her at last to the bedside.

"He's not very well, I'm afraid, and I don't think you should stay more than a few minutes this time."

Phyllis Horton had to use her imagination to recognise the figure in the bed as her husband. Hardly anything of him could be seen. Apart from one bloodshot eye, his head was entirely swathed in bandages, as were those of the other three occupants in the ward. Even the pyjamas were not his own.

"Oh Binkie," she said, "why weren't you in Scotland?"

"mmmm ... eee ... eheh ..." said the Brigadier, his mummified head falling back weakly onto the pillow, "mmm ... er ... er ... er ..."

It was too much for poor Phyllis Horton. Tearfully, she took his hand: "Don't try to talk now darling. You just get some sleep, and I'll be back first thing in the morning."

On the way out the Sister revived her with a cup of tea and provided a little comfort. The Brigadier was not in any immediate danger, but he had had a bad shock and, at his age, he would need to be watched for a day or two. His jaw had been broken and was wired up, which accounted for his curious turn of phrase. Other than that, his cuts and bruises would heal in time. What he most needed now was rest.

She took another taxi home and sank into her chair with a feeling that the day was somehow not quite real. A stiff Scotch revived her a little, then she rose and started packing a few of his things in readiness for the morning.

Jolyon Horton had inherited all of his father's *gravitas*, and none of his charm. Middle-aged at twenty, he had early shown an interest in politics and, after the usual long apprenticeship of unwinnable contests, was presently, as he liked to put it, candidate in a parliamentary by-election for the Conservative interest. His considerable height would have lent him sufficient presence, had it not been offset by a rather too obvious corpulence and a manner of studied superiority better suited to a class and generation long since fallen into desuetude. Pompous was the word most often applied to him, and it was a measure of his self-absorption that he alone remained wholly unaware of it.

The campaign was not going well. His agent said it lacked lustre, that it was boring, that it required an "issue". The problem had been that there were few issues of the 20th century upon which a man of the likes of Jolyon Horton could expatiate with any degree of conviction. He had tried AIDS, but these attempts foundered on his evident distaste; the mismanagement of the capital could too easily be laid at the door of his own party; the question of education was considered too dangerous for one whose own ambitions in that field had been limited to a proficiency in classical Greek.

Therefore, when the candidate telephoned to make his excuses for that evening on the grounds that his father had been injured by a bus, great was the rejoicing at campaign headquarters. The buses represented a rich vein of discontent which could endlessly be mined. They travelled in convoys and were never on time. They drove at top speed through large puddles, drenching pedestrians and washing cyclists into gutters. They belched stinking fumes into the ventilation systems of adjacent vehicles and made deafening noises during news broadcasts. In short, there was hardly a citizen in the capital who had not cause to add a voice to any clamour which could be raised.

It was unfortunate, in a way, that the Brigadier had survived the accident, but doubtless he was sufficiently injured, and much could be made of his continuing suffering. The public relations machine wheeled rapidly into action. Photographs of a younger and more vigorous Brigadier were purloined from the flat at Fulham. Copy was written extolling his long service in foreign parts, his idyllic marriage and grieving spouse. Whole paragraphs were quoted verbatim from the doctors, and finally, permission having been obtained with some difficulty from the hospital, a reporter from an evening paper, with photographer in tow, was invited to the bedside at Hampstead.

These arrangements occupied most of the Tuesday afternoon. Early on Wednesday morning the press arrived at the hospital shortly after Phyllis Horton. Naturally they were overjoyed to find a faithful wife tending the stricken hero. The flashgun popped from every angle, causing the patient exquisite agony. The reporter, refusing to believe that the Brigadier's speech impediment had purely mechanical origins, wrote that "a spokesman at the hospital" suspected that the shock might have precipitated a stroke.

With a great deal of bustle and noise and bumping of the bedstead, they completed their business, and suddenly, in a whooping gaggle, rushed down the stairs and were gone, leaving a bewildered Phyllis mewling plaintively beside her stupefied husband.

The story made the lunchtime edition, and the newspaper gave special prominence to the role of the bus in the catastrophe, having had for some time a particular interest in transport arrangements in the capital. Little could be gleaned from the photograph in the hospital, which showed only what looked like a pile of linen, but the earlier one of the healthy patient was easily recognisable, and this began a new and unfortunate train of events.

The Hampstead and Highgate Express is an august organ of the twin parishes on either side of Hampstead Heath. In normal circumstances it would not stoop to lifting a story from another paper, but on this occasion its intelligence sources had failed, the Brigadier having been registered in the hospital as a resident of Fulham. However, a bright young reporter, seeing the photograph of a well-known face, abandoned his lunch and made some rapid investigations, soon finding himself connected to the campaign office of Jolyon Horton, which was naturally anxious to oblige by providing additional prints and extra copy. Thus, that week's edition of the paper carried prominently on the front page a slightly different version of the story, with the emphasis on the local element, and with an enlargement of the Fulham photograph occupying pride of place.

The consternation that weekend in the various hostelries of Hampstead was profound. Those in Heath Street clubbed together with one in Flask Walk to start a collection, postponing a decision on whether to spend the result on a wreath or a libation. A man with a hat was despatched to obtain further and better particulars, and returned to report that the Brigadier was speechless and dying. Some lunch-timers grew maudlin towards the evening and spilt tears into their beer. All about the parish there pervaded a sense of disaster and dismay.

On the Saturday morning Phyllis Horton, unaware of this local excitement, arrived too early from Fulham and was given a chair outside the ward while the patients were rearranged and made presentable. She found another woman already established there, and was surprised to see that the latter had in her hand a page of a newspaper with her own photograph of the Brigadier upon it. She was a pleasant looking woman, in her early sixties at a guess, with untidy grey hair and an air of calm resourcefulness shining from friendly grey eyes. A stranger might have remarked that the two were not unlike.

After a few moments during which nothing was said, Phyllis's puzzlement was giving way to embarrassment. Extending her hand, she broke the silence: "How do you do."

"Hello," said the other, "I'm Mary Horton."

Phyllis was nonplussed. The Brigadier had never told her very much about his family, but could he really have failed to mention a sister, or even a brother's wife, or was this someone more remote?

"How very nice of you to come," she said, gesturing to the article. "I'm Phyllis Horton, the Brigadier's wife."

It was the turn of the other to look astounded.

"But that's impossible," she exclaimed. "I've been ..."

A dreadful suspicion suddenly struck both of the women at once. They stared at each other in disbelief.

"I think you and I had better go and have a cup of tea somewhere," said Mary.

Without further ado the pair left the hospital and, after a brief search, found a tea shop at the foot of the hill. Having ordered a pot and something to eat, Mary broke the ice: "I'm very much afraid that we are about to give each other some nasty shocks," she said. "Let's try to stay calm and not say anything which either of us would regret." She covered Phyllis's hand with her own.

Phyllis nodded dumbly, but made no reply. After a short pause, Mary continued: "I married Benedict Horton in Kenya in 1948."

"And he married me in Reigate in 1956!" exclaimed Phyllis, colouring to the roots of her hair.

They sat staring at each other. These revelations took some taking in. In the silence, on both sides, all sorts of puzzling happenings over the years suddenly began to become clearer. The strange stories of intelligence work which he was not allowed to explain. The continual absences long after he should have retired. The mysterious trips to Scotland.

And Mary was thinking: "Crafty old devil! All these years!"

Mind you, after the early years, she had rather come to enjoy having a semi-detached husband. His weekly absences gave her a freedom which few wives could boast, and they also made the time they spent together more enjoyable. Also, she had to admit, there had been occasions when her own inclinations had strayed in other directions, so there was no point in pretending outrage.

Anyway, as a husband he could not be faulted, if you ignored this one unusual lapse, that is. She wouldn't have him different for the world. "But heavens!" she thought, "what on earth are we going to do about *this* ludicrous situation?"

And Phyllis was thinking: "Then I suppose I've never been married! . . . Silly old goat . . . what's he think he's doing? . . . Don't suppose it makes much difference, really, these days . . . but what happens now? . . . Is he going to have to stay away for good?"

The possibility of losing him brought her up short, but she thrust the thought aside. "And what about Jolyon? . . . he must be illegitimate! . . . My God . . . this will ruin his career . . . how dreadful!" But, as the thought arose, so an image of her portly son appeared in her mind's eye and a gremlin on her shoulder whispered, "Pompous prat". She was aware that this was an unworthy thought, and possibly it was the sudden shock, but suddenly she had an overpowering urge to giggle.

She caught Mary's eye, and did giggle, and suddenly, the two women were convulsed with hysterical laughter, rolling about in the tea shop helplessly, clutching each other's hands, tears streaming down their faces, gasping for breath.

By the time the spasm had subsided, a degree of mutual understanding had developed, and the beginnings of a real affection. This was obviously a matter of concern to both of them, and, whatever happened, they would have to find a way forward together, before the outside world forced a conclusion unwelcome to both.

So they settled down to discuss the situation. They established, first, the manner of the deception over the years; the sharing out of each week; the variable routine, never more than three days, never less than two; the convincing accounts of time spent away. They spent an hour on the last year alone. If nothing else, there was much to admire in the sheer perfection of the operation, and the meticulous attention to detail which it had involved.

Nevertheless, when the hour was over, and they thought they had covered the ground, there remained at the back of Phyllis's mind, a niggling question-mark over something on which she could not quite put her finger.

In a happier vein, they reminisced on his performance as a husband; the never-forgotten anniversaries and birthdays, the prompt payment of expenses and allowances, the unfailing consideration and attention to feminine eccentricities, the fun he could be on outings and holidays.

Altogether, the Brigadier came out of the examination rather well. Neither woman heretofore had ever had to call her affection into question and, much to their astonishment, under this most severe test, they found that it was not much shaken in either case. Their marriages had been secure and comfortable, and both set great store by the personal freedom these curious arrangements provided.

After much hesitation and soul-searching, they together came to the conclusion, surprising to them both, that if it were possible, they would be quite happy to allow their lives to carry on much as before.

Nevertheless, the Brigadier was not going to be allowed to get away entirely scot-free. They ordered another pot of tea and set about devising a strategy.

They ought to have known better. Hampstead is infested with long-eared scribblers, and a few of them have a liking for tea.

As the two women left the tearoom early in the afternoon, the doubt which had been nagging at Phyllis suddenly surfaced. She confided it to Mary in a whisper. Seconds later, passing pedestrians gaped at the sight of two sober and respectable matrons clasping the hospital railings and doubled up in a fit of hysterical laughter.

Imagine the sense of outrage and despair at campaign headquarters on the following morning when they discovered that the most lurid of the Sunday tabloids, with the studied hypocrisy peculiar to election coverage, had penned and published the following item across its front page:

TORY LOVE CHILD IN POLL SHOCK

A BY-ELECTION in a London borough was thrown into turmoil yesterday when it was revealed that Tory candidate Jolyon Horton **IS A BASTARD.**

Not news to his mum, and not to us!—eh Jolly ole son?

Labour candidate Sid Pickings said " The Tory Party is full of them, but I'm fighting a clean campaign."

Mother, Phyllis "Horton" was not available for comment.

Polling day is Thursday.

Jolyon had barely finished his breakfast when the phone started ringing.

"What's this mean?" His agent's voice was tight with anxiety.

"What's what mean?" retorted Jolyon crossly. He did not read the tabloids.

Not for the first time, his agent wanted to kick him. "The papers have got hold of some story that—not to put too fine a point on it—your father and mother weren't married."

"That's completely absurd ... ridiculous! ... absolutely typical! ... toads! ... guttersnipes! ... which papers? ... where?" Jolyon was spluttering.

The agent read the piece over the phone. Jolyon's outrage

was palpable. "Who wrote this? ... I'll sue! ... where did it come from? ... A damnable lie ... I'm coming right over."

He took a cab and arrived at the office in a lather of rage, jowls aquiver, bulbous eyes popping.

His agent was unimpressed. "Look, Jolyon, sometimes they make mistakes, but on a thing like this? ... they're just not that stupid."

"Whose side are you on?" Jolyon bellowed, "We can't let them get away with this! It's outrageous ... bloody proles ... my God, I'll have them for this! ... my mother ..."

He grabbed the phone and dialled furiously. "No reply. She must be at the hospital. We'll have to see my father. God's blood! I'm going to hit them with everything there is!"

He dialled again, this time his solicitor. "That you, Marcus? I have to see you at once ... yes, I know it's Sunday, but this can't wait ... matter of libel ... in the paper today ... preposterous allegation ... what? ... they accuse me of being illegitimate! Dammit, I'm fighting an election, don't you understand? ... Right, I'll be there in ten minutes."

He snatched up his paper and dashed out into the street, agent at his heels.

"For God's sake calm down," panted the agent, "If you meet anyone in this state they'll make mincemeat of you."

"Oh, shut up," raged Jolyon, as another cab drew up. They clambered on board and raced west towards Putney.

"mmm ... eheheheh ... nnntts," said the swaddled corpse. If one bloodshot eye could be said to express astonishment, fear and perplexity all at once, then that eye was the Brigadier's, as it darted from side to side at the two women on either side of his bed. "mmm ... zzz," said its owner.

Phyllis took out a knitting needle and gave him a poke in the buttock.

'Ahrrr ... eeeee!" said the corpse.

Through a hole in the bandages Mary tweaked a hair poking out from his nose.

"Ngngng," said the corpse, and the eye closed. The sight of a trickling tear softened the women's resolve.

"You've got a lot of explaining to do," said Mary.

"And do it you shall," said Phyllis.

"And soon," said Mary, "They are unbuttoning you this afternoon."

"Nnnnn ..." said the corpse.

Just then a team of doctors, nurses and students bustled into the ward and made for the Brigadier's bed. The Sister motioned the women to withdraw. Phyllis followed Mary out. They settled into an earnest whispered conversation in the lobby outside the lift.

Barely an hour later, the foyer on the ground floor was once again thrown into confusion by the invasion of a noisome swarm of journalists, this time from half a dozen dailies with their photographers, led by a panting and quivering Jolyon. His agent and solicitor brought up the rear. They made a formidable clamour as they rushed yelling past the desk, pushing and shoving in their anxiety to be first up the stairs or into the lift. Within minutes the whole concatenation had burst into the ward and were milling round the bed, where the consultant had just begun the removal of the bandages, clicking and shouting and doing their best to elbow the hospital staff out of the way.

The consultant was not going to put up with this. A commanding presence and a fierce eye had them corralled within minutes in a heaving mass in a corner of the ward. At the front of this stood Jolyon, quaking with anxiety. The procedure seemed to take an age. Miles of bandages and bits of sticking plaster had to be undone. First appeared a tuft of hair, followed by a piece of forehead still covered in gauze. Then an ear with a fragment of cheek. Jolyon trembled, and his solicitor whispered in his ear: "Keep control of yourself. You can't be too careful in front of this lot."

Round and round the bandages went. The suspense was affecting everyone. Slowly, more and more of the head appeared until, at length, only gauze remained. This the consultant, with infinite care, gradually removed.

A frisson ran through the assembled company. Jolyon took a step forward and came to a sudden halt. "But that's not my father," he gasped.

As the dejected Jolyon stumped woodenly down the stairs into political oblivion, the impervious hacks tumbled noisily past to their next assignment. In their haste, the vanguard almost collided with two brown-coated figures struggling with a laundry basket on a landing. A volley of curses sent the pair scurrying for cover, and the pack continued, unheeding, on its way.

In a flat near Brunswick Square, overlooking the sea at Hove, Isobel Horton gazed fondly out of her drawing-room window at the distinguished figure of her husband, making his way home along the front. The slight limp which was a legacy of the accident only added interest to what she felt was still a very handsome picture.

She turned from the window and arranged his pipe and tobacco next to his chair. To these she added a glass of whisky and a bucket of ice: then she set out the bridge table with its pads and pencils. It was so very agreeable that Mary and Phyllis were able to make up a four each week on the first night of her turn, now they that both lived so near. She made some small adjustments in the kitchen, and was ready with a smile to greet the Brigadier as his key turned in the lock.

My Life as a Girl in a Men's Prison

KATE PULLINGER

I can feel myself changing at night. Alone, in my cell—it's such a cliché, but it's true, it is my actual situation. I live in a cell in a closed unit, in a prison within a prison; but at night I feel the changes taking place and this is something that no one—not even me—can control. And they are letting me get away with it, they are letting me do it, which is the astounding thing. They, the authorities—another cliché, I know—can't stop me now, it's too late.

Like Esmerelda the English teacher, Kelsey lives in London; that is, he lived in London before *It* happened. *It* is what Kelsey calls the accident, the event, the thing that happened that got Kelsey locked away. Another queer-bashing gone wrong—Kelsey ended up the murderer instead of the murderee—in old London town, under the shadow of the gleaming, phallic Canary Bird thing. "The Canary's stopped singing," Kelsey used to say to John in the kitchen after those Canadian business brothers went bankrupt. "Ooh," he would continue, looking out of the window of their flat, "I hate that fucking thing." Secretly this was not true; Kelsey and John rather admired the colossus. It made them think about what it might be like to live in New York, far away from the grimiest end—the grimy east end—of a filthy old city.

Now Kelsey lives in prison, but Esmerelda still lives in the city. She works in the prison and for her it is part of London; she travels there on a bus down the long, bereft, empty-shop-windows high street. But Kelsey and the other inmates in the closed wing are not in the city any longer, not in the world any longer in fact. They are in the closed wing, the segregation unit, on Rule 43: they are the nonces, the sex beasts, the scum.

Esmerelda teaches English in the prison; she was made redundant when the Putney secondary school where she worked was amalgamated with a secondary school in Tooting. Tooting—nothing to toot about there as far as she could see. Esmerelda misses teaching teenage girls, she misses the single-sex environment of the secondary girls' school. The prison is, of course, a single-sex environment also, but the other sex, the opposite one, men. And yet there is Kelsey, Kelsey who is neither here nor there; perhaps Esmerelda's nostalgia for girls is part of the reason why she finds herself drawn to Kelsey now.

London is full of prisons; Esmerelda learned this when she began working in one. They are part of the unseen, unnoticed structure of the city like Underground ventilation shafts and sewers. Spot one and you start seeing them everywhere. Wormwood Scrubs—oh, the very name makes Esmerelda shudder. Holloway. Pentonville. Wandsworth. Brixton. Brrr.

The masculinity of the place is palpable; the air is thick with maleness. Esmerelda thinks she can actually feel it on her skin. The prison smells like a huge locker room that somehow ended up inside an even larger greasy spoon, sweat and socks mixed with custard and frying mince. And tobacco—a dense fogbank of cigarette smoke builds up during the course of the day. They all smoke, all the men, everyone single one of them, except Kelsey.

Kelsey somehow manages to remain nicotine-free, sweetened.

There are twenty of us in this unit, twenty of us lowest of the low, a layer of scum twenty men thick. They're not so bad, the others. I don't mind them. We're all just a little misunderstood. Well, actually, we're all massively misunderstood, in fact, none of us understand it ourselves really. But we get on okay, we watch each other's backs to a certain extent; it's all right so long as no one from out there can get to us with their home-made weapons, "shanks"—bent nails, metal chair legs, etc. They're all so butch out there in the open wings, it's frightening; but butch is the wrong word, those kinds of words don't work in here.

Esmerelda goes down to the segregation unit once a week to teach an English class. Kelsey doesn't come to her class yet, but Esmerelda has been told about him by an officer and by a governor grade as well. "He likes to iron, does our Kelsey," said the Governor. "He irons everything down there in the seg unit. Ironed shirts, ironed socks, they even have bloody ironed sheets down there. And it's weird," he continued while Esmerelda smiled and nodded, "Kelsey is changing. Right before our very eyes, he is changing. His hair is different now and well," the Governor paused, his eyes looking beyond the bars for the right word, "it's uncanny, really, it is."

The other men in the seg unit did not discuss Kelsey, and Esmerelda did not ask questions about him. The other men—mostly rapists, child abusers and men accused of sodomy—were reading Thomas Hardy and the class held long discussions about fate that Esmerelda found fascinating. Fate seemed to be something they knew about; fate and coming to a bad end. They engaged with Hardy on a completely different level from teenaged school girls, and this made Esmerelda read Hardy differently as well. When she was in prison Esmerelda found the rest of her life faded away; it was as though life started and finished at the prison gates. London was not really out there at all, the prison floated somewhere in outer space.

Outside the closed unit, in the Education block and on the open wings, things were not quite so extreme. One of her students, a man who could recite Coleridge's "Rime of the Ancient Mariner" in its entirety—a lifetime's work— described his cell to her as part of an oral exam one day. "And I have a view," he concluded.

"What?" said Esmerelda.

"From the top of B-Wing, where my cell is, I have a view. I can see London from up there. I can see some council flats, some garages, and the back of the high street."

Esmerelda smiled. "That's London all right," she said.

"You don't know what a relief it is," he continued, "to know that while I'm stuck in here, out there people are hanging up their laundry."

"Ahh, London," said another man, "I miss it. I miss the dirty old town. Brilliant, isn't it? Where do you live, Miss?"

"Archway," replied Esmerelda.

"Ahh, the big old arch over Highgate Road. What I wouldn't do for a ride in a taxi under that just now," the prisoner sighed. "Highgate Cemetery—I've got my plot sorted already."

"Oh?" said Esmerelda. "Speaking of plots—" and she brought up Thomas Hardy again.

When Kelsey came to Esmerelda's seg unit English class for the first time he walked in smelling of roses, St James Park summer roses, Esmerelda thought. He took a seat alongside the other men. He had very curly and blond long hair, blue

blue eyes, full pouting lips, and bad skin. "I'm sorry I've missed
the first few classes, Miss," he said politely. "I had prior engagements."

The other men smirked. "Oh, you're engaged now are you Kelsey?" one of them asked.

"No," said Kelsey, a kind of Princess Diana at a charity dinner smile across his face, "but I am terribly, awfully, busy."

Esmerelda needed a few moments to recover from the impact of Kelsey's entrance. Her silence was filled by the other prisoners; they always had plenty to say. Kelsey gazed at Esmerelda, she could feel his steady eyes upon her. "Where'd you get your shoes, Miss?" he asked eventually.

"Covent Garden."

"Oh that dump," he replied, smiling.

The class went on, Esmerelda's composure returned. Kelsey had done all the reading, and he was smart; she could see he would be a good student. They finished on time and the other men got up to leave, the sound of banging trays and officers outside the door. Kelsey walked up to where Esmerelda was sitting on the edge of a table. He leaned over and whispered, "I've got an English degree." His breath smelt of mint.

"What are you doing studying for a GCSE?"

"Boredom, you see. I'd rather talk about Thomas Hardy than mop floors all day. And besides, I'd heard you were nice. There's not a lot of women around here, you might have noticed. It's important to make the most of every opportunity."

Esmerelda left the prison at 4:30 that afternoon. Outside workers, education people, probation, etc. left at the same time every day; after that the prison fell almost silent for a moment before the evening racket began. As she left Esmerelda imagined Kelsey in his cell; as she left Kelsey imagined Esmerelda on her way home. He stood on his bed and looked out through his cell window into the tiny seg exercise yard. It was raining and the London sky was very low. Kelsey had a theory, one he used to expound upon with John, that the reason there were so few skyscrapers in London was that in the winter the sky was too low. "There's hardly room for a five floor block of flats," he'd say looking out the kitchen window as he did the washing-up, "let alone a skyscraper. The Canary Bird has completely disappeared today."

Esmerelda took the bus home. That evening she stayed in by herself and watched TV. The milk had gone sour so she ate a bowl of dry cereal instead. The phone did not ring. As she cleaned her face to get ready for bed she remembered Kelsey's skin. It must be the hormones she thought, although she didn't know why, no one had said anything about hormones.

Which am I: a nonce, a sex beast, or scum? Hmm. Nonce maybe, that seems the most likely. Perhaps I should change my name to Nancy when the time comes, forget Kitty, the girl I used to be. Nance, I'll be used to that. In here I'm just Kelsey, of course, number L651254—yet another cliché. I'll have to write a book when I get out: My Life as a Girl in a Men's Prison.

I'll have to write a book, thought Esmerelda before she went to sleep: *My Life as a Girl in a Men's Prison.*

Later that week when Esmerelda was getting ready to go teach her seg unit English class, she found herself staring in the bathroom mirror. A new haircut, she thought, that's what I need. A new face. A complete new body. She ran her fingers through her hair and then put on more make-up than usual.

In class the men were noisy and reluctant to work. Kelsey came in late, wearing a neck-scarf that appeared to have been torn from a prison sheet. When Esmerelda looked from his neck to his face she found he was looking at her. Kelsey shrugged and smiled apologetically, "A girl's got to make some attempt, doesn't she?" The other men hissed and jeered half-heartedly. Esmerelda blushed. The class continued.

The weeks went by. The season changed in its oblique London way. In prison time passes like water in the Thames, slow, murky, inevitable, taking forever to get to the sea. Kelsey missed his lover John. John missed Kelsey. Kelsey felt he had been wrongly convicted and sentenced. These are things suitable for understatement only. The Canary Bird opened its doors to sightseers in a bid to pay for its own feed.

Esmerelda continued to teach English. She gave assignments. Her classes worked toward taking their exams. Kelsey continued to change. One day Esmerelda thought she could see a hint of breasts beneath his carefully pressed prison shirt. Kelsey came up to her after class, in the few moments before the officers came to shoo everyone away. "I'm worried," he said.

"What about?"

"My orals. I'm not very strong on oral exams."

"You speak perfectly well, Kelsey."

"Not in exams. I want to practise. When can I see you?"

Esmerelda was a little surprised. No one in the seg unit had ever asked her for extra help. Men on the open wings asked for extra help all the time, but they didn't down here. She was accustomed to coming into the closed unit and then being able to leave.

"Can you come tomorrow?" Kelsey could see Esmerelda hesitating. "Please?"

Esmerelda consulted her diary. "I have half an hour tomorrow morning before lock-up."

"Good," said Kelsey. "I'll see you then."

The next morning while Esmerelda was getting ready to go

to work, she went to the bathroom to pick up her lipstick. She put some on, and then put the tube into her purse. In the mirror her make-up looked fine, she was wearing enough. She picked up her mascara, her eye-liner, her eyebrow pencil. She rummaged through the make-up bag she kept beside the sink and found some eye shadow, other shades of lipstick, an old pair of false eyelashes. She picked up the entire bag and put it into her purse.

Esmerelda got down to the seg unit a little early; Kelsey was waiting for her. They walked past the cells on the way to the interview room, where it's a bit more quiet, Kelsey said. They embarked on a practice exam; Esmerelda opened her purse to find her notes. She brought out the make-up bag instead.

Cleanser, moisturiser, foundation, toner, powder, blush: Kelsey looked best with a dark brown eye-liner, black mascara, his eyebrows darkened and made thick. Esmerelda found it easy to touch him. He tilted his face back and let himself be touched. They consulted the mirror in her compact. Kelsey knew more about make-up than Esmerelda; this did not surprise either of them. "But your skin . . ." said Esmerelda.

"I know. It's all the things I've been taking. For the change—as though I'm bloody menopausal already," he laughed. "My skin's gone all funny. But apparently it will clear up again."

"What's going to happen?" asked Esmerelda.

"Well, I suppose I'll have to go to a women's prison some time soon." Esmerelda held her breath, but Kelsey smiled and said, "That will be weird. In all of London I'll bet I'm the only girl in a men's prison."

"You're not a girl yet," said Esmerelda.

"Well," said Kelsey, "nearly."

In the Courtyard
of the Moneylenders

JOHN TURNER

Arnold looked up at the big iron gates which climbed above him into the clear October sky. It was quiet in the Temple gardens. There were always foreigners about, but not too many of his people. It was quite warm for the time of year, the sun was shining, it looked nice. He would like to go in and lie on a bench, take his boots off and let the breeze cool his feet. It was Sunday and the Salvation Army minibus would be around when it was dark with hot coffee and something to eat. He'd go down the back of the Savoy, they normally made a stop in Temple Place and then he'd go over the bridge to the Hole in the Wall. He might get some more there.

Through the wrought iron bars he could see a pavilion, beyond the bandstand, opening onto the grass. Big white words were painted on its walls, he could have read them once. In the shelter was a green bench, the sun shone in and flooded it with light. He could sit there, sheltered from the wind, until the day slid away behind the trees. It was a lovely day, but the wind had a bite to it and that clear sky would bring a frost tonight. Yes, the air was cold and it carried the smell of fallen leaves. The days were getting short. It would soon be winter. How he hated the cold darkness of winter.

Arnold thought all this while standing in front of the entrance. He did one thing at a time. He thought or he ate or he walked. He had done his thinking, now he walked through into the ornamental gardens and along the sunlit path. He would eat later, he hoped, because his stomach was already hurting. Each activity was as slow and painful as all the rest. Age, alcohol, cold and disease had brought him to this.

On the move, he shuffled one foot past the other, eyes downcast, restlessly scanning the ground. He had no idea what London's skyline looked like, show him the new Charing Cross station or the Lloyd's building and he wouldn't have a clue what he was looking at. If you kept your eyes down, you might find treasure and you didn't get into any trouble. The yuppy drunks pushed you out of the way and the Law watched you go by, but, normally, you got no hassle and there was no knowing what you might pick up.

A young woman sat in the shelter, reading a newspaper, where the sun shone. He hadn't been able to see her from the road and he hovered outside in the shade. He looked at the floor, at the toes of his boots, at the mud-caked, frayed ends of his trousers and would not meet the woman's eyes. He knew they'd be fixed on him, full of pity or hate. People always did that. They asked questions. He didn't know what they wanted him to do or say and so he stared at the ground. She wouldn't stay long, they never did.

With biting words about his smell and living on the dole, the woman swept away, leaving him the place in the sun. As he settled down, he felt comfortable, with his world close around him.

His bottle, hard and round, was secure in an inner pocket, wrapped round with rags to keep it safe. It felt reassuringly heavy. The lid of his tobacco tin bulged with plenty. The warmth of the sun soaked through his coat, he relaxed, but he wasn't safe yet. He didn't dare take his boots off and he couldn't yet let go of his hold on his mind. The woman might have gone to fetch security to drive him out.

Minutes passed and thoughts of guards, policemen and park keepers faded. Through half closed eyes he saw the sun sparkling on the Thames. It could have been a river of gin. He shut his eyes and drew in air, hoping that his nose could recreate the illusion. It was too long ago since he'd drunk gin and he opened his eyes again, disenchanted. The river still sparkled, but like water, without attraction.

A crumpled piece of coloured paper rolling down the wind, caught his eye and he moved with the swiftness of a striking snake. Astonishing speed if one remembered his laboured walking. A floppy sole shot out and smothered the paper. He didn't move another muscle. A woman strode towards him along the path and he watched her from under heavy-lidded eyes. He didn't think it was the same one who had been in the shelter when he came, but he couldn't be sure, they all looked alike. He sat with his head bent forward, still, listening to the tapping heels approaching. His heart beat like a tamping machine, piling a strange prickling sensation onto his indigestion.

He was sure it was money, but if he moved to pick it up, she might see. She might say it was hers. It might be the same woman, it might be hers. No, it wasn't hers, it was his, but she would say he stole it. The heels went by without breaking their rhythm and the gardens fell quiet. With a quick glance around to make sure there was no one else to see, he bent down to tie the lace of his boot. Another quick look and then, with a movement like a swooping hawk, he had the note in his hand which flew on into the safety of his pocket. Let anyone say that it wasn't his now.

His heart was racing with excitement and he leant back against the wall with his eyes closed, savouring the joy of possession. He felt the need for a drink to celebrate. Snuggling the old brown bottle in the shadows between him and the corner, he bent down and stole a mouthful. He had to be careful, if the coppers saw him they would be down on him like a pack of dogs and drive him out of his place in the sun.

The golden spirit burned his stomach, it eased all pain and made life feel good. No hunger, no cold, no thirst and no need to move. He cleared his mind of all aggravation, all thoughts left him and he closed his eyes to doze against the wall.

A cloud passed across the sun and instantly the warmth was gone from the shelter. The sunshine was an illusion, it was nearly winter. The sun came again in a few minutes, as warm as it had been before, but Arnold had a fleeting thought of death that left him frightened.

Stealing another glance to ensure that he was alone, he drank again from his bottle. At the same time, he let the hand in his pocket crumple and smooth the little square of paper nestling against his thigh. Here was a bed for the night down Great Peter Street, away from the killing frost, a drink when the bottle ran dry, soft food which didn't need to be hunted down and stolen away or hung around all night for.

His fingers played guessing games with the note through holes in his glove. Suddenly his mouth was dry and the sharp contraction of his stomach made him wet himself. It seemed too small. What if it were foreign or one of those token things? Again his heart speeded up and he drew his mittened fist out into the open. He forced himself to look around before he opened his finger the merest fraction. Not a flicker of expression crossed his face, but deep down he smiled.

There was the Queen's head, they couldn't put that on rubbish. It was money, one of those pretty new ten pound notes. He closed his fist and returned it among his coats. He tried to concentrate. He could vaguely remember Duffer Charlie saying something about fake tenners when he was dossing in Lincoln's Inn Fields last week or was it John the Irishman or was it yesterday?

No, it wasn't yesterday, yesterday the council had put up a fence around the Fields and thrown them all out. He'd lost his box and spent last night roughing it, always on the move, trying to keep warm. The frost had nigh on killed him. The police had picked him up in Kingsway. They must have thought he was dead or they'd have left him. They gave him a sandwich and a cup of tea. That was the last thing he'd had to eat.

He had another drink, scratched through his matted beard and dozed again contentedly. The sun moved round and he awoke in the shade, shaking with the cold, or was it the pain in his chest? He'd have to move on soon, he thought. He didn't dare spend another night on the pavement. He had time for a smoke before he moved on, he slid around the bench to hold onto the last patch of the sunlight. Reaching for his tobacco tin, he sorted himself out a dog end, a good long one with lipstick on the end. Women always smoked the best. He'd only one match left and that was a split one. With the money he could buy himself matches, perhaps even cigarettes. He couldn't remember the last time he had bought a packet of cigarettes. He used to once, he used to buy them all the time. He could buy some more cider and something to liven it up. He might even buy some gin.

Doubt swept across his mind, what if it wasn't real money? It might not buy anything. He began to panic, he didn't know what to do, who to ask. There was no one he could trust not to cheat him. Everyone would lie to him, try to steal it from him. If he took it into a shop, they'd tell him that it wasn't worth anything. They always cheated him in shops. Every one cheated him, lied to him and stole from him.

The sun slipped back behind the clouds hanging low over the Houses of Parliament and the air turned chill. The cold would normally have been enough to turn off his brain and send him shuffling on his way, but the turmoil in his head was now in control. He thought and thought about who he could ask, until his head spun. The Captain at the Sally Ann wouldn't lie or cheat or steal. Or would he? He might, if it were a lot of money. He was a bloke like all the rest.

No, not the Captain. He vaguely remembered the time when he was still allowed in the hostel. The other Charlie, Twopenny Charlie, came in with a tenner he'd found. He said he'd earned it washing up, but the Captain knew he'd found it. He told Charlie that he should take it to the lawshop. He preached what was right, but he didn't take it off him. He knew what everybody knew, Charlie wouldn't give it up.

When Charlie was bashed in the night, the Captain had them all out of their beds and went through their packs. He found it too and gave it back to Twopenny Charlie, saying it was more Charlie's than anyone else's. He'd told Charlie what was right and left it up to his conscience. But what if the Captain was short, God knows, they didn't pay him much. Arnold didn't know if he could trust the Captain.

The sun was going, almost gone. It flickered fitfully among the bare branches of the trees on the Embankment and had lost its warmth. The air was still now and the last leaves fell straight down, to rattle on the grass. He gathered his coats about him, took another drink and put the bottle safe while he applied himself to lighting the cigarette. There was a numbness in his fingers. He broke the frail match and when he tried to strike it again, it flared and was instantly gone.

Where did it go, where was the sun going, where was he going? Across the gardens, a bell sounded, they would be closing soon. The pain in his chest rose back into his consciousness. It was worse than ever. It stopped him breathing.

In panic, he wrenched himself to his feet and hurried towards the street, moaning in agony and fear. He had to get to the hostel, there was a sick room there, they'd get a doctor to look at him. Tears ran down his cheeks, washing furrows in the grime. The bell came nearer and then moved away again. The gardens were closing and he would be locked in, but he had to rest.

He hunched against a tree and fought for breath, waiting for the pain to ease. There was a sense of death laying heavily on him. No one cared for an old man, in pain and alone. They didn't even know his name. It would be the law that found him. Some fresh faced kid would wrinkle up his nose and get out his notebook, but he wouldn't know him or care. He'd tell the sergeant. The sergeant knew him. He'd say, "so old Arnold croaked at last," and he'd write it in a book.

Arnold . . . Oh God, he couldn't remember his own second name. The sergeant would phone the Sally Ann and the Captain would tell him. No, he wouldn't, he'd say, "poor old Arnold, no, I don't know his other name, no, I don't know where he came from." He'd say a quick prayer and then forget him. The Captain was too busy worrying about the living to bother about the dead.

"They must know me," Arnold shouted aloud. "I was a soldier. I remember, I drove a bus, a big red bus, a million people rode on my bus. They know who I am. Somebody must know me."

Terror twisted him up inside, swamping all the pain. "They won't know me. They'll walk by and they won't even look at me, like they did with old . . ." the name had gone ". . . when she dropped dead in the street. They say she laid there all morning and nobody stopped. It'll be the same for me. They'll dig a hole and put me in and no one will know my name.

"I'm Arnold, Arnold Seagrave," he shouted as the memory

came back. He reached out towards a man who happened to be passing, hurrying towards the underground station, "Arnold Seagrave."

The man said nothing. He glowered at him for his intrusion and brushed the sleeve of his Savile Row suit, even though Arnold hadn't managed to touch him.

"Arnold Seagrave," the old man whispered, "of Walworth. I drove a bus. A 73, but you don't want to remember."

The gloom crowded in. The Embankment seethed with activity, but in the gardens it was all quiet. "Arnold Seagrave," he muttered over and over to himself as he shuffled frantically towards the gate. He hung onto his identity grimly. In the misty depths of memory he could see a flight of stairs above a barber's shop. There was a tattooist, even though he couldn't remember where. He would find him, the money would pay to have his name tattooed on his arm and then they would know who he was when he couldn't remember any more himself. When he died, someone would be able to write his name down in a book, just to show that he had been there at all.

In a reflex action, he touched his pocket for reassurance. It was gone. His bottle had gone. He searched every pocket and then again. Someone had stolen it. No, he'd put it down in the shelter when he tried to light the cigarette.

He turned and shuffled back into the nearly dark. He knew that he wouldn't be able to get back to the shelter and return before the gate clanged shut. He wouldn't be able to climb over it. He would be trapped, but he had no choice.

The last of the security men at the last of the gates looked back over his domain to check that everything was in order. He could see nothing moving, it was totally still.

Acacia Avenue

KIRSTY SEYMOUR-URE

I stumble off the bus clutching the baby under one arm and the pushchair under the other. Two middle-aged, motherly women get off too and start muscling in, and I feel unusually grateful now for this neutral contact. They help me strap Joseph into his seat, cooing and clucking at his little moon face. One of them adjusts his scarf and mittens, the other pulls up the buggy's transparent waterproof hood against the threatening rain. The bus churns exhaust into our faces.

"There now. You want to watch he doesn't catch cold," says the first woman, shivering and pulling her green anorak tight around her.

"Nasty weather for him to be out in," says the other, and looks at me as if it's my fault the temperature's suddenly dropped below zero. It is, after all, spring.

I say politely, "Yes, well, thanks very much for your help," and Joseph watches them silently, droopy-eyed. "Goodbye," I say firmly, and start pushing the baby down the street. I have no idea where I'm going.

Some way along, when I'm sure the two women aren't following us, I stop and fumble in my pocket for the map. It's a page torn from the A–Z and I have some difficulty locating my position on it. Eventually I realise we're not where we should be: in my anxiety not to go too far, I have got off the bus several stops early. I mutter curses under my breath. The baby stares up at me blankly from behind his transparent shield.

"Never mind, Joseph," I tell him. "We'll walk it. It can't be far."

The route is easy in the grid-patterned streets: so many streets down, turn left, so many streets along, turn right: Acacia Avenue, number 38. Gritting my teeth, I set off. There are few people out on this grey day, though on the main road the traffic is a ceaseless jerky flow. I walk mechanically, hardly aware of my surroundings, another terrible anony-mous suburb of south London that is at once familiar and utterly alien; the small neat front gardens, frosted glass in the front doors, a glimpse of gas fires flickering like real coals behind the net curtains. The small second car for the wife; the car port that designates real success. It is all here, as it is anywhere else. This is where Lisa grew up. I am numb with cold and residual grief.

As I walk I'm thinking of what I'm going to say to Lisa's parents. They are expecting me, but they don't know who I am; they are not expecting Joseph. They are not expecting anything.

Should I just come out with it all at once, on the doorstep? "Mr and Mrs Coe? I spoke to you on the phone. Yes: David. Your daughter's lover. And this is Joseph, your daughter's baby; but I'm not the father. Oh, and one other thing. Lisa's dead."

That ought to take care of it.

It starts to rain, a steady relentless drizzle that will probably keep going for the next couple of months. It doesn't make any difference to me. How could it? I glance down at the baby. He is serenely asleep, warm and dry, his little bobble hat pulled down over his ears. At times I think that I will not be able to give him up: there is something addictive about his presence, the smile that he reserves for me only, the absolute trust that he gives me, the surprising grip of his tiny fingers. I don't know if this is love. Is it simply that he is Lisa's child? My last link to her. I know I shall have to give him up.

We walk past Laburnum Gardens, Jasmine Road, Daffodil Way. I can't believe these street names. How do streets get their names? Who chooses them? There's a section of north London where the streets are called, charmingly, after Shakespearean characters; Cressida, Miranda, Prospero, Lysander. Why? Is there a naming committee consisting of people with nutty obsessions? "I think it's time we had obscure East European cities." "How about ancient South American cult deities?" Well, I rather fancy flowering shrubs myself." "Come on, now you're being silly."

And on I plod through the rain. Lisa's parents. Perhaps I should wait till we're inside, till I've been offered and accepted the obligatory cup of tea, till we've sat down on the three-piece suite, huddled round the switched-off telly that will be there glaring like a baleful one-eyed household god. "There's something I have to tell you. It's bad news, I'm afraid."

That was what the doctor said to me, as I stood by the maternity wing vending-machine. Chocolate, crisps, peanuts, sweets: I was overdosing on junk food, running on sugar, high on E-numbers. There was nowhere in the hospital that sold alcohol; perhaps that was just as well.

"It's bad news, I'm afraid," the doctor said in a voice of terrible gentleness.

I waited for the Mars Bar to fall into my hand.

"She's dead, isn't she?"

"The baby survived. The baby's fine. It's a little boy." The doctor's hesitant face blurring in front of me, his hand pressing down on my shoulder. "Sit down, David. Drink this."

And my cry, my long cry of despair. Then, viciously: "I

don't care about the baby, it's not mine, I didn't want her to have it. I wish it had died." Which was all true.

The doctor, refusing me the satisfaction of looking shocked, murmured soothingly, "I understand, David." And I see now that perhaps he did. It was his job, after all.

All my memories of Lisa have pain in them, but at the time we were happy.

How can I say that? We were miserable; though in different ways. It is only looking back that I perceive those months as happy. She had become pregnant in an absurd manner, which made me, though I had no right to be, extremely angry. Can I tell her parents this? She hadn't seen her parents for months. They disapproved of what they termed her "way of life", by which they meant the fact that she didn't have a proper job, didn't want to get married and settle down in a little house in the suburbs, didn't want—I screw my face up at the irony—to have children.

Joseph's father was a man on the run.

Can I say this to her parents?

"He was a wanted man, Mr and Mrs Coe. He was—a murderer."

It was the kind of melodrama that Lisa would have appreciated. In fact, it was more or less this that drew her to Anton in the first place.

Over the pink linen tablecloth of an Italian restaurant in Soho, he had leaned towards her, fixed her with his piercing blue eyes (as she described them afterwards) and said softly, "There is something you must know." Lisa held her breath in anticipation. Anton lowered his voice. He said: "I have killed a man."

An extreme, seductive statement; a statement of grandeur and import and danger: there are not many occasions in a life when such statements are handed to you. Can you throw them away? Lisa thought not. She thought that to waste them was verging on the criminal.

No, you fall in love with them.

She put down her spaghetti fork, let out her breath in a silent whistle, gazed at Anton with sparkling eyes, flushed cheeks. "Have you really? Is it true?"

He nodded slowly. "Yes. It is true." Can he have remained unmoved by her excitement?

The waiter came and poured more wine. The candle flickered on the table. The restaurant and the other diners faded into the background. "Tell me!" demanded Lisa, shivering with delight. "Who did you kill? Why? Tell me how it happened."

"Are you sure you want to know?" asked Anton.

This is the point at which, if it had been me instead of Lisa, I would have said, No. No, I don't want to know. This is the point at which I would have walked out. She said: Tell me.

I push Joseph's chair into a bus shelter for a moment to check the map. Crocus Crescent? Unbelievable but true. Right there in front of me. Despite the cold, I decide to pause for a quick cigarette. "Sorry, Joseph, but it's a question of sanity," I mutter; but in the event my fingers are too numb to manipulate the match. Joseph has woken and is gazing around him with a marked lack of interest. "I don't blame you," I tell him. "But don't worry, it's probably not as bad as it looks. Imagine it in summer. All your little neighbourhood pals. Your new parents will buy you ice-cream and a trike and take you to the multiplex." Joseph remains impassive. "Yes, I see your point," I say. Impulsively I bend down and unzip the rainhood and peer in at him. He bestows one of his rare, grave smiles upon me and struggles to free a mittened hand. I help him and he puts his hand up to touch my cheek, which is streaming with rainwater. He looks at his wet fingers in wonder. I have a horrible feeling that I'm going to cry. "Come on, pull yourself together," I say out loud. I zip the hood back together and carry on walking. There is still some way to go.

"Mr and Mrs Coe. Approximately one year ago, on a day rather warmer than today, your daughter is approached by a young man in the street. He is foreign, German to be precise, and he asks her for directions in rather sexily accented English. (I have this on good authority.) Your daughter, being the trusting and helpful individual that she is, offers to show this stranger around. Why? Because she is bored. She is wandering about on her own in central London and she's bored. (Mr and Mrs Coe, you are doubtless aware of your daughter's somewhat, er, capricious nature.) The German wishes to see the Docklands development that he has heard so much about, he wants to be whisked along on the famous Light Railway, his ultimate desire is to visit Canary Wharf.— Well, the famous Railway is, famously, not running, but they take a river-bus instead, which the German finds enchanting—though probably not as enchanting as he finds your daughter. They stroll around parts of the site through clouds of dust, piles of cement, men in hard hats dangling from half-constructed buildings. They step over rusty girders, twisted pipes, oddly shaped perspex blocks that seem to have no function. Mr and Mrs Coe, the German holds out his hand to your daughter and she takes it. Envision her face, lit up, imagine that smile . . ."

Finally they came to Canary Wharf. Walking hand in hand up the approach road that was built with cars in mind, they felt as if they were walking onto a film set. Everything was on a different scale, inhuman, suprahuman. The tower soared above them, unimaginably huge, so tall that as they watched, a whirring helicopter had to fly round than over it. In awe, Anton and Lisa stood below and looked up, up, up. They

watched the racing clouds and the setting sun reflected endlessly in the thousand panes of glass. They walked around the
landscaped piazza with its caged, strapped-in saplings, careful low hedges, the cold fountains whose spray blew in their
faces as they passed; and above it all, a looming presence, the
extraordinary tower. Anton said, "It is like something you
cannot believe in." "But you have to," said Lisa.

What happened then? I don't know. Lisa didn't tell me
how they got back from Docklands to the West End.
Presumably it's not important. The next bit of the story takes
place in the Italian restaurant—Greek Street, was it? Frith
Street? One of those little roads that run north/south in that
part of Soho. It's warm, they have strolled in the spring
evening, mingling with tourists and shoppers and business-
folk; they've looked at the rather tame hookers draped in
peepshow doorways; they've paused beneath the Raymond
Revue Bar's neon sign. They have jostled their way among
the fruit-and-veg stalls of Berwick Street market and
breathed in the rich organic nature of its smells, incongruous
in the fumy centre of town. They are footsore from the miles
of concrete they have trodden: relieved to sit down at the
pink-clothed table and order a bottle of wine and relax. They
gaze over the bread-basket at each other and see in each
other's eyes curiosity, happiness and light.

Yet there is something melancholy about her companion
that intrigues Lisa, a certain intensity, as if he sees things that
are hidden from others. She says to him, "Are you unhappy,
Anton?"

And that was when Anton told her that he had killed a
man.

He was not a murderer, not as such, Lisa said to me. The
man died in a fight. "Huh, a street brawler," I said in disgust.

"No, it wasn't like that," she said defensively. "Anton was
helping some friends who were being attacked by a group of

those, you know, neo-Nazis, in a bar. Well, one of them died. But he died later, in hospital, and it's not even certain that it was Anton who hit him."

I shook my head. "Why did you believe this guy?"

She said quietly, "He seemed to be worth believing."

After the neo-Nazi's death, Anton, wanted for questioning by the police, left Germany and came to England—"fled the country by night!" said Lisa, high on romance. He spent a couple of days wandering alone around London; then he met Lisa. "If he was innocent, why did he flee?" I asked bitterly.

Finally, we come to Sycamore Drive, though I see no evidence of sycamores in any of the careful gardens or municipally pruned trees. This is where we turn left. "Nearly there now, Joseph," I murmur. I'm feeling more and more scared as Mr and Mrs Coe become ever nearer, ever more tangible. Could I simply thrust Joseph into their arms and run? Attach a note to his ankle giving his name, his favourite foods and his preferred song at bedtime? If only I could be certain I will not weep.

After dinner, they walked down to the Thames. The night air was still soft and warm. They held hands and walked like lovers. They crossed the river by the Hungerford Footbridge, pausing halfway across to look downriver at the skyline; dwarfed dome of St Paul's, the mingling of glass towers and church spires, the bizarre pink and blue glow of the Lloyd's building. A long barge chugged slowly below them, heading towards the sea with its cargo of waste. The buses crossing Waterloo Bridge were solid rectangles of light; floodlit, the South Bank complex looked quite romantic, the Festival Hall like a huge ocean-going liner ready to slip its moorings, the boxy concrete National Theatre clear and crisp as a giant sugar-cube. Sketching a vague gesture in the air, Lisa murmured, "I love this—", and Anton smiled and said, "Yes, it is beautiful, your city."

They walked along the river for some way on the south bank, the concrete walkway lit by electrified Victorian gas-lamps entwined with wrought-iron serpents. When they stopped they leant on the railing and watched the turmoiled muddy water rushing past below. "You know," said Anton, "your Thames is clean again, there are fish in it. This is no mean feat for a city river."

"How did you know that?" asked Lisa.

He brushed her hair away from her face and regarded her seriously; he kissed her gently. Then he looked at his watch, which was still on German time, and said, "It is getting late."

She didn't want to go home. "Not all that late," she said. "Do you want a drink? I know somewhere that's still open."

"I must go back," he said.

Disappointed, she said, "Well, shall I walk you to your hotel?"

"I mean, I must go back to Germany."

"Back to Germany? Why? Won't they be looking for you? What if they send you to prison?"

He nodded, looking at her sadly. "I know. But I must go back and turn myself in. It is the only thing to do." From the river came the sprightly hoot of a tugboat and a barge's mournful reply.

"No!" Lisa cried.

He looked at her steadily and she held his gaze. Then she said in a voice urgent with emotion, "Anton, stay here. Stay here with me. Marry me, take my name. Start a new life, here, with me."

He shook his head. "It is impossible, my Lisa. I must go back and face the consequences of what I have done."

At that she became angry. "Do you have to be so goddamn honest? You didn't meant to do it. It wasn't your fault." A couple strolling by looked at them curiously and Lisa lowered her voice. "It might not even have been you that killed that—thug."

"I have to go back," he repeated.

And seeing that he was not going to change his mind, Lisa asked, "When?"

"Tomorrow," Anton said.

When Lisa was telling me all this, I said then, "Well, whatever else he was, at least he had a certain kind of honour." She gave me a filthy look. "He was honourable in everything he did," she said, and I did not reply, "Yes, except in getting you pregnant and then disappearing without a second thought."

Where did they go for their midnight tryst, for their one night of passion, their few hours of love? Lisa would never tell me, I don't know why. Was it back to the comfort and warmth of her flat, or did they creep, giggling and embarrassed, up to his room in a seedy hotel? Or—given the warmth of the night—did they find some sheltered and secluded spot in one of London's private parks and curl up there like two forsaken animals, finding a deep well of love and forgiveness beneath the stars and a curtain of smog? This last—the open air, the elements—would have appealed to Lisa's romantic nature, and I like to think that it is what they did, despite my own dismay at the idea of such behaviour. And then did Anton slip off into the mist at dawn without disturbing her; or did they both wake early and aching, and head up into town to find a café for breakfast? I like to imagine them huddled at a formica-topped table warming themselves on chipped china mugs of steaming coffee from an urn, lost in their own little world as burly shiftworkers come and go on either side of them. Whatever my own feelings towards Lisa and Anton, I have to do them the courtesy of allowing these few invented moments of love the dignity of pathos in my mind.

But she told me the details of their moment of parting. They stood in the echoing halls of Victoria Station—was it a Sunday, or too early for commuters?—and held on to each other, (her flesh bruising from the strength of his grip). Pigeons swooped under their artificial sky. Tramps were picking themselves up for another day on the streets. Anton and Lisa said goodbye without words or tears, and she watched him walk away. He got on a train without a ticket, bound for Dover, and Lisa said to me afterwards, laughing, "He probably got arrested on that train and is still here languishing in jail for not paying his fine!"

When she found she was pregnant she came to me. Old faithful. We went to a pub in Soho and drank whisky, shouting above the jukebox to make ourselves heard. The pub was crowded with pre-theatre drinkers and we were squashed uncomfortably up against a wall near the loos. That was when Lisa told me the whole story, not bothering to keep her voice down for privacy; enjoying, even, the sense of performance.

"You're mad," I said to her, when it seemed she'd finished. "What about AIDS?"

"I trusted him," she said. Then she added, "I'm pregnant."

I sighed heavily. "Oh, Jesus. Presumably you're not intending to have it?"

"I want to keep it," she told me. "I want you to help me. I need you, David."

When I say I was Lisa's lover I mean it in a very specific way. I mean that I was her lover in every way but sexually. I mean that I loved her. I could have slept with her—she would have allowed that—but I didn't want her mere assent. I wanted her love. I wanted what, incomprehensibly, she had given Anton.

"Why?" I asked her, later on that same night, when the

pub had quietened down and we were sitting at a table in a shadowy corner, slightly drunk. "Why do you want his baby? What was it about him? What was it about that evening?"

She said to me, "I can't describe the thrill that went through me—that is still echoing through me—when he said those words. *I have killed a man.* It made my heart leap, my blood race. God, it was pure *sex*, David." She paused, glanced at me, and then continued, "It was as if I had not been fully alive before that point. I just knew that nothing like this would ever happen again to me." She looked down, as if embarrassed, which was unlike her. I knocked back my whisky and went to get another round. She didn't love me, but she needed me; she had fallen in love with a moment, and it wasn't my moment.

Nobody's fault.

I agreed to help her—what else could I do? We would move in together and she would have the baby and I would say it was mine. *I have killed a man.* By the end of the evening my heart was breaking.

The pregnancy was complicated. Lisa hadn't expected the discomfort, the tiredness, the pains. Everything irritated her, including me. I brought her cakes from Patisserie Valerie and anchovy-stuffed olives from Camisa's delicatessen, but she wouldn't touch my offerings. She refused to tell her parents about the pregnancy. "They'll know soon enough," she snapped. She had infrequent, bored, bland conversations about the weather with them on the phone. Her suppressed anger seemed out of proportion, but I had learnt not to probe.

She wouldn't let me be with her during her labour, but when the contractions started she gave a cry of terror. "David, don't let them take me in there, I'm going to die!" I stroked her hair and said, "No, you're not, don't be silly.

People don't die in childbirth any more." I believed this. I thought that it was true.

After the long night, the doctor came towards me. "It's bad news, I'm afraid."

He took me to see her body. I was horrified. Androgynous beings in green overalls and facemasks were clearing the blood and mess away from between her legs like dripping lumps of meat. There was blood everywhere. The doctor was confused. "I'm sorry," he said, "they should have had her cleaned up by now." He led me out again hastily, and then went back to say something to the nurses. After that, I remember nothing.

It's still raining, not hard, but the wet is seeping through my layers of clothing. Joseph wriggles in his pushchair. I stop and lean down towards him. I whisper, "Oh, God, what are we going to do?" We are so near now. Honeysuckle Road, Lilac Court. The next one is Acacia Avenue. I turn down it, push the buggy slowly, noticing that one of the wheels has started squeaking. I read the house numbers. Thirty-four, thirty-six. It's a nice road, like all of them round here. Neat, trim, inoffensive, quiet. Thirty-eight. The car in the drive is a red Sierra. The front door is painted red. What does that mean? I lean on the little gate for a moment before opening it. The net curtains twitch. Mr and Mrs Coe? There's something I have to tell you . . . It's bad news, I'm afraid.

I push the chair up the path to the front door, and look at Joseph, hoping he will smile. I lift my hand to press the bell, but the door is already opening.

Lunching with the Anti-Christ

MICHAEL MOORCOCK

In memorium, Horst Grimm

Begg Mansions,
Sporting Club Square

The Editor,
Fulham & Hammersmith Telegraph,
Bishops Palace Avenue,
London W14

13th October 1992

Sir,

SPIRIT OF THE BLITZ

It is heartening to note, as our economy collapses perhaps for the last time, a return to the language and sentiments of mutual self-interest. London was never the kindest of English cities but of late her cold, self-referential greed has been a watchword around the world. Everything we value is threatened in the name of profit.

I say nothing original when I mourn the fact that it took the Blitz to make Londoners achieve a humanity and heroism they never thought to claim for themselves and which no one expected or demanded of them!

Could we not again aspire to achieve that spirit, without the threat of Hitler but with the same optimistic courage? Can we not, in what is surely an hour of need, marshall what is best in us and find new means of achieving that justice, equity and security for which we all long? The existing methods appear to create as many victims as they save.

Yours faithfully, Edwin Begg,
former vicar of St Odhran's, Balham.

HEAR! HEAR! says the Telegraph. This week's Book Token to our Letter of the Week! Remember, your opinions are important to us and we want to see them! A £5.00 Book Token for the best!

ONE

My First Encounter With the Clapham Anti-
Christ; His Visions & His Public Career; His
Expulsion from the Church & Subsequent
Notoriety; His Return To Society & Celebrity
as a Sage; His Mysterious & Abrupt
Departure Into Hermitage; His Skills in the
Kitchen.

"SPIRIT OF THE BLITZ" (a sub-editor's caption) was the
last public statement of the Clapham Antichrist.

Until I read the letter at a friend's I believed Edwin Begg
dead some twenty years ago. The beloved TV eccentric had
retired in the 1950s to live as a recluse in Sporting Club
Square, West Kensington. I had known him intimately in the
60s and 70s and was shocked to learn he was still alive. I felt a
conflicting mixture of emotions, including guilt. Why had I
so readily accepted the hearsay of his death? I wrote to him at
once. Unless he replied to the contrary I would visit him on
the following Wednesday afternoon.

I had met Begg first in 1966 when as a young journalist I
interviewed him for a series in the *Star* about London's
picturesque obscurities. Then too I had contacted him after
reading one of his letters to the *Telegraph*. The paper, still a
substantial local voice, was his only source of news, delivered
to him weekly. He refused to have a telephone and
communicated mostly through the post.

I had hoped to do a few paragraphs on the Antichrist's
career, check a couple of facts with him and obtain a short,
preferably amusing, comment on our Fab Sixties. I was

delighted when, with cheerful courtesy, Edwin Begg had agreed by return to my request. In a barely legible old-fashioned hand he invited me to lunch.

My story was mostly drafted before I set off to see him. Research had been easy. We had half a filing drawer on Edwin Begg's years of notoriety, first before the War then afterwards as a radio and early TV personality. He had lived in at least a dozen foreign cities. His arguments were discussed in every medium and he became a disputed symbol. Many articles about him were merely sensational, gloating over alleged black magic rites, sexual deviation, miracle-working, blasphemy and sorcery. There were the usual photographs and also drawings, some pretending to realism and others cruel cartoons: the Clapham Antichrist as a monster with blazing eyes and glittering fangs, architect of the doom to come. One showed Hitler, Stalin and Mussolini as his progeny.

The facts were pretty prosaic; in 1931 at the age of 24 Begg was vicar of St Odhran's, Balham, a shabby South London living where few parishioners considered themselves respectable enough to visit a church and were darkly suspicious of those who did. The depression years had almost as many homeless and hungry people on the streets as today. Mosley was gathering a more militant flock than Jesus and those who opposed the Fascists looked to Oxford or the secular left for their moral leadership. Nonetheless the Reverend Begg conscientiously performed his duty, offering the uncertain comforts of his calling to his flock.

Then quite suddenly in 1933 the ordinary hard-working cleric became an urgent proselytiser, an orator. From his late Victorian pulpit he began preaching a shocking message urging Christians to act according to their principles and sacrifice their own material ambitions to the common good, to take a risk on God being right, as he put it. This Tolstoyan exhortation eventually received enough public attention to make his sermons one of London's most popular free attractions from Southwark to Putney, which of course brought him the attention of the famous Bermondsey barrackers, the disapproval of his establishment and the closer interest of the press.

The investigators the Church sent down heard a sermon touching mainly on the current state of the Spanish Republic, how anarchists often acted more like ideal Christians than the priests, how people seemed more willing to give their lives to the anarchists than to the cause of Christ. This was reported in *Reynolds News*, tipped off that the investigators would be there, as Begg's urging his congregation to support the coming Antichrist. The report was more or less approving. The disapproving church investigators, happy for a lead to follow, confirmed the reports. Overnight, the Reverend Edwin Begg, preaching his honest Christian message of brotherly love and equity under the law, became the Clapham Antichrist, Arch Enemy of British Decency, Proud Mocker of All Religion and Hitler's Right Hand, a creature to be driven from our midst.

In the course of a notoriously hasty hearing Edwin Begg was unfrocked, effectively by public demand. In his famous defence Begg confirmed the general opinion of his guilt by challenging the commission to strip itself naked and follow Christ, if they were indeed Christians! He made a disastrous joke: and if they were an example of modern Christians, he said, then after all he probably was the Antichrist!

Begg never returned to his vicarage. He went immediately to Sporting Club Square. Relatives took him in, eventually giving him his own three-roomed flat where it was rumoured he kept a harem of devil-worshipping harlots. The subsequent Siege of Sporting Club Square in which the *News of the*

World provoked a riot causing one near-fatality and thousands of pounds worth of damage was overshadowed by the news of Hitler's massacre of his stormtroopers, the SA. Goebbels' propaganda became more interesting and rather more in the line of an authentic harbinger of evil, and at last Edwin Begg was left in peace.

Usually attached to a circus or a fair and always billed as 'Reverend' Begg, The Famous Clapham Antichrist! he began to travel the country with his message of universal love. After his first tours he was never a great draw since he disappointed audiences with urgent pleas for sanity and the common good and never rose to the jokes or demands for miracles, but at least he had discovered a way of making a living from his vocation. He spent short periods in prison and there were rumours of a woman in his life, someone he had mentioned early on, though not even the worst of the Sundays found evidence to suggest he was anything but confirmed in his chastity.

When the War came Edwin Begg distinguished himself in the ambulance service, was wounded and decorated. Then he again disappeared from public life. This was his first long period of seclusion in Begg Mansions until suddenly on 1 May, 1949, encouraged by his cousin Robert in BBC Talks, he gave at 9.45 pm on the Home Service the first of his Fireside Observer chats.

No longer the Old Testament boom of the pulpit or the sideshow, the Fireside Observer's voice was level, reassuring, humorous, a little sardonic sometimes when referring to authority. He reflected on our continuing hardships and what we might gain through them if we kept trying—what we might expect to see for our children. He offered my parents a vision of a wholesome future worth working for, worth making a few sacrifices for, and they loved him.

He seemed the moral spirit of the Festival of Britain, the

best we hoped to become, everything that was decent about being British. An entire book was published proving him the object of a plot in 1934 by a Tory bishop, a Fascist sympathiser, and there were dozens of articles, newsreels and talks describing him as the victim of a vicious hoax or showing how Mosley had needed a scapegoat.

Begg snubbed the Church's willingness to review his case in the light of his new public approval and continued to broadcast the reassuring ironies which lightened our 1950s darkness and helped us create the golden years of the 1960s and 70s. He did not believe his dream to be illusory.

By 1950 he was on television, part of the *Thinkers' Club* with Gilbert Harding and Professor Joad, which every week discussed an important contemporary issue. The programme received the accolade of being lampooned in *Radio Fun* as *The Stinker's Club* with Headwind Legg which happened to be one of my own childhood favourites. He appeared, an amiable sage, on panel games, quiz shows, programmes called *A Crisis of Faith* or *Turning Point* and at religious conferences eagerly displaying their tolerance by soliciting the opinion of a redeemed antichrist.

Suddenly, in 1955, Begg refused to renew all broadcasting contracts and retired from public life, first to travel and finally to settle back in Begg Mansions with his books and his journals. He never explained his decision and then the public lost interest. New men with brisker messages were bustling in to build utopia for us in our lifetime.

Contenting himself with a few letters mostly on parochial matters to the Hammersmith *Telegraph*, Edwin Begg lived undisturbed for a decade. His works of popular philosophy sold steadily until British fashion changed. Writing nothing after 1955, he encouraged his books to go out of print. He kept his disciples, of course, who sought his material in increasingly obscure places and wrote to him concerning his uncanny understanding of their deepest feelings, the ways in which he had dramatically changed their lives, and to whom, it was reported, he never replied.

The first Wednesday I took the 28 from Notting Hill Gate down North Star Road to Greyhound Gardens. I had brought my *A–Z*. I had never been to Sporting Club Square before and was baffled by the surrounding network of tiny twisting streets, none of which seemed to go in the same direction for more than a few blocks, the result of frenzied rival building work during the speculative 1880s when developers had failed to follow the plans agreed between themselves, the freeholder, the architect and the authorities. The consequent recession ensured that nothing was ever done to remedy the mess. Half-finished crescents and abrupt cul-de-sacs, odd patches of wasteland, complicated rights of way involving narrow alleys, walls, gates and ancient pathways were interrupted, where bomb damage allowed, by the new council estates, totems of clean enlightenment geometry whose erection would automatically cause all surrounding social evils to wither away. I had not expected to find anything quite so depressing and began to feel sorry for Begg ending his days in such circumstances, but turning out of Margrave Passage I came suddenly upon a cluster of big unkempt oaks and cedars gathered about beautiful wrought-iron gates in the baroque oriental regency style of Old Cogges, that riot of unnatural ruin, the rural seat of the Beggs which William the Goth remodelled in 1798 to rival Strawberry Hill. They were miraculous in the early after-noon sun: the gates to paradise.

The square now has a preservation order and appears in international books of architecture as the finest example of its kind. Sir Hubert Begg, its architect, is mentioned in the same breath as Gaudi and Norman Shaw, which will give you some notion of his peculiar talent. Inspired by the fluid aesthetics of the *fin-de-siècle* he was loyal to his native brick and fired almost every fancy from Buckingham clay to give his vast array of disparate styles an inexplicable coherence. The tennis courts bear the motifs of some Mucha-influenced smith, their floral metalwork garlanded with living roses and honeysuckle from spring until autumn: even the benches are on record as one of the loveliest expressions of public *art nouveau*.

Until 1960 there had been a black chain across the Square's entrance and a porter on duty day and night. Residents' cars were never seen in the road but garaged in the little William Morris cottages originally designed as studios and running behind the eccentrically magnificent palaces, which had been Begg's Folly until they survived the Blitz to become part of our heritage. When I walked up to the gates in 1966 a few cars had appeared in the gravel road running around gardens enclosed by other leafy ironwork after Charles Rennie Mackintosh, and the Square had a bit of a shamefaced seedy appearance.

There were only a few uniformed porters on part-time duty by then and they too had a slightly hangdog air. The Square was weathering one of its periodic declines, having again failed to connect with South Kensington during a decade of prosperity. Only the bohemian middle classes were actually proud to live there, so the place had filled with actors, music hall performers, musicians, singers, writers, cheque-kiters and artists of every kind, together with journalists, designers and retired dance instructresses, hair-dressers and disappointed legatees muttering bitterly about any blood not their own, for the Square had taken refugees and immigrants. Others came to be near the tennis courts maintained by the scs Club affiliated to nearby Queen's.

Several professionals had apartments in Wratislaw Villas. The courts never went down and neither did the gardens which were preserved by an endowment from Gordon Begg, Lord Mauleverer, the botanist and explorer, whose elegant vivarium still pushed its flaking white girders and steamy glass above exotic shrubbery near the Mandrake Road entrance. Other examples of his botanical treasures, the rival of Holland's flourished here and there about the Square and now feathery exotics mingled with the oaks and hawthorn of the original Saxon meadow.

Arriving in this unexpected tranquillity on a warm September afternoon when the dramatic red sun gave vivid contrast to the terracotta, the deep greens of trees, lawns and shrubbery, I paused in astonished delight. Dreamily I continued around the Square in the direction shown me by the gatehouse porter. I was of a generation which enthused over Pre-Raphaelite paint and made Beardsley its own again, who had bought the five shilling Mackintosh chairs and sixpenny Muchas and ten bob Lalique glass in Portobello Road to decorate Liberty-oriental pads whose fragrant patchouli never disguised the pungent dope. They were the best examples we could find in this world to remind us of what we had seen on our acid voyages.

To my father's generation the Square would be unspeakably old-fashioned, redolent of the worst suburban pretension, but I had come upon a gorgeous secret. I understood why so few people mentioned it, how almost everyone was either enchanted or repelled. My contemporaries, who thought "Georgian" the absolute height of excellence and imposed their stern developments upon Kensington's levelled memory, found Sporting Club Square hideously "Victorian"—a gigantic, grubby whatnot. Others dreamed of the day when they would have the power to be free of Sporting Club Square, the power to raze her and raise their fake Le Corbusier mile-high concrete in triumph above the West London brick.

I did not know, as I made my way past great mansions of Caligari Tudor and Kremlin De Mille, that I was privileged to find the Square in the final years of her glory. In those days I enjoyed a wonderful innocence and could no more visualise this lovely old place changing for the worse than I could imagine the destruction of Dubrovnik.

Obscured, sometimes, by her trees, the mansion apartments of Sporting Club Square revealed a thousand surprises. I was in danger of being late as I stared at Rossettian gargoyles and Blakean caryatids, copings, gables, corbels of every possible stamp yet all bearing the distinctive style of their time. I was filled with an obscure sense of epiphany.

In 1886, asymmetrical Begg Mansions was the boldest expression of modernism, built by the architect for his own family use, for his offices and studios, his living quarters, a suite to entertain clients, and to display his designs, accommodation for his draughts- and crafts-people whose studios in attics and basements produced the prototype glass, metal, furniture and fabrics which nowadays form the basis of the V&A's extraordinary collection. By the 1920s after Hubert Begg's death the Square became unfashionable. Lady Begg moved to Holland Park and Begg Mansions filled up with the poorer Beggs who paid only the communal fee for general upkeep and agreed to maintain their own flats in good condition. Their acknowledged patron was old Squire Begg, who had the penthouse. By 1966 the building was a labyrinth of oddly twisting corridors and stairways, unexpected landings reached by two old oak and copper cage elevators served by their own generator, which worked on an eccentric system devised by the architect and was always going wrong. Later I learned that it was more prudent to walk the six flights to Edwin Begg's rooms but on that first visit I got into the lift, pressed the stud for the sixth floor and was taken up without incident in a shower of sparks and rattling brass to the ill-lit landing where the Antichrist himself awaited me.

I recognised him of course but was surprised that he seemed healthier than I had expected. He was a little plumper and his bone-white hair was cropped in a self-administered pudding-basin cut. He was clean-shaven, pink and bright as a mouse, with startling blue eyes, a firm rather feminine mouth and the long sharp nose of his mother's Lowland Presbyterian forefathers. His high voice had an old-fashioned Edwardian elegance and was habitually rather measured. He reminded me of a Wildean *grande-dame*, tiny but imposing. I was dressed like most of my Ladbroke Grove peers and he seemed pleased by my appearance, offering me his delicate hand, introducing himself and muttering about my good luck with the lift. He had agreed to this interview, he said, because he'd been feeling unusually optimistic after playing the new Beatles album. We shared our enthusiasm.

He guided me back through those almost organic passages until we approached his flat and a smell so heady, so delicious that I did not at first identify it as food. His front door let directly onto his study which led to a sitting room and bedroom. Only the dining room seemed unchanged since 1900 and still had the original Voysey wallpaper and furniture, a Henry dresser and Benson copperware. Like many reclusive people he enjoyed talking. As he continued to cook he sat me on a sturdy Wilson stool with a glass of wine and asked me about my career, showing keen interest in my answers.

"I hope you don't mind home cooking," he said. "It's a habit I cultivated when I lived on the road. Is there anything you find disagreeable to eat?"

I would have eaten strychnine if it had tasted as that first meal tasted. We had mysterious sauces whose nuances I can still recall, wines of exquisite delicacy, a dessert which contained an entire orchestra of flavours, all prepared in his tiny perfect 1920s "modern" kitchenette to one side of the dining room.

After we had eaten he suggested we take our coffee into the bedroom to sit in big wicker chairs and enjoy another wonderful revelation. He drew the curtains back from his great bay window to reveal over two miles of almost unbroken landscape all the way to the river with the spires and roofs of Old Putney beyond. In the far distance was a familiar London skyline but immediately before us were the Square's half-wild communal gardens and cottage garages, then the ivy-covered walls of St Mary's Convent, the Convent School sports field and that great forest of shrubs, trees and memorial sculptures, the West London Necropolis, whose Victorian angels raised hopeful swords against the ever-changing sky. Beyond the cemetery was the steeple of St Swithold's and her churchyard, then a nurtured patchwork of allotments, some old alms cottages and finally the sturdy topiary of the Bishop's Gardens surrounding a distant palace whose Tudor dignity did much to inspire Hubert Begg. The formal hedges marched all the way to the bird sanctuary on a broad, marshy curve where the Thames approached Hammersmith Bridge, a medieval fantasy.

It was the pastoral and monumental in perfect harmony which some cities spontaneously create. Edwin Begg said the landscape was an unfailing inspiration. He could dream of Roman galleys beating up the river cautiously alert for Celtic war-parties or Vikings striking at the Bishop's Palace leaving flames and murder behind. He liked to think of other more contemplative eyes looking on a landscape scarcely changed in centuries. "Hogarth, Turner and Whistler amongst them.

Wheldrake, writing *Harry Wharton*, looked out from this site when staying at the Sporting Club Tavern and earlier Augusta Begg conceived the whole of *The Bravo of Bohemia* and most of *Yamboo; or, The North American Slave* while seated more or less where I am now! Before he went off to become an orientalist and London's leading painter of discrete seraglios James Lewis Porter painted several large landscapes which show market gardens where the allotments are, a few more cottages, but not much else has changed. I can walk downstairs, out of the back door, through that gate, cross the convent field into the graveyard, take the path through the church down to the allotments all the way to the Bishop's Gardens and be at the bird sanctuary within half-an-hour, even cross the bridge into Putney and the Heath if I feel like it and hardly see a house, a car or another human being!" He would always stop for a bun, he said, at the old Palace Tea Rooms and usually strolled back via Margrave Avenue's interesting junkyards. Mrs White, who kept the best used bookshop there, told me he came in at least twice a week.

He loved to wake up before dawn with his curtains drawn open and watch the sun gradually reveal familiar sights. "No small miracle, these days, dear! I'm always afraid that one morning it won't be there." At the time I thought this no more than a mildly philosophical remark.

For me he still had the aura of a mythic figure from my childhood, someone my parents had revered. I was prepared to dislike him but was immediately charmed by his gentle eccentricity, his rather loud plaid shirts and corduroys, his amiable vagueness. The quality of the lunch alone would have convinced me of his virtue!

I was of the 1960s, typically idealistic and opinionated and probably pretty obnoxious to him but he saw something he liked about me and I fell in love with him. He was my ideal father.

I returned home to rewrite my piece. A figure of enormous wisdom, he offered practical common sense, I said, in a world ruled by the abstract sophistries and empty reassurances heralding the new spirit of competition into British society. It was the only piece of mine the *Star* never used, but on that first afternoon Edwin Begg invited me back for lunch and on almost every Wednesday for the next eight years, even after I married, I would take the 28 from the Odeon, Westbourne Grove to Greyhound Gardens and walk through alleys of stained concrete, past shabby red terraces and doorways stinking of rot until I turned that corner and stood again before the magnificent gates of Sporting Club Square.

My friend kept his curiosity about me and I remained flattered by his interest. He was always fascinating company, whether expanding on some moral theme or telling a funny story. One of his closest chums had been Harry Lupino Begg, the music hall star, and he had also known Al Bowlly. He was a superb and infectious mimic and could reproduce Lupino's patter by heart, making it as topical and fresh as the moment. His imitation of Bowlly singing "Buddy, Can You Spare a Dime" was uncanny. When carried away by some amusing story or conceit his voice would rise and fall in rapid and entertaining profusion, sometimes taking on a birdlike quality difficult to follow. In the main however he spoke with the deliberate air of one who respected the effect of words upon the world.

By his own admission the Clapham Antichrist was not a great original thinker but he spoke from original experience. He helped me look again at the roots of my beliefs. Through him I came to understand the innocent intellectual excitement of the years before political experiments turned one by one into tyrannical orthodoxies. He loaned me my first Kropotkin, the touching *Memoirs of an Anarchist*, and helped me understand the difference between moral outrage and social effect. He loved works of popular intellectualism. He was as great an enthusiast for Huxley's *The Perennial Philosophy* as he was for Winwood Reade's boisterously secular *Martyrdom of Man*. He introduced me to the interesting late work of H.G. Wells and to Elizabeth Bowen. He led me to an enjoyment of Jane Austen I had never known. He infected me with his enthusiasms for the more obscure Victorians who remained part of his own living library and he was generous with his books. But no matter how magical our afternoons he insisted I must always be gone before the BBC broadcast Choral Evensong. Only in the dead of winter did I ever leave Sporting Club Square in darkness.

Naturally I was curious to know why he had retired so abruptly from public life. Had he told the church of his visions? Why had he felt such an urgent need to preach? To risk so much public disapproval? Eventually I asked him how badly it had hurt him to be branded as the premier agent of the Great Antagonist, the yapping dog as it were at the heels of the Son of the Morning. He said he had retreated from the insults before they had grown unbearable. "But it wasn't difficult to snub people who asked you questions like 'Tell me, Mr Begg, what does human blood taste like?' Besides, I had my Rose to sustain me, my vision ..."

I hoped he would expand on this but he only chuckled over some association he had made with an obscure temptation of St Anthony and then asked me if I had been to see his cousin Orlando Begg's *Flaming Venus*, now on permanent display at the Tate.

Though I was soon addicted to his company, I always saw him on the same day and time every week. As he grew more comfortable with me he recounted the history of his family and Sporting Club Square. He spoke of his experiences as a young curate, as a circus entertainer, as a television personality, and he always cooked. This was, he said, the one time he indulged his gourmet instincts. In the summer we would stroll in the gardens or look at the tennis matches. Sitting on benches we would watch the birds or the children playing. When I asked him questions about his own life his answers became fuller, though never completely unguarded.

It was easy to see how in his determined naïveté he was once in such frequent conflict with authority.

"I remember saying, my dear, to the magistrate—Who does not admire the free-running, intelligent fox? And few, no matter how inconvenienced, begrudge him his prey which is won by daring raiding and quick wits, risking all. A bandit, your honour, one can admire and prepare against. There is even a stirring or two of romance for the brigand chief. But once the brigand becomes a baron that's where the balance goes wrong, eh, your honour? It gets unfair, I said to him. Our sympathies recognise these differences so why can't our laws? Our courts make us performers in pieces of simplistic fiction! Why do we continue to waste so much time? The magistrate said he found my last remark amusing and gave me the maximum sentence."

Part of Edwin Begg's authority came from his vivacity. As he sat across from me at the table, putting little pieces of chicken into his mouth, pausing to enjoy them, then launching off onto a quite different subject, he seemed determined to relish every experience, every moment. His manner offered a clue to his past. Could he be so entertaining because he might otherwise have to confront an unpleasant truth? Anyone raised in a post-Freudian world could make that guess. But it was not necessarily correct.

Sometimes his bright eyes would dart away to a picture or

glance through a window and I learned to interpret this fleeting expression as one of pain or sadness. He admitted readily that he had retreated into his inner life, feeling he had failed in both his public and private missions. I frequently reassured him of his value, the esteem in which he was still held, but he was unconvinced.

"Life isn't a matter of linear consequences," he said. "We only try to make it look like that. Our job is not to force grids upon the world but to achieve harmony with nature."

At that time in my life such phrases made me reach for my hat, if not my revolver, but because I loved him so much I tried to understand what he meant. He believed that in our terror we imposed perverse linearity upon a naturally turbulent universe, that our perceptions of time were at fault since we saw the swirling cosmos as still or slow-moving just as a gnat doubtless sees us. He thought that those who overcame their brute terror of the truth soon attained the state of the angels.

The Clapham Antichrist was disappointed that I was not more sympathetic to the mystical aspects of the alternative society but because of my familiarity with its ideas was glad to have me for a devil's advocate. I was looking for a fast road to utopia and he had almost given up finding any road at all. Our solutions were wrong because our analysis was wrong, he said. We needed to rethink our fundamental principles and find better means of applying them. I argued that this would take too long. Social problems required urgent action. His attitude was an excuse for inaction. In the right hands there was nothing wrong with the existing tools.

"And what are the right hands, dear?" he asked. "Who makes the rules? Who keeps them, my dear?" He ran his thin fingers through hair which became a milky halo around his earnest face. "And how is it possible to make them and keep them when our logic insists on such oppressive linearity? We took opium into China, dear, and bled them of their silver. Now they send heroin to us to lay hands upon our currency! Am I the only one enjoying the irony? The Indians are reclaiming the Southwestern United States in a massive migration back into the old French and Spanish lands. The world is never still, is it, my dear?"

His alert features were full of tiny signals, humorous and anxious, enquiring and defiant, as he expanded on his philosophy one autumn afternoon. We strolled around the outer path enjoying the late roses and early chrysanthemums forming an archway roofed with fading honeysuckle. He wore his green raglan, his yellow scarf, his hideous turf accountant's trilby, and gestured with the blackthorn he always carried but hardly used. "The world is never still and yet we continue to live as if turbulence were not the natural order of things. We have no more attained our ultimate state than has our own star! We have scarcely glimpsed any more of the multiverse than a toad under a stone! We are part of the turbulence and it is in turbulence we thrive. Once that's understood, my dear, the rest is surely easy? Brute warfare is our crudest expression of natural turbulence, our least productive. What's the finest? Surely there's no evil in aspiring to be our best? What do we gain by tolerating or even justifying the worst?"

I sat down on the bench looking the length of a bower whose pale golds and browns were given a tawny burnish by the sun. Beyond the hedges was the sound of a tennis game. "And those were the ideas which so offended the Church?" I asked.

He chuckled, his face sharp with self-mockery. "Not really. They had certain grounds I suppose. I don't know. I merely suggested to my congregation after the newspapers had begun the debate, that perhaps only through Chaos and

Anarchy could the Millennium be achieved. There were after all certain clues to that effect in the Bible. I scarcely think I'm to blame if this was interpreted as calling for bloody revolution, or heralding Armageddon and the Age of the Antichrist!"

I was diplomatic. "Perhaps you made the mistake of overestimating your audiences?"

Smiling he turned where he sat to offer me a reproving eye. "I did not overestimate them, my dear. They underestimated themselves. They didn't appreciate that I was trying to help them become one with the angels. I have experienced such miracles, my dear! Such wonderful visions!"

And then quite suddenly he had risen and taken me by my arm to the Duke's Elm, the ancient tree which marked the border of the larger square in what was really a cruciform. Beyond the elm were lawns and well-stocked beds of the cross's western bar laid out exactly as Begg had planned. Various residents had brought their deckchairs here to enjoy the last of the summer. There was a leisurely good-humoured holiday air to the day. It was then, quite casually and careless of passers-by, that the Clapham Antichrist described to me the vision which converted him from a mild-mannered Anglican cleric into a national myth.

"It was on a similar evening to this in 1933. Hitler had just taken power. I was staying with my Aunt Constance Cunningham, the actress, who had a flat in D'Yss Mansions and refused to associate with the other Beggs. I had come out here for a stroll to smoke my pipe and think over a few ideas for the next Sunday's sermon which I would deliver, my dear, to a congregation consisting mostly of the miserably senile and the irredeemably small-minded who came to church primarily as a signal to neighbours they believed beneath them ...

"It was a bloody miserable prospect. I have since played

better audiences on a wet Thursday night in a ploughed field
outside Leeds. No matter what happened to me I never
regretted leaving those dour ungiving faces behind. I did my
best. My sermons were intended to discover the smallest
flame of charity and aspiration burning in their tight little
chests. I say all this in sad retrospect. At the time I was
wrestling with my refusal to recognise certain truths and find
a faith not threatened by them.

"I really was doing my best, my dear." He sighed and
looked upward through the lattice of branches at the
jackdaw nests just visible amongst the fading leaves. "I was
quite agitated about my failure to discover a theme
appropriate to their lives. I wouldn't give in to temptation
and concentrate on the few decent parishioners at the
expense of the rest." He turned to look across the lawns at
the romantic rococo splendour of Moreau Mansions. "It was
a misty evening in the Square with the sun setting through
those big trees over there, a hint of pale gold in the haze and
bold comforting shadows on the grass. I stood here, my dear,
by the Duke's Elm. There was nobody else around. My vision
stepped forward, out of the mist, and smiled at me.

"At first I thought that in my tiredness I was hallucinating.
I'd been trained to doubt any ecstatic experience. The scent
of roses was intense, like a drug! Could this be Carterton's
ghost said to haunt the spot where he fell to his death,
fighting a duel in the branches after a drunken night at
Begg's? But this was no young duke. The woman was about
my own height, with graceful beauty and the air of peace I
associated with the Virgin. My unconventional madonna
stood in a mannish confident way, a hand on her hip, clearly
amused by me. She appeared to have emerged from the earth
or from the tree. Shadows of bark and leaves still clung to
her. There was something plant-like about the set of her
limbs, the subtle colours of her flesh, as if a rose had become

human and yet remained thoroughly a rose. I was rather frightened at first, my dear.

"I'd grown up with an Anglicanism permitting hardly a hint of the Pit, so I didn't perceive her as a temptress. I was thoroughly aware of her sexuality and in no way threatened by it or by her vitality. After a moment the fear dissipated, then after a few minutes she vanished and I was left with what I could only describe as her inspiration which led me to write my first real sermon that evening and present it on the following Sunday."

"She gave you a message?" I thought of Jeanne D'Arc.

"Oh, no. Our exchange was wordless on that occasion."

"And you spoke of her in church?"

"Never. That would have been a sort of betrayal. No, I based my message simply on the emotion she had aroused in me. A vision of Christ might have done the same. I don't know."

"So it was a Christian message? Not anti-Christian?"

"Not anti-religious, at any rate. Perhaps, as the bishop suggested, a little pagan."

"What brought you so much attention?"

"In the church that Sunday were two young chaps escorting their recently widowed aunt, Mrs Nye. They told their friends about me. To my delight when I gave my second sermon I found myself with a very receptive congregation. I thanked God for the miracle. It seemed nothing else, my dear. You can't imagine the joy of it! For any chap in my position. I'd received a gift of divine communication, perhaps a small one, but it seemed pretty authentic. And the people began to pack St Odhran's. We had money for repairs. They seemed so willing suddenly to give themselves to their faith!"

I was mildly disappointed. This Rose did not seem much of a vision. Under the influence of drugs or when overtired I had experienced hallucinations quite as elaborate and inspiring. I asked him if he had seen her again.

"Oh, yes. Of course. Many times. In the end we fell in love. She taught me so much. Later there was a child."

He stood up, adjusted his overcoat and scarf and gave his stick a little flourish. He pointed out how the light fell through the parade of black gnarled maples leading to the tennis courts. "An army of old giants ready to march," he said. "But their roots won't let them."

The next Wednesday when I came to lunch he said no more about his vision.

TWO

A Brief History of the Begg Family & of Sporting Club Square

In the course of my first four hundred lunches with the Clapham Antichrist I never did discover why he abandoned his career but I learned a great deal about the Begg family, its origins, its connections and its property, especially the Square. I became something of an expert and planned a monograph until the recent publication of two excellent Hubert Begg books made my work only useful as an appendix to real scholarship.

Today the Square, on several tourist itineraries, has lost most traces of its old unselfconscious integrity. Only Begg Mansions remains gated and fenced from casual view, a defiantly private museum of human curiosities. The rest of the Square has been encouraged to maximise its profitability. Bakunin Villas is now the Hotel Romanoff. Ralph Lauren for some time sponsored D'Yss Mansions as a fashion gallery. Beardsley Villas is let as company flats to United Foods, while the council (which invested heavily in BBIC) took another building, the Moorish fantasy of Flecker Mansions, as offices. There is still some talk of an international company "theme-parking" Sporting Club Square, running commercial tennis matches and linking it to a television soap. Following the financial scandals involving Begg Belgravia International and its associate companies, the Residents' Association has had some recent success in reversing this progress.

When I visited Edwin Begg in 1992, he welcomed me as if our routine had never been broken. He mourned his home's decline into a mere fashion, an exploitable commodity instead of a respected eccentricity, and felt it had gone the way of the Chateau Pantin or Derry & Toms famous Roof Garden, with every feature displayed as an emphatic curiosity, a sensation, a mode, and all her old charm a wistful memory. He had early on warned them about these likely consequences of his nephew's eager speculations. "Barbican wasn't the first to discover what you could do in a boom economy with a lick of paint, a touch of brass and a good story, but I thought his soiling of his own nest a remote chance, not one of his first moves! The plans of such people are generally far advanced before they achieve power. When they strike you are almost always taken unawares, aren't you, dear? What cold, patient dreams they must have."

He derived no satisfaction from Barbican Begg's somewhat ignoble ruin but felt deep sympathy for his fellow residents hopelessly trying to recover their stolen past.

"It's too late for us now and soon it won't matter much, but it's hard to imagine the kind of appetite which feeds upon souls like locusts on corn. We might yet drive the locust from

Michael Moorcock

our field, my dear, but he has already eaten his fill. He has taken what we cannot replace."

Sometimes he was a little difficult to follow and his similes grew increasingly bucolic.

"The world's changing physically, dear. Can't you feel it?" His eyes were as bright a blue and clear as always, his pink cheeks a little more drawn, his white halo thinner, but he still pecked at the middle-distance when he got excited, as if he could tear the truth from the air with his nose. He was clearly delighted that we had resumed our meetings. He apologised that the snacks were things he could make and microwave. They were still delicious. On our first meeting I was close to tears, wondering why on earth I had simply assumed him dead and deprived myself of his company for so long. He suggested a stroll if I could stand it.

I admitted that the Square was not improving. I had been appalled at the gaudy golds and purples of the Hotel Romanoff. It was, he said, currently in receivership, and he shrugged. "What is it, my dear, which allows us to become the victims of such villains, time after time! Time after time they take what is best in us and turn it to our disadvantage. It's like being a conspirator in one's own rape."

We had come up to the Duke's Elm again in the winter twilight and he spoke fondly of familiar ancestors.

Cornelius van Beek, a Dutch cousin of the Saxon von Beks, had settled in London in 1689, shortly after William and Mary. For many Europeans in those days England was a haven of relative enlightenment. A daring merchant banker, van Beek financed exploratory trading expeditions, accompanying several of them himself, and amassed the honourable fortune enabling him to retire at sixty to Cogges Hall, Sussex. Amongst his properties when he died were the North Star Farm and tavern, west of Kensington, bought on the mistaken assumption that the area was growing more respectable and where he had at one time planned to build a house. This notorious stretch of heath was left to van Beek's nephew, George Arthur Begg who had anglicised his name upon marriage to Harriet Vernon, his second cousin, in 1738. Their only surviving grandson was Robert Vernon Begg, famous as Dandy Bob Begg and ennobled under the Prince Regent.

As financially impecunious as his patron, Dandy Bob raised money from co-members of the Hellfire, took over the old tavern at North Star Farm, increased its size and magnificence, entertained the picaro captains so they would go elsewhere for their prizes, ran bare-knuckle fights, bear-baitings and other brutal spectacles, and founded the most notorious sporting establishment of its day. Fortunes were commonly lost and won at Begg's; suicides, scandals and duels no rarity. A dozen of our oldest families spilled their blood in the meadow beneath the black elm, and perhaps a score of men and women drowned in the brook now covered and serving as a modern sewer.

Begg's Sporting Club grew so infamous, the activities of its members and their concubines such a public outrage, that when the next William ascended, Begg rapidly declined. By Victoria's crowning the great dandy whom all had courted had become a souse married into the Wadhams for their money, got his wife Charlotte pregnant with male twins and died, whereupon she somewhat boldly married his nephew Captain Russell Begg and had three more children before he died a hero and a colonel in the Crimea. The twins were Ernest Sumara and Louis Palmate Begg, her two girls were Adriana Circe and Juliana Aphrodite and her youngest boy, her favourite child, was Hubert Alhambra born on January 18th 1855 after his father's fatal fall at Balaclava.

A youthful disciple of Eastlake, by the late 1870s Hubert

Begg was a practising architect whose largest single commission was Castle Bothwell on the shores of Loch Ness (his sister had married James Bothwell) which became a victim of the Glasgow blitz. "But it was little more than a bit of quasi-Eastlake and no rival for instance to the V&A," Edwin Begg had told me. He did not share my admiration for his great-uncle's achievement. "Quite frankly, his best work was always his furniture." He was proud of his complete bedroom suite in Begg's rather spare late style but he did not delight in living in "an art nouveau wedding cake". He claimed the Square's buildings cost up to ten times as much to clean as Oakwood Mansions, for instance, at the western end of Kensington High Street. "Because of the crannies and fancy mouldings, those flowing fauns and smirking sylphs the late Victorians found so deliciously sexy. Dust traps all. It's certainly unique, my dear, but so was Quasimodo."

Hubert Begg never struggled for a living. He had married the beautiful Carinthia Hughes, an American heiress, during his two years in Baltimore and it was she who suggested he use family land for his own creation, tearing down that ramshackle old firetrap, The Sporting Club Tavern, which together with a smallholding was rented to a family called Foulsham whom Begg generously resettled on prime land, complete with their children, their cow, their pig and various other domestic animals, near Old Cogges.

The North Star land was cleared. North Star Square was named but lasted briefly as that. It was designed as a true square with four other smaller squares around it to form a sturdy box cross, thus allowing a more flexible way of arranging the buildings, ensuring residents plenty of light, good views and more tennis. Originally there were plans for seven tennis courts. By the 1880s tennis was a social madness rather than a vogue and everybody was playing. Nearby

Queens Club was founded in Begg's shadow. Begg's plans were altogether more magnificent and soon the projected settlement blossomed into Sporting Club Square. The name had a slightly raffish, romantic reference and attracted the more daring young people, the financiers who still saw themselves as athletic privateers and who were already patrons to an artist or two as a matter of form.

Clients were encouraged to commission favourite styles for Begg to adapt. He had already turned his back on earlier influences, so Gothic did not predominate, but was well represented in Lohengrin Villas which was almost an homage to Eastlake, commissioned by the Church to house retired clergy who felt comfortable with its soaring arches and mighty buttresses. Encouraged by the enthusiasm for his scheme, the architect was able to indulge every fantasy, rather in the manner of a precocious Elgar offering adaptations of what Greaves called, in *The British Architect*, "Mediterranean, Oriental, Historical and Modern styles representing the quintessence of contemporary taste." But there were some who even then found it fussy and decadent. When the Queen praised it as an example to the world Begg was knighted. Lady Carinthia, who survived him by many years, always credited herself as the Square's real procreator and it must be said it was she who nudged her husband away from the past to embrace a more plastic future.

Work on Sporting Club Square began in 1885 but was not entirely completed until 1901. The slump of the 1890s destroyed the aspirations of the rising bourgeoisie, who were to have been the likely renters; Gibbs and Flew had bankrupted themselves building the Olympia Bridge, and nobody who still had money felt secure enough to cross into the new suburbs. Their dreams of elevation now frustrated, the failed and dispossessed took their new bitter poverty with them into the depths of a North Star development doomed never to rise and to become almost at once a watchword for social decrepitude, populated by loafers, psychopaths, unstable landladies, exploited seamstresses, drunkards, forgers, beaten wives, braggarts, embezzlers, rat-faced children, petty officials and prostitutes who had grown accustomed to the easy prosperity of the previous decade and were now deeply resentful of anyone more fortunate. They swiftly turned the district into everything it remained until the next tide of prosperity lifted it for a while, only to let it fall back almost in relief as another generation lost its hold upon life's ambitions. The terraces were occupied by casual labourers and petty thieves while the impoverished petite bourgeoisie sought the mews and parades. North Star became a synonym for wretchedness and miserable criminality and was usually avoided even by the police.

By 1935 the area was a warren to rival Notting Dale, but Sporting Club Square, the adjoining St Mary's Convent and the churchyard, retained a rather dreamy, innocent air, untouched by the prevailing mood. Indeed locals almost revered and protected the Square's tranquillity as if it were the only thing they had ever held holy and were proud of it. During the last war the Square was untouched by incendiaries roaring all around, but some of the flats were already abandoned and then taken over by the government to house mostly Jewish political exiles and these added to the cosmopolitan atmosphere. For years a Polish delicatessen stood on the corner of North Star Road; it was possible to buy all kinds of kosher food at Mrs Green's grocery, Mandrake Terrace, and the Foulsham Road French patisserie remained popular until 1980 when Madame Stejns retired. According to Edwin Begg, the war and the years of austerity were their best, with a marvellous spirit of cooperation everywhere. During the war and until 1954 open air concerts were regularly performed by local musicians and an excellent theatrical group was eventually absorbed into the Lyric until that was rationalised. A song, *The Rose of Sporting Club Square*, was popular in the 1930s and the musical play it was written for was the basis of a Hollywood musical in 1940. The David Clazier Ensemble, perhaps the most innovative modern dance troupe of its day, occupied all the lower flats in Le Gallienne Chambers.

Edwin Begg was not the only resident to become famous with the general public. Wheldrake's association with the old tavern, where he spent two years of exile, is well known. Audrey Vernon lived most of her short life in Dowson Mansions. Her lover, Warwick Harden, took a flat in Ibsen Studios next door and had a door built directly through to her bedroom. John Angus Gilchrist the mass murderer lived here but dispatched his nearest victim three miles away in Shepherd's Bush. Others associated with the Square, sometimes briefly, included Pett Ridge, George Robey, Gustav Klimt, Rebecca West, Constance Cummings, Jessie Matthews, Sonny Hale, Jack Parker, Gerald Kersh, Laura Riding, Joseph Kiss, John Lodwick, Edith Sitwell, Lord George Creech, Angela Thirkell, G.K. Chesterton, Max Miller, Sir Compton Mackenzie, Margery Allingham, Ralph Richardson, Eudora Welty, Donald Peers, Max Wall, Dame Fay Westbrook, Graham Greene, Eduardo Paolozzi, Gore Vidal, Bill Butler, Jimi Hendrix, Jack Trevor Story, Laura Ashley, Mario Amayo, Angela Carter, Simon Russell Beale, Ian Dury, Jonathan Carroll and a variety of sports and media personalities. As its preserves were stripped, repackaged and sold off during the feeding frenzy of the 1980s only the most stubborn residents refused to be driven from the little holdings they had once believed their birthright, but it was not until Edwin Begg led me back to his bedroom and raised the newly-installed blind that I understood the full effect of his nephew's speculations. "We do not rest, do we," he said, "from mortal toil? But I'm not sure this is my idea of the new Jerusalem. What do you think, dear?"

They had taken his view, all that harmony. I was consumed with a sense of unspeakable outrage! They had turned that beautiful landscape into a muddy wasteland in which it seemed some monstrous, petulant child had scattered at random its filthy Tonka trucks and Corgi cranes, Portakabins, bulldozers in crazed abandon, then in tantrum stepped on everything. That perfect balance was destroyed and the tranquillity of Sporting Club Square was now forever under siege. The convent was gone, as well as the church.

"I read in the *Telegraph* that it required the passage of two private member's bills, the defiance of several preservation orders, the bribery of officials in thirteen different government departments and the blackmailing of a cabinet minister just to annex a third of the cemetery and knock down the chapel and almshouses," Begg said.

Meanwhile the small fry had looted the cemetery of its saleable masonry. Every monument had been chiselled. The severed heads of the angels were already being sold in the antique boutiques of Mayfair and St Germaine-des-Prés. Disappointed in their share of this loot, others had daubed swastikas and obscenities on the remaining stones.

"It's private building land now," said Begg. "They have dogs and fences. They bulldozed St Swithhold's. You can't get to the Necropolis, let alone the river. Still, this is probably better than what they were going to build."

The activities of Barbican Begg and his associates, whose enterprises claimed more victims than Maxwell, have been discussed everywhere, but one of the consequences of BBIC's speculations was that bleak no-man's-land standing in place of Edwin Begg's familiar view. The legal problems of leases sold to and by at least nine separate companies means that while no further development has added to the Square's decline, attempts to redress the damage and activate the Council's preservation orders which they ignored, have failed through lack of funds. The project, begun in the name of freedom and civic high-mindedness, always a mark of the scoundrel, remains a symbol and a monument to the asset-stripped 80s. As yet only Frank Cornelius, Begg's close associate, has paid any satisfactory price for ruining so many lives.

"Barbican was born for that age." Edwin Begg drew down the blind against his ruined prospect and sat on his bed, his frail body scarcely denting the great Belgian pillows at his back. "Like a fly born to a dungheap. He could not help himself, my dear. It was his instinct to do what he did. Why are we always surprised by his kind?"

He had grown weak but eagerly asked if I would return the following Wednesday when he would tell me more about his visions and their effect upon his life. I promised to bring the ingredients of a meal. I would cook lunch. He was touched and amused by this. He thought the idea great fun.

I told him to stay where he was. It was easy to let myself out.

"You know," he called as I was leaving, "there's a legend in our family. How we protect the Grail which will one day bring a reconciliation between God and Lucifer. I have no Grail to pass on to you but I think I have its secret."

THREE

Astonishing Revelations of the Clapham
Antichrist; Claims Involvement in the Creation
of a New Messiah; His Visions of Paradise &
Surrendering His Soul for Knowledge; Further
Description of the Sporting Club Square
Madonna; Final Days of the Antichrist; His
Appearance In Death.

"Perhaps the crowning irony," said the Clapham Antichrist
of his unfrocking, "was how devoted a Christian I was then! I
argued that we shouldn't wait for God or heroes but seek our
solutions at the domestic level. Naturally, it would mean
empowering everyone, because only a thoroughly enfran-
chised democracy ever makes the best of its people. Oh, well,
you know the sort of thing. The universal ideal we all agree
on and never seem to achieve. I merely suggested we take a
hard look at the systems we used! They were quite evidently
faulty! Not an especially revolutionary notion! But it met
with considerable antagonism as you know. Politics seems to
be a war of labels, one slapped on top of another until any
glimmer of truth is thoroughly obscured. It's no wonder how
quickly they lose all grip on reality!"

"And that's what you told them?"

He stood in his dressing gown staring down at a Square
and gardens even BBIC had failed to conquer. The trees were
full of the nests crows had built since the first farmers hedged
the meadow. His study, with its books and big old-fashioned
stereo, had hardly changed but had a deserted air now.

I had brought the ingredients of our lunch and stood in my street clothes with my bag expecting him to lead me to the kitchen, but he remained in his window and wanted me to stay. He pointed mysteriously towards the Duke's Elm and Gilbert's War Memorial, a fanciful drinking fountain that had never worked.

"That's what I told them, my dear. In the pulpit first. Then in the travelling shows. Then on the street. I was arrested for obstruction in 1937, refused to recognise the court and refused to pay the fine. This was my first brief prison sentence. Eventually I got myself in solitary.

"When I left prison I saw a London even more wretched than before. Beggars were everywhere. Vagrants were not in those days tolerated in the West End, but were still permitted in the doorways of Soho and Somers Town. The squalor was as bad as anything Mayhew reported. I thought my anger had been brought under control in prison but I was wrong. The obscene exploitation of the weak by the strong was every-where displayed. I did whatever I could. I stood on a box at Speakers' Corner. I wrote and printed pamphlets. I sent letters and circulars to everyone, to the newspapers, to the BBC. Nobody took me very seriously. In the main I was ignored. When I was not ignored I was insulted. Eventually, holding a sign in Oxford Street, I was again arrested but this time there was a scuffle with the arresting policeman. I went into Wormwood Scrubs until the outbreak of the Blitz when I was released to volunteer for the ambulance service. Well, I wasn't prepared to return to prison after the War and in fact my ideas had gained a certain currency. Do you remember what Londoners were like then, my dear? After we learned how to look after ourselves rather better than our leaders could? Our morale was never higher. London's last war was a war the people won in spite of the authorities. But some-where along the line we gave our achievements over to the politicians, the power addicts. The result is that we now live in rookeries and slum courts almost as miserable as our 19th century ancestors', or exist in blanketed luxury as divorced from common experience as a Russian Tsar. I'm not entirely sure about the quality of that progress, are you? These days the lowest common denominators are sought for as if they were principles."

"You're still an example to us," I said, thinking to console him.

He was grateful but shook his head, still looking down at the old elm as if he hoped to see someone there. "I'll never be sure if I did any good. For a while, you know, I was quite a celebrity until they realised I wasn't offering an anti-Christian message and then they mostly lost interest. I couldn't get on with those Jesuits they all cultivated. But I spoke to the Fabians twice and met Wells, Shaw, Priestley and the rest. I was very cheerful. It appeared that I was spreading my message. I didn't understand that I was merely a vogue. I was quite a favourite with Bloomsbury and there was talk of putting me on Radio Luxembourg. But gradually doors were closed to me and I was rather humiliated on a couple of occasions. I hadn't started all this for fame or approval, so as soon as I realised what was happening I retired to the travelling shows and seaside fairgrounds which proliferated in England in the days before television.

"Eventually I began to doubt the value of my own pronouncements, since my audiences were dwindling and an evil force was progressing unchecked across Europe. We faced a future dominated by a few cruel dictatorships. Some kind of awful war was inevitable. During my final spell in clink I made up my mind to keep my thoughts to myself and consider better ways of getting them across. I saw nothing wrong with the message, but assumed myself to be a bad medium. In my free time I went out into the Square as much as I could. It was still easy to think there, even during the War."

He took a step towards the window, almost as if he had seen someone he recognised and then he shrugged, turning his head away sharply and pretending to take an interest in one of his Sickerts. "I found her there first, as you know, in 1933. And that one sight of her inspired a whole series of sermons. I came back week after week, but it always seemed as if I had just missed her. You could say I was in love with her. I wanted desperately for her to be real. Well, I had seen her again the evening I was 'unfrocked'. Of course I was in a pretty terrible state. I was praying. Since a boy I always found it easy to pray in the Square. I identified God with the Duke's Elm—or at least I visualised God as a powerful old tree. I never understood why we placed such peculiar prohibitions on how we represented God. That's what they mean by 'pagan'. It has nothing to do with one's intellectual sophistication. I was praying when she appeared for the second time. First there was that strong scent of roses. When I looked up I saw her framed against the great trunk and it seemed a rose drew all her branches, leaves and blooms together and took human form!"

His face had a slight flush as he spoke. "It seemed to me I'd been given a companion to help me make the best use of my life. She had that vibrancy, that uncommon beauty; she was a sentient flower.

"Various church examiners to whom I explained the vision understood my Rose either as an expression of my own unstable mind or as a manifestation of the devil. It was impossible for me to see her as either.

"She stepped forward and held out her hand to me. I had difficulty distinguishing her exact colours. They were many and subtle—an unbroken haze of pink and green and pale gold—all the shades of the rose. Her figure was slim but it wasn't easy to tell where her clothes met her body or even which was which. Her eyes changed in the light from deep emerald to violet. In spite of her extraordinary aura of power, her manner was almost hesitant. I think I was weeping as I went to her. I probably asked her what I should do. I know I decided to continue with my work. It was years before I saw her again, after I'd come out of prison for the last time."

"But you did see her again?"

"Many times. Especially during the Blitz. But I'd learned my lesson. I kept all that to myself."

"You were afraid of prison?"

"If you like. But I think it was probably more positive. God granted me a dream of the universe and her ever-expanding realities and I helped in the procreation of the new messiah!"

I waited for him to continue but he turned from the window with a broad smile. He was exhausted, tottering a little as he came with me to the kitchen and sat down in my place while I began to cook. He chatted amiably about the price of garlic and I prepared the dishes as he had taught me years before. This time, however, I was determined to encourage him to talk about himself.

He took a second glass of wine, his cheeks a little pinker than usual, his hair already beginning to rise about his head in a pure white fog.

"I suppose I needed her most during the War. There wasn't much time for talk, but I still came out to the Duke's Elm to pray. We began to meet frequently, always in the evenings before dark, and would walk together, comparing experience. She was from a quite different world—although her world sort of included ours. Eventually we became lovers."

"Did she have a name?"

"I think so. I called her the Rose. I travelled with her. She took me to paradise, my dear, nowhere less! She showed me the whole of Creation! And so after a while my enthusiasm returned. Again, I wanted to share my vision but I had become far more cautious. I had a suspicion that I made a mistake the first time and almost lost my Rose as a result. When my nephew, who was in BBC Talks, offered me a new pulpit I was pretty much ready for it. This time I was determined to keep the reality to myself and just apply what I had experienced to ordinary, daily life. The public could not accept the intensity and implications of my pure vision. I cultivated an avuncularity which probably shocked those who knew me well. I became quite the jolly Englishman! I was offered speaking engagements in America. I was such a show-off. I spent less and less time in the Square and eventually months passed before I realised that I had lost contact with my Rose and our child! I felt such an utter fool, my dear. As soon as I understood what was happening I gave everything up. But it was too late."

"You haven't seen her since?"

"Only in dreams."

"What do you believe she was? The spirit of the tree?" I did my best to seem matter-of-fact, but he knew what I was up to and laughed, pouring himself more wine.

"She is her own spirit, my dear. Make no mistake."

And then the first course was ready, a *paté de foie gras* made by my friend Loris Murrail in Paris. Begg agreed that it was as good as his own. For our main course we had Quantock veal in saffron. He ate it with appreciative relish. He had not been able to cook much lately, he said, and his appetite was reduced, but he enjoyed every bite. I was touched by his enthusiasm and made a private decision to come regularly again. Cooking him lunch would be my way of giving him something back. My spirits rose at the prospect and it was only then that I realised how much I had missed his company.

"Perhaps," he said, "she was sent to me to sustain me only when I most needed her. I had thought it a mistake to try to share her with the world. I never spoke of her again after I had told the bishop about her and was accused of militant paganism, primitive nature-worship. I saw his point of view but I always worshipped God in all his manifestations. The bishop seemed to argue that paganism was indistinguishable from common experience and therefore could not be considered as a religion at all!"

"You worshipped her?"

"In a sense, my dear. As a man worships his wife."

I had made him a *tiesen sinamon* and he took his time with the meringue, lifting it to his lips on the delicate silver fork which Begg's Cotswold benches had produced for Liberty in 1903. "I don't know if it's better or worse, dear, but the world is changing profoundly you know. Our methods of making it safe just aren't really working any more. The danger of the simple answer is always with us and is inclined to lead to some sort of Final Solution. We are affected by turbulence as a leaf in the wind, but still we insist that the best way of dealing with the fact is to deny it or ignore it. And so we go on, hopelessly attempting to contain the thunder and the lightning and creating only further confusion! We're always caught by surprise! Yet it would require so little, surely, in the way of courage and imagination to find a way out, especially with today's wonderful computers?"

I had been depressed by the level and the outcome of the recent British election and was not optimistic. He agreed. "How we love to cling to the wrecks which took us onto the rocks in the first place. In our panic we don't even see the empty lifeboats within easy swimming distance."

He did not have the demeanour of a disappointed prophet.

He remained lively and humorous. There was no sense of defeat about him, rather of quiet victory, of conquered pain. He did not at first seem disposed to tell me any more but when we were having coffee a casual remark set him off on a train of thought which led naturally back to that most significant event of his life. "We aren't flawed," he said, "just as God isn't flawed. What we perceive as flaws are a reflection of our own failure to see the whole." He spoke of a richly populated multiverse which was both within us and outside us. "We're all reflections and echoes, one of another, and our originals, dear, are lost, probably forever. That was what I understood from my vision. I wrote it in my journal. Perhaps, very rarely, we're granted a glimpse of God's entire plan? Perhaps only when our need is desperate. I have no doubt that God sent me my Rose."

I am still of a secular disposition. "Or perhaps," I suggested, "as God you sent yourself a vision?"

He did not find this blasphemous but neither did he think it worth pursuing. "It's much of muchness, that," he said.

He was content in his beliefs. He had questioned them once but now he was convinced. "God sent me a vision and I followed her. She was made flesh. A miracle. I went with her to where she lived, in the fields of colour, in the far ether. We were married. We gave birth to a new human creature, neither male nor female but self-reproducing, a new messiah, and it set us free at last to dwell on that vast multiplicity of the heavens, to contemplate a quasi-infinity of versions of ourselves, our histories, our experience. That was what God granted me, my dear, when he sent me my Rose. Perhaps I was the antichrist, after all, or at least its parent."

"In your vision did you see what became of the child?"

He spoke with lighthearted familiarity, not recalling some distant dream but describing an immediate reality. "Oh, yes. It grew to lead the world upon a new stage in our evolution.

I'm not sure you'd believe the details, my dear, or find them very palatable."

I smiled at this, but for the first time in my life felt a hint of profound terror and I suppressed a sudden urge to shout at him, to tell him how ridiculous I considered his visions, a bizarre blend of popular prophecy and alchemical mumbo-jumbo which even a New Age traveller would take with a pinch of E. My anger overwhelmed me. Though I regained control of it he recognised it. He continued to speak but with growing reluctance and perhaps melancholy. "I saw a peculiar inevitability to the process. What, after all, do most of us live for? Ourselves? And what use is that? What value? What profit?"

With a great sigh he put down his fork. "That was delicious." His satisfaction felt to me like an accolade.

"You're only describing human nature." I took his plate.

"Is that what keeps us on a level with the amoeba, my dear, and makes us worth about as much individual affection? Come now! We allow ourselves to be ruled by every brutish, greedy instinct, not by what is significantly human in our nature! Our imagination is our greatest gift. It gives us our moral sensibility." He looked away through the dining room window at the glittering domes of Gautier House and in the light the lines of his face were suddenly emphasised.

I had no wish ever to quarrel with him again. The previous argument, we were agreed, had cost us both too much. But I had to say what I thought. "I was once told the moment I mentioned morality was the moment I'd crossed the line into lunacy," I said. "I suppose we must agree to understand things differently."

For once he had forgotten his usual courtesy. I don't think he heard me. "Wasn't all this damage avoidable?" he murmured. 'Weren't there ways in which cities could have grown up as we grew up, century adding to century, style to style, wisdom to wisdom? Isn't there something seriously wrong with the cycle we're in? Isn't there some way out?"

I made to reply but he shook his head, his hands on the table. "I saw her again, you know, several times after the birth. How beautiful she was! How much beauty she showed me! It's like an amplification, my dear, of every sense! A discovery of new senses. An understanding that we don't need to discard anything as long as we continue to learn from it. It isn't frightening what she showed me. It's perfectly familiar once you begin to see. It's like looking at the quintessential versions of our ordinary realities. Trees, animals—they're there, in essence. You begin to discover all that. The fundamental geometry's identified. Well, you've seen this new math, haven't you?"

He seemed so vulnerable at that moment that for once I wasn't frank. I was unconvinced by what I judged as hippy physics made possible only by the new creative powers of computers. I didn't offer him an argument.

"You can't help but hope that it's what death is like," he said. "You become an angel."

He got up and returned slowly to his dusty study, beckoning me to look out with him into the twilight gathering around the trees where crows croaked their mutual reassurances through the darkening air. He glanced only once towards the old elm then turned his head away sharply. "You'll think this unlikely, I know, but we first came together physically at midnight under a full moon as bright and thin and yellow as honesty in a dark blue sky. I looked at the moon through those strong black branches the moment before we touched. The joy of our union was indescribable. It was a confirmation of my faith. I made a mistake going back into public life. What good did it do for anyone, my dear?"

"We all made too many easy assumptions," I said. "It wasn't your fault."

"I discovered sentimental solutions and comforted myself with them. Those comforts I turned to material profit. They became lies. And I lost her, my dear." He made a small, anguished gesture. "I'm still waiting for her to come back."

He was scarcely aware of me. I felt I had intruded upon a private moment and suggested that I had tired him and should leave. Looking at me in surprise but without dispute he came towards me, remarking in particular on the saffron sauce. "I can't tell you how much it meant to me, my dear, in every way."

I promised to return the following Wednesday and cook. He licked his pink lips in comic anticipation and seemed genuinely delighted by the prospect. "Yum, yum." He embraced me suddenly with his frail body, his sweet face staring blindly into mine.

I had found his last revelations disturbing and my tendency was to dismiss them perhaps as an early sign of his senility. I even considered putting off my promised visit, but was already planning the next lunch when three days later I took a call from Mrs Arthur Begg who kept an eye on him and had my number. The Clapham Antichrist had died in his sleep. She had found him at noon with his head raised upon his massive pillows, the light from the open window falling on his face. She enthused over his wonderful expression in death.

About the authors

Kate Clanchy lives in the East End.

Patrick Cunningham was born in Ireland and works in publishing.

Sue Gee is a freelance writer and editor and a counsellor for the Medical Foundation for the Care of Victims of Torture. She has published three novels, *Spring Will Be Ours*, *Keeping Secrets* and *The Last Guests of the Summer*. She also co-edited an anthology, *Coming Late to Motherhood*.

Roy Heath is a leading Guyanese novelist who has lived in London for many years. His work includes *The Murderer*, winner of The Guardian Fiction Prize, and *The Shadow Bride*.

Maggie Hewitt is an oral history worker in the East End of London, working with individuals and groups who have been under-represented historically.

Tobias Hill has twice won first prize in the Mary and Alfred Wilkins National Poetry Competition, and has had poetry published in several anthologies and magazines.

R. L. Huntress is an American journalist working in London.

Alison Love works as a freelance in public relations. Her only previous prize for writing was two bottles of olive oil for a satirical poem about Inspector Morse.

Shena Mackay is a novelist and short story writer who is a perceptive and hugely entertaining observer of urban life. Her latest books are *Dunedin*, a novel, and *The Laughing Academy*, a collection of stories.

Michael Moorcock, described by Angela Carter as 'the master storyteller of our time', is an award-winning writer of science fiction and satire. His recent work includes the novel, *Mother London*, an epic tale of the city over the last fifty years, and *Jerusalem Commands*, the third in the Colonel Pyat quartet.

Kate Nivison was a secondary school teacher in London and in Nigeria and Zambia. She now writes full time and has had stories published in a number of women's magazines.

Clare Palmier is working on a performance which takes place in a swimming pool, with divers, gospel singers, musicians and synchronised swimmers.

D. A. J. Pearson is a supply teacher. He based his story on his experiences when he worked as a park-keeper.

Kate Pullinger is a Canadian writer who has lived in London since 1982. She won the City Limits Short Story Competition, and then published her acclaimed short story collection, *Tiny Lies*. Her latest novel is *Where Does Kissing End?*, and she is currently one of the first in a new national initiative to place Writers in Residence in prisons.

David Rogers has had several stories published and has been runner-up in two competitions.

Joanna Rosenthall is a psychotherapist at the Tavistock Institute. She has had several stories published before.

Kirsty Seymour-Ure was born and brought up in Canterbury, but has lived in London since 1988. She works in publishing.

James Sinclair was born in South Africa. He is a consultant and lecturer in European Community Law.

John Turner is an Environmental Health Officer and has worked on Salvation Army soup runs.

Tom Wakefield has published a collection of short stories, *Drifters*, novels, *Mates*, *The Discus Throwers*, *The Variety Artistes*, *Lot's Wife* and *War Paint*, and a childhood autobiography, *Forties' Child*. He is editor of *The Ten Commandments*, a collection of short stories, and wrote (with Francis King and Patrick Gale) *Secret Lives*, a trio of novellas.

SHORTLISTED STORIES

DAISYHEAD   *Brooke Auchincloss-Foreman*
THEY MIGHT HAVE FLOATED   *Alan Bisset*
BIRYANI JUNCTION   *Stefan Boltzmann*
LONDON FLING   *Richard F Bradford*
CANARY SONGS   *Adrian Burnham*
BIRD-BRAINED   *James Cressey*
GROWING OLD IN THE CITY   *W A Harbinson*
JULIANNA   *Vivian Hassan-Lambert*
PHOTO   *Rebecca Hesketh-Pritchard*
SOUTH OF THE BORDER   *Natasha Hughes*
THE PIETERSON BLUE   *Daniel Jamieson*
LURID   *Michael Kowalski*
NEIGHBOURS FROM HELL   *Linda Hone*
FOOT SOLDIERS OF SAINT MAMMON   *Maria Munro*
BROTHER'S FOWL   *Jeremy Page*
COME OUT, COME OUT WHEREVER YOU ARE
   Anita Naoko Pilgrim
A SIMPLE LON ON STORY   *Robert Porter*
THE OBSERVER   *Lara Rabinowitz*
PICNIC AT THE ANGEL   *S Rafferty*
THE JOCASTA COMPLEX   *Glenda Richards*
FALLING   *Peter Michael Rosenberg*
LONDON STANDARD   *Richard Statham*
THE PACKAGE   *Steve Tasane*
THE PHOTOGRAPHER   *Rebecca Vincenzi*
BAD WILLIAM AND THE BLACK MERCEDES   *Maria Wickens*